Praise for *Love Me* by (

"Keillor's forte . . . is hitting those wry, eyebrow-arching notes that ring true no matter who you are or where you're from. . . . Sharp humor doesn't always have a heart, yet for all its sly satire and deadpan zingers, *Love Me* is surprisingly touching. . . . [It] succeeds as light-footed fun, or as social comedy . . . Keillor had me laughing." —*The New York Times Book Review*

"If Mr. Keillor's Lake Wobegon books purport to tell the true stories of a fictional town, *Love Me* tells wonderfully fictional stories of a true town. . . . Mr. Keillor is deliciously clever in his parodies of New York's literati, losing none of his trademark wit in the move from Midwest to Manhattan."
—*The Wall Street Journal*

"A hilarious satire of just about everything in the early twenty-first century worth poking fun at. . . . Like his Midwestern literary predecessor Mark Twain, [Keillor] despises whatever is sanctimonious, self-righteous and disingenuous, going after every sacred cow he can find, with a gleeful but never ill-natured abandon. . . . *Love Me* is unfailingly engaging. Keillor has the great gift of making just about any situation funny by celebrating the very human foibles he is skewering. . . . *Love Me* is Garrison Keillor's funniest and most ambitious novel to date."
—*The Washington Post Book World*

"*Love Me* is in part love story, but it is also a very funny riff, an almost surreal spooling out of American idiom in the great tradition of James Thurber and S. J. Perelman."
—*The Boston Sunday Globe*

"Keillor's latest novel has as much style as Jean Paul Gaultier's fall collection, and it's even funnier. . . . Bottom Line: Love it."
—*People*

"The charms of *Love Me* are in its flights of doggerel, its high-brow slapstick, its hero's hapless gumption and bemused lyricism. They make one want to know Larry better."
—*Boston Herald*

"Keillor demonstrates his extraordinary satirical gifts . . . with verve, wit and empathy for human foibles."
—*Times Union* (Albany)

"True to form, Keillor creates lovable characters, lets us listen in on their neuroses, puts them into unbelievable situations, and makes us want to believe them for the sheer enjoyment of the tale. . . . [H]ilarious."
—*Richmond Times-Dispatch*

"Keillor's inimitable gift for delicately layering humor and honesty, pathos and absurdity, is on full display here. He can write like he's spreading honey with a straight-edge razor."
—*St. Petersburg Times*

"[F]unny, bittersweet. . . . Garrison Keillor tickles the funny bone."
—*The News & Observer* (Raleigh)

"[C]atchy, quick . . . witty and self-deprecating in true Garrison Keillor fashion."
—*Herald-Tribune* (Sarasota, FL)

"Sweet and touching."
—*The Wichita Eagle*

"Wholly entertaining throughout."
—*The Grand Rapids Press*

"With his trademark droll humor, Keillor exposes the foibles of human nature and pokes fun at our more absurd conventions. The icing on the cake is the use of some obviously autobiographical material from Keillor's publishing experiences in this wry send-up of literary life."
—*Publishers Weekly*

PENGUIN BOOKS

# LOVE ME

Garrison Keillor is the creator of Lake Wobegon and the host and writer of the Saturday-night radio show *A Prairie Home Companion*, on the air since 1974. He is the author of thirteen books including *New York Times* bestsellers *Lake Wobegon Summer 1956*, *Wobegon Boy*, and *Lake Wobegon Days*, and editor of the anthology *Good Poems*. He is a resident of St. Paul, Minnesota, and a member of the Academy of American Arts & Letters. He was born in Anoka, Minnesota, in 1942.

# GARRISON KEILLOR

## LOVE ME

PENGUIN BOOKS

PENGUIN BOOKS

Published by the Penguin Group

Penguin Group (USA) Inc., 375 Hudson Street, New York, New York 10014, U.S.A.
Penguin Books Ltd, 80 Strand, London WC2R 0RL, England
Penguin Books Australia Ltd, 250 Camberwell Road,
    Camberwell, Victoria 3124, Australia
Penguin Books Canada Ltd, 10 Alcorn Avenue, Toronto, Ontario, Canada M4V 3B2
Penguin Books India (P) Ltd, 11 Community Centre,
    Panchsheel Park, New Delhi – 110 017, India
Penguin Group (NZ), cnr Airborne and Rosedale Roads,
    Albany, Auckland 1310, New Zealand
Penguin Books (South Africa) (Pty) Ltd, 24 Sturdee Avenue,
    Rosebank, Johannesburg 2196, South Africa

Penguin Books Ltd, Registered Offices:
80 Strand, London WC2R 0RL, England

First published in the United States of America by Viking Penguin,
a member of Penguin Group (USA) Inc. 2003
Published in Penguin Books 2004

10  9  8  7  6  5  4  3  2  1

PUBLISHER'S NOTE
This is a work of fiction. Names, characters, places, and incidents either are the product of
the author's imagination or are used fictitiously, and any resemblance to actual persons,
living or dead, business establishments, events, or locales is entirely coincidental.

THE LIBRARY OF CONGRESS HAS CATALOGED THE HARDCOVER EDITION AS FOLLOWS:
Keillor, Garrison.
    Love me / Garrison Keillor.
       p.   cm.
    ISBN 0-670-03246-8 (hc.)
    ISBN 0 14 20.0499 5 (pbk.)
       1. Saint Paul (Minn.)—Fiction.   2. Advice columnists—Fiction.
    3. Married people—Fiction.   I. Title.
    PS3561.E3755L68    2003
    813'.54—dc21        2003052540

Printed in the United States of America
Designed by Carla Bolte

*To the memory of*

**MARY GUNTZEL**
1945–1998

*A friend of the helpless.*

As you travel day by day
Along your earthly way
Of the faces that you see
Love Me.
On the dark and stormy plain,
In the wind and sleet and rain,
Not a friendly house or tree,
Just Me.
I know you could do better
If you shopped around.
I'm just an old dead letter
Waiting in the lost and found.
I'm not smart or debonair,
Not the answer to a prayer,
But here's my simple plea:
O darling
My darling,
Love Me.

—The Make Rites

(Cunningham/Rasmussen; 1965, Midway Music, Inc. BMI.
Used by permission.)

LOVE ME

# Prologue

Once I was young and virtually indestructible and now I am an old married guy on a January morning on Sturgis Avenue in St. Paul sniffing the wind and taking my vitamins. Six A.M. It's pitch-black out. Fresh coffee in the air. I take vitamin C, E, B complex, lysine, cod-liver oil, echinacea, with orange juice, which eases the pills down the gullet. I do a few leg stretches, forty crunches, twenty push-ups, a dozen curlies, on the living room floor. I don't want to struggle when I go to get out of a car. And if tonight my queen should reach over from her side of the bed and draw me to her, I intend to be capable of knighthood.

I look out the kitchen window to get my bearings. St. Paul sits on a bend in the Mississippi, and from my window I see the giant illuminated 1 on the First National Bank downtown and the light in the cupola on the great dome of the Cathedral of St. Paul high on the hill above us. The cathedral sits up there overlooking downtown along with the stately mansions of Summit Avenue that we show to tourists, where James J. Hill, the Empire Builder, resided and next door, the Hampls who made Hamm's beer, and the lumbering Weyerhaeusers, the O'Briens, the Pearsons of Pearson's Nut Goodies, the MacDonald and McNeil families who founded 3M, and the domiciles of their vice presidents and their spoiled children. Sturgis Avenue is a long way down from Summit and Ramsey Hill. Down here are the mechanics and millhands, the laundry workers, the ladies of the cafeterias. Up there the liquor stores stock twenty-year-old single-malt Scotch from the Orkneys and the grocery sells goat yoghurt and eight different kinds of oregano and coffee beans from

Costa Rica and in the coffee shops you hear Haydn and people talking about Henry James. Down here people buy Old Overshoe bourbon and season their food with salt and the coffee comes in cans and in the coffee shops people talk about their sister whose husband beat the shit out of her and took off for South Dakota. If it were up to me, I'd be living on Ramsey Hill by sundown tonight, but my wife is a Democrat and I lost that fight a long time ago.

Next door is the house of Mr. Ziegler, who died in September of aimlessness, now owned by a hard-working young couple who don't smile when they see me. Apparently they don't know I'm a former famous author and I write the twice-weekly "Mr. Blue" column in the Minneapolis *Star Journal* (**Romance going sour? Boyfriend acting weird? Wife ignoring you? Ask Mr. Blue.**) They are delivery truck drivers, judging by their dark brown convict uniforms. **Dear Mr. Blue, My wife and I live next door to an older man who is always staring over our way. Should we say something? Suspicious.** Dear Suspicious, It can't hurt.

I attained old married guyhood despite some outstanding bad behavior on my part and an unsuccessful lunge at fame and riches a long time ago. There was a fairly popular novel, *Spacious Skies,* and an apartment at the Bel Noir on Central Park West in New York and an office at *The New Yorker* with a drawing on the wall above my desk that James Thurber scrawled there years ago with a carpenter's pencil. A thoughtful dog with a harpy standing over him, saying, "I know what you're thinking and the answer is No, No, No." J. D. Salinger's office was down the hall and J. F. Powers's and S. J. Perelman's. John Updike smiled at me in the hallways. Calvin Trillin took me to lunch. The great editor William Shawn became a pal of mine. Him and me went barhopping and got so soused we had to hold each other up. God, I loved that man. We played golf and sailed his boat, the *Shawnee,* through the Verrazano Narrows and out to sea and fished for grouper. I was in New York for six years and Iris almost divorced me, on grounds of emotional distance, but then I wrote a wretched second novel, *Amber Waves of Grain*, which bombed so badly she took pity on me and called off the dogs. I came down with a brutal case of writer's block. Wrote one sentence of *Purple Mountains' Majesty* and quit. The sentence was: "He and the Mrs. dreamed of alabaster cities but here they were in St. Paul and what could they do but cry in their soup?" Couldn't write worth beans.

She almost divorced me again after I shot the publisher of *The New Yorker* (an accident, sort of). He lay on the floor of the Oak Room at the Algonquin Hotel, quietly discoloring the carpet, and said, quietly, "You'll never write for my magazine again, Larry Wyler," and expired. I left New York the next day and returned to St. Paul, to a studio apartment on Ramsey Hill, and cooled my heels there until Iris was willing to take me back.

So I am basically okay. When people ask me, that's what I tell them. "You're sure looking good," they say, which they never said twenty years ago when I did look good, but never mind. I'm sixty. Brown hair, low medium IQ, big feet and sloping shoulders, the face of a ladies' shoe salesman, about a quart low in the charm department, and nothing to be done about it. Boo hoo for me. Hurray for monogamy.

Shortly, I'll take coffee and the *Times* up to Iris, the mistress of the house, as she soaks in a hot bath, suds up to her neck, a rolled-up towel behind her head, listening to *Morning Edition* from NPR. And an hour later, she'll appear downstairs good and pissed off at the Republicans for their treacheries. This bodes well for the day. We'll eat our bran flakes and bananas and she'll say something short and sharp about our shallow doctrinaire president and pick up her battered briefcase and hike to work downtown. Meanwhile, I stay home and write my column for the lovelorn. **Dear Mr. Blue, He used to be**

**a young stallion taking me to heights of wild passion and then he turned into Eeyore, all moody and needy.** In the afternoon, I take a nap and scribble on a legal pad what I hope will become this book and I chop vegetables for supper. Iris comes home at 6. We eat. We go for our nightly constitutional, a two-mile circuit along West 7th past the old Czech lodge hall and the Day By Day Café, the porn shop and the magic store and the funeral parlor, and the half-mile trek across the High Bridge over the Mississippi to Cherokee Heights and back. Even on the bitterest cold nights when the arctic blast bites you in the shorts, she insists we do the Death March over the frozen Father of Waters—"It's good for you," she mutters through her ski mask, and I guess it is. It seems to settle the meal and pacify our minds and we arrive at some tender if inconclusive understanding of each other and come home and read ourselves into a pleasant drowsy state and so to bed.

Perchance to some nobility or else straight to sleep and the nobility of dreams. And then it's 6 A.M. again.

~~~~

Today Mr. Blue has a letter from **Lonely** asking how a woman who hates the bar scene can find a good man. And there's **Frustrated,** who asks if he should stick with his programmer job or fly to Stockholm and pursue the woman he met at her farewell party two weeks ago. The Swedish girl. She didn't say she loved him but there definitely was something between them and he can't get her out of his mind. And then there is **Uncertain,** who responded to a personals ad *(Seek sex buddy. No grief artists, drama queens, memoir writers, Dylan fans, or people in recovery. I am a fattycakes & two-fisted drinker & UB2. Acne a plus.)* and met a large lonely man who came into her life like a bad case of psoriasis. He wants to borrow money so he can go back to technical college. Should she lend it to him? Surely not, but I am in no position to scorn her, or **Frustrated** either. I have my own flaws.

1. Arrogance. Glorying in the dopiness of others. Taking a piggy pleasure in hearing nice things said about me no matter how fatuous.
2. Restlessness. The reckless urge to abandon ship and move on and thus stay a step ahead of defeat.
3. An ungrateful heart. The expectation of gifts.
4. Alcohol. Too much of it. The inevitable stupidity. (I have cut out No. 4 for now and that leaves three to deal with. Sorry. Forgot No. 5. Dishonesty.)

I go to fetch the *Times* from the front step and there is fresh snow, so I grab a broom and sweep the steps and the front walk. I like January. Christmas is put away and the cold air wakes a man up and kills off delusions of grandeur. I am sober this morning. It has been two and a half years.

Dark figures stumble through the dark toward the bus stop on West 7th, an old man in a beat-up denim jacket. **Dear Mr. Blue, I want to quit my custodial job and move to Florida but Mother needs me here. She is 95 and I am 72. What to do? I am freezing to death.** And a young couple not holding hands, her shivering violently in a cheap leather jacket, hands in her pockets, him solemn-faced, sleepy, earrings, head shaved. I'm guessing they live together and she is angry about the three years she's invested in him. **Dear Mr. Blue, My girlfriend is mad because I'm not all that thrilled about the idea of us buying a house. I like things the way they are. She keeps saying, "What if I get pregnant?" As if this were an option. I'm 28 and don't know what I want to do except buy a new guitar and write more songs. Why the sudden rush to buy a house? And silverware**

**patterns? I don't get it. Confused.** Hey, it's only life, son. It can crowd in on a guy fast. Don't buy the house if you don't want to. Pray for clarification. I say a prayer for you now as you walk past me. Pray for me in return.

~~~~

This morning, as I have for two and a half years, I stepped out of the shower and felt lucky. Stepped on the scale. 195. Brushed my teeth and toweled my thatch of thin hair and anointed myself with Tango deodorant and put on jeans and black T-shirt and asked God to forget my transgressions and give me a cheerful and attentive heart and headed for the kitchen to make coffee.

Let us speak about the importance of separate bathrooms. The wise old couple cherish their individual rights and one is the right not to be crowded. I am a man who awakens in a convivial mood, apt to shuffle off to Buffalo and sing about the red, red robin who comes bob-bob-bobbin' along. Her Ladyship does not. She rises as if from open-heart surgery. She should not be jostled or spoken to until she gathers her faculties. This requires the *Times* and a cup of strong coffee. She sits in her bath, eyes closed, tendrils of brown hair trailing into the water, freckled arms folded over dappled breasts, organizing the world—the Holy Trinity, the Four Points of the Compass, the Seven Cardinal Virtues, the schools of the Western Collegiate Hockey Association, the avenues of Minneapolis, *Aldrich, Bryant, Colfax, Dupont, Emerson, Fremont, Girard.* When I tiptoe in, she reaches up for the paper and the cup of coffee and says, "Thank you. Good morning, " and I am dismissed.

I am loathe to write about her, our life, my sins. I dislike revealing what must be revealed here. I love secrecy. I would love to live invisibly with Iris and let the dust settle on us until we are hauled off to the glue factory.

Communication is an injurious thing in marriage. A person

should never ever discuss the marriage if it can be avoided. Sometimes in a weak moment you blurt out something—"You never understood me!" for example—and it becomes your albatross. "What did you mean when you said she has never understood you," says the therapist, who hopes you will say more and throw some more sand in the pistons, all the more work for him at $150 an hour. Don't answer the question. Keep all dark thoughts to yourself. Be cheerful. Tell the therapist to peddle his papers somewhere else. You can deal with your own problems by the time-tried method of shutting up and letting them pass.

One thing that kept our marriage together was a mutual distaste for Republicans. Nixon fuming about the Jews and Reagan weaving his little MGM fables and the Ivy rednecks George I and George II and their servitude to the obscenely rich. Without this gallery of rogues, we might've been history a long time ago.

It also helps that I'm not drunk.

I don't want to but I will tell the truth to the best of my ability as a step toward sobriety. I sincerely apologize if this offends you, dear reader.

# 1 &#x1F41D;   We Met at the U

I met Iris O'Blennis in choir when I was twenty. We were juniors at the University of Minnesota, 1963. She was in social work, I was an English major. Choir met MTW 3–4:30 in the musty basement of Northrop Auditorium. I took my place among the baritones and stood behind a pale shining alto with short brown hair and long neck and that was her. **Dear Mr. Blue, I am too shy to talk to girls.** Sing to them then. Join a choir. Pick out the girl you want and stand behind her and blend your voice with hers, gently, reverently, in tune, as if lifting her by the waist, and this will excite her and also create trust. Animals mate by ear, so do people. People mate in choir all the time in Minnesota. We are a choral state. Our director, Bruno Phillips, was rehearsing us in *The Passion According to St. Matthew,* and I leaned forward and looked down the front of her silk blouse and saw her pale freckled breasts resting in their white hammock and my baritone heart swoll up, as did my baritone pants.

> April is in my mistress's face,
> And July in her heart hath place.
> Within her bosom lies September,
> And that's the one that I remember.

I was thrilled to stand within inches of her and smell her and brush against her bare arms as we swung off together in *"O Mensch, bewein dein' Sünde gross,"* breathing in unison, my voice a buttress and sounding board.

I followed her like a dog. She ran with a crowd of poets and literati who camped in the corner of the Shevlin Hall cafeteria and said airy things about jazz and sex and revolution and I sat studying her and entertaining lustful thoughts, working up the courage to ask her to come with me to a movie—**O Mr. Blue, how do you do that?** You do it by doing it, sir.—and then one day in May, I was witness to a horrible traffic accident (CAR JUMPS CURB, SLAYS FAMILY OF 4) and an hour later I stood dumbly in choir, weeping, as the apostles cried out for the soldiers to let Jesus go—"*Lasst ihn! Haltet! Bindet nicht!*" and I swayed forward and put my right hand on her bare shoulder and she turned and smiled up at me. And afterward asked me what was wrong. And I told her.

It was on the West River Road. I was sitting on the grass, reading *Dubliners*, and a car jumped the curb and mowed down the four picnickers. Bodies strewn like dolls on the grass and the Buick Dynaflow smashed into an elm tree and the driver was wandering around, an old man, confused, needing to "get to Dorothy's" and pleading with the dead to get out of his way. The bodies covered with picnic blankets. The crowd of relentless gawkers. The Elvis lookalike priest giving last rites. Fresh gawkers arriving by the minute. *What happened?* Car went out of control. *Anybody hurt?* No, they're all dead. Four people gone, evaporated like a song.

We lay side by side on the grass in front of Northrop looking up at the white clouds and I told her all about it.

She took my hand and pressed it to her cheek.

"I am glad you're alive," she said. "Life is so precious, we have to savor every moment." And she scootched over and kissed me on the mouth, a sisterly kiss that lasted longer than intended and sort of flared up into something passionate and noble, her tongue searching my mouth, and then she touched my pants and I about passed out for joy.

Odd fish that I am, I didn't speak to her for a couple weeks. I skipped the kaffeeklatsch. Too much to say and no idea how to say it. So I made as if we'd never met. And my disregard paid off.

After the big performance in May of the *Passion*, I emerged from Northrop Auditorium and there she was, waiting, and said, "When are we going to make love?" We headed for her apartment on 8th Street SE above the Rexall drugstore and I followed her up the stairs. Why not? Two magnificent things in one day. The apartment was tidy, spare, a white kitchen table and two chairs, a row of clay pots, a sheaf of dry milkweed in a vase, a pine bookcase, a poster of Uncle Sam pointing his finger (I WANT YOU TO WORK FOR PEACE & JUSTICE), a big bed with a blue chenille cover. She lit a dozen candles on the windowsill and put the Bach cello suites on the record player. I sat on the bed. "The bathroom is down the hall if you need to use it," she said. What would I use it for? I didn't know. Was it my job to get a condom out of the medicine cabinet? I went into the bathroom, rinsed my face, stared at it in the mirror. Tried to look handsomer. No condoms in the cabinet. She lay on the bed. She said, "I honestly believe that people who love Bach are good people." We kissed. She tasted of blackberries. I took off my shoes and socks. She lay my hand against her tremoring breast and I unbuttoned her shirt and she slipped out of her jeans and I took off mine. I kissed the pale slope of her belly with the little indentations from the elastic like the ghostly skyline of an alabaster city. The lush valley below. The birthplace of civilization.

The doorbell rang a nasty ring and she jumped up. "It's the landlord! He said he was going to check the toilet!" So I pulled on my pants and tried to look businesslike, went to the door, and it was a hollow-eyed man who wanted to discuss prophecies in Scripture. His handshake was damp. Perspiration shone on his brow. No easy matter getting rid of him, he was so jazzed on the idea that I stood at the threshold of a great spiritual turning point, and I hemmed and hawed about being busy and then I told him the truth: "I can't talk

to you now, I am about to get laid, sir." He didn't understand *get laid*.
"I am about to fornicate with a young woman." He backed away,
quite mournful but promising to pray for me, and I returned to the
bedroom feeling oddly depleted. The imminence of the Last Judgment and all. Fornication did not seem like a good idea, with those
avenging angels poised to descend, the Antichrist, Armageddon, the
seven-headed beast, the whore of Babylon and so forth. I put a Sina-
tra record on to get me in a secular mood. I thought, Oh boy, what if
I can't—and that was a fatal thought to have right at that point. My
penis shrank to the size of a tassel. It hung down like a defeated flag,
like Florida. It forgot what it was there for. The minutemen lay down
their rifles, the redcoats took Concord and Lexington. Meade turned
tail in the face of Pickett's charge and Gettysburg went gray and
Lincoln fled Washington, disguised as a washerwoman. The U.S.
Marines surrendered Iwo Jima. The Washington Monument melted
like wax. I went to the bathroom and tried some little twirling and
stretching exercises. *Fourscore and seven inches long, our forefa-
thers brought forth on this continent a great rebirth of the penis, for
the penis, by the penis.* Finally, I lay on Iris's bed and turned my face
to the wall. After years of gigantic involuntary erections in high
school hallways whenever a girl came within three feet, now on this
historic occasion when I am naked with a naked woman, God takes
the lead out of my pencil.

"Do you want me to leave?" I said.

"I want you to stay the night."

"What for?"

"To be with me." She nestled her head against my neck. "It's no
big deal," she said.

"You're telling me," I said.

She lay, holding me. She was sweet. A social worker is used to
dealing with silly predicaments. She fixed a frittata for supper and
got out her Scrabble board and let me beat her. We lay curled to-

gether in the dark. "I love your voice," she said. "You put so much feeling into the baritone part."

The candles flickered on the windowsill, my cigarette burned in the tuna-fish can, a still small voice said, "This is where you belong. Don't mess this up."

On the night before the choir took off on our eastern tour, I took her to hear Doc Evans's Dixieland jazz band play in the courtyard of Walker Art Center, Iris in her white summer dress, me in my chinos and sport coat. We sat on the cool grass by a hedge and she glanced at my crotch and said, "There are holes in your pants." Which there were. You could see London and France. "You must've brushed against something with acid on it."

I ignored this and lit a cigarette. It was a perfect summer night in the North, a hot clarinet, a crowd of lovers in the dark, smoking, lying on the grass and on each other, engines revving, stoplights turning green all over town, every song about sex, none about wise career choices, all about kissing and feeling your heart go boom, and meanwhile the summer breeze is blowing through the holes in my pants, which definitely are getting bigger. We head back to her apartment and I take off the pants and we go to bed and make love. So sweet and true. And the next morning, we're on the bus heading for Madison, South Bend, Cleveland, Syracuse, and New York City. I'm sitting next to Iris and she dozes with her head on my shoulder. Everyone can look at us and see: *They're a couple. They sleep together.* Sex written all over us.

We were all pumped up for the tour. This was no rinky-dink thing, *The Bobbsey Twins Sing Bach*, this was a real kick-ass choir. We're serious about this in Minnesota. We do choir as well as anybody in the world. We were brought up for it. Stood in Zion Lutheran with folks who never said boo in real life, and the organ played *"Ein feste burg ist unser Gott"* and my God, a cathedral of sound rose up through the floorboards and out your scalp, the Sacred Harmonic Convergence of the Blessed Are the Meek, and now in a packed hall in Cleveland we sing the *St. Matthew Passion*, and there are tears glittering in the front row, noses are blown, stunned faces, and again in Syracuse—just as Bruno Phillips has told us, "We are going to sing so that they will remember this for the rest of their lives. There is no other reason to do it, folks, none"—and two nights later, at Holy Trinity Lutheran Church on Central Park West in New York City. Oh, my God. Our driver missed the exit on the Thruway and wound up on the New Jersey Turnpike and then it took two hours to turn around and come through the Lincoln Tunnel and into Manhattan, Bruno Phillips sitting tall and composed behind the driver, and in the anxiety of arriving late, we forgot to be nervous about our New York debut, we just hustled off the bus and peed and combed our hair, and filed onto the stage twenty minutes late and the audience gave us a standing ovation. There were standees in back, people sitting in the aisles. We sang the best *St. Matthew* of our lives and those New Yorkers wept openly—old Broadway actresses, crooked financiers, admen, Jewish socialists, atheists, fingers stained yellow from tobacco, breath redolent of gin and vermouth—they were transformed into angels by J. S. Bach's faith in Christ's sacrifice and they rose to their feet and drenched us in applause and shouts and we stood and soaked in it. People shouting "Thank you" and "God bless you." (A Minneapolis audience would've turned and walked out and gotten in their cars and driven home and turned on the news, but never mind.) So we sang "Children of the Heavenly Father" for an encore. And then the "Hallelujah Amen." The applause wore us out. We walked off in a daze and Iris and I wandered into Central Park in the dark, into the Sheep Meadow and stood holding hands and I asked her to marry me. "Tonight?" she said. No, I said, when we get home. "Sounds good to me," she said.

> Let us not to the marriage of people who know what they want
> Admit impediments. Love doesn't vary
> Like you might change your hair style from pixie to bouffant
> Or throw away your swimsuit in January.
> Oh no, it is an ever fixéd mark
> That looks on tempests and is never shaken.
> It laughs at death and gooses statues in the park
> And loves a cheeseburger with extra bacon.
> Love's not time's fool though rosy lips and cheeks
> Get all wrinkly and veiny and saggy and gnarly.
> Love alters not with its brief hours and weeks
> So don't give up on it, Charley.
> If this be a big mistake and we wind up hissing and snarling
> There is nobody I'd rather be wrong with than you, my darling.

I knew so little about her. She was a good person, a good alto. A true-blue feminist and Democrat out to save the world like her heroes Dorothea Dix and Jane Addams and Elizabeth Cady Stanton and also a Golden Gophers hockey fan who leaped to her feet when the team scored and whooped and yelled and sang "Minnesota, Hats Off to Thee" and shouted out the *Rah rah rah for Ski-u-Mah*. Her father was a Lutheran minister from Wisconsin, so she knew the power of principled blockheads to drive you nuts, and her maternal grandfather led the plumbers out on strike in 1915 crying, "If they won't pay a living wage, let them shit in the streets!" so she also knew the power of united action to bring about change. She got her degree in social work and was hired by Lutheran Social Services as a caseworker and discovered her calling in life, which was to rescue old people from the ravages of longevity. She became the Susan B. Anthony of demented geezerdom. She was a great woman. She went out one day to track down somebody's lost grandpa, and found him living in filth in a plywood shack near the Dayton's Bluff freight yard. He'd been a mover and shaker in the Republican party, a federal judge for twenty-five years, a patron of the arts, a man who once dined with Ike at the White House, and now he was filthy and out of his mind, and she roped him in and brought him to the hospital and made sure that his needs were attended to and that the newspapers wouldn't find out, and took the afternoon off and married me, at the courthouse in Hudson, Wisconsin, August 4, 1966, with a bouquet of dandelions in her hand. No fancy wedding for her because the expense was ridiculous and what did we need it for? Dandelions are fine.

We called our parents from a coffee shop and gave them the big news. My father said, "What did you go and do that for?" He was miffed, but then he always is. My mother said, "I hope you'll be happy" in a tone of voice that said, *Six months. A year at most.* They were on their way to play in the 3M Parade of Plaid golf tournament. My parents live in their own little world. May to October at Dellwood, winters in Palm Beach. They golf eighteen holes three or four times a week and attend a cocktail party every single night and in their pink lady and martini haze are honestly not aware that some people do not have two homes. We don't talk except when absolutely necessary and we haven't come to that point yet.

We attended Iris's dad's church in Hopkins that Sunday and he introduced us from the pulpit and people clapped and he had us come up front for a special blessing and then he preached on fruitfulness. It was a twenty-five-minute sermon and all through it I thought about how nice it would be to get back into Iris's pants. The Rev. and Mrs. O'Blennis took us to dinner at the Tremont and the Rev was still revved up about fruitfulness; he asked Iris if she had a bun in the oven. She said no. "What do you do, if I may ask?" he said to me. "I am a writer, sir," I said. "I'm working on a novel." For all the work I had done on that novel, I might as well have said, "I am working on a cure for the common cold," but he seemed satisfied with my being a novelist and keeping busy novelizing. They were sweet old birds. He said to the Missus, "Well, it's a big occasion, our little girl going off and getting married," and he ordered a bottle of red wine and they got slightly potted and then he had a big glass of tawny port and I thought he might burst into song. "When can you two come up to the cabin?" he cried. The Missus fussed over the fact that Iris was keeping her last name, which was customary among young progressive women in those days. Her mother worried, "How does Larry feel about that? What's wrong with Wyler?" Larry felt fine about that and everything else. Had no dough and no great prospects, but I had the girl, and that was good enough for me.

## 2 🌿 Salad Days

We lived in a string of one-bedroom apartments in southeast Minneapolis, and I washed dishes, worked in a mailroom, tended kids at a day camp, and at night I stayed up late, writing short stories with characters who talked like my sweet Iris—who said, "Ya, shur," and "What kinda deal is that?" "Well, all right then." *Anyhoo. Sounds good.* I worked at nothing jobs by day and spent the evenings at my Selectric. She and I made love more or less constantly but nobody in my stories ever did, they mostly sulked. Sometimes they got in a car and drove around. I tried out pen names: *Lawrence Wyler, Carson Wyler, Wyler Lawrence.* And then (unconsciously) signed my real name, Larry Wyler, to one that *The Carleton Miscellany* bought and there I was. It took me five years to get three stories published in little literary magazines with no readers. I sat *rap-tap-tapping* until 3 or 4 A.M. and smoking many many Pall Mall cigarettes and praying, *O dear God, please give me a success. Don't make me live my life as a nobody. I am terrified of monotony. Let me be a somebody. That's all I'm asking. That's it. Make me the Turgenev of the Tundra, the Prairie Proust, the Poor Man's Maupassant. Don't let me die a schnook.* I woke every morning in a prayerful state and Iris went off to help old people in pee-stained pants who were pushing their shopping carts around, combing the Dumpsters for collectibles. She was their champion. She was a bulldog on the phone. She was good at harassment. She stood up to the big cheeses in the blue suits. She fought for the underdog. After someone had been in a fight with Iris, he wasn't anxious to go again. The mayor, for one. He was a slippery little sucker with a big pickerel smile and a quick hand and he'd grab your elbow and massage your back and murmur endearments in your ear even as he was planning how to dispose of your body. A one-time antiwar radical who became a liberal Democrat and then a Republican. He slid across the floor playing his squeezebox and loved anybody within ten feet of him and was in complete agreement with the last five things anybody told him and he kept his promises for up to one half-hour. He was a Smile on Wheels and 100 percent Content Free. When he slipped his hand around Iris and told her how much he admired her and her work in the community— work he had tried to sabotage in every way he could—she said, "Norm, if you don't quit doinking around, I am going to cut you a new asshole." His smile faded. He turned away and he found somebody else to love for fifteen seconds.

~~~~

You don't talk like that in Minnesota. But she did. And then she came home and fixed tuna hotdish or her famous Not So Bad Beans with ground beef and ketchup and onions and Worcestershire and was her own sweet self. She kept in touch with her old pals from the U, Bob and Sandy and Katherine and Frank. She took up the recorder and played in the Macalester Groveland Early Music Consort. She read Doris Lessing. We subscribed to *Whole Earth* and attended Pete Seeger concerts and joined Common Cause and believed in people of all races and religions working together to make a decent world. We believed that, deep down, people really are good. Or she did. And I believed in her.

She was big on birthdays and anniversaries. She told me once, "I would forgive you if you decided to be a Republican but I couldn't if you forgot my birthday. So don't." So every March 8, we celebrated with supper at Vescio's and a U of M hockey game and I wrote her a poem. *Happy birthday, dear Iris. I would write it on stone or papyrus. My heart is on fire since I met you in choir, and it's either romance or a virus.*

~~~~

Every July we made the pilgrimage to her parents' cottage on Cross Lake north of Brainerd, a family shrine crammed with historic furniture. The authentic original linoleum floor that Grandpa Guntzel laid in 1924. The novels of Booth Tarkington and Cornelia Otis Skinner and Ernestine Gilbreth Carey. Antique dinnerware and a broad assortment of forks and spoons. Embroidered dish towels that deserved to be in the National Museum of Washing & Drying. Iris's craft projects from grade school. We sunned on the sandbar and fished for bluegills and sunnies and fried them up in cornmeal and drank gin and tonic, which the Rev referred to as "a beverage," and we put vodka in his, instead of gin. He couldn't bear arguments. Politics was not for the dinner table. He and the Missus took a long walk after supper—"so you young people can be to yourselves"—and that was so we could have sex. There was a stuffed lynx named Walter which, whenever somebody farted, they looked at and said, "Cut that out." And a jar you put a quarter in for every cuss word and at the end of summer, the 75 cents (or a dollar) went toward ice cream cones at the superette. Iris liked to stand in the open door just before the place was locked up on Labor Day and say, "Any vandal who breaks in here, goddamn the goddamn son-of-a-bitch to fucking hell, the ice cream's on me."

Every August 4, we observed our wedding anniversary with a canoe trip on the St. Croix. My frugal wife fixed an elaborate picnic lunch of fresh guacamole and cold roast sirloin, rare, on kaiser rolls, an Oregon Pinot Noir, chocolate ice cream. We lunched on an island upstream from Stillwater, got a nice buzz, napped in the shade, and paddled on to Hudson, our destiny, site of our marriage. Every August, this was a sacred day.

On the last Saturday in August we put on our shorts and Gopher T-shirts and went to the Minnesota State Fair for the ritual trek through the Swine, Cattle, Horse and Sheep Barns, the Chicken Pavilion, to the Tilt-a-Whirl, Big Jiggle, the Giant Slide, the John Deere exhibit, blue-ribbon preserves and cakes in the Home Activities Building, the fine art show, and we bought four corn dogs with mustard and a bag of miniature doughnuts, which we ate on the double Ferris wheel, and then went home, satisfied, foot-sore, smelling of grease.

And on September 7, we celebrated my birthday by staying in bed all morning. We had our coffee in bed and read the paper and talked and nuzzled and dozed and necked and at 11:30 we made love and at noon we got up. Larry Day. A grand occasion.

~~~~

A fact: I was born on September 7, 1942, exactly nine months after the Japanese bombed Pearl Harbor, which shows you that people do react to international crises in different ways. Some folks sit and fret about the future and others go upstairs and create the future and we are the product of their optimism.

And in a burst of optimism, Iris and I put a down payment on a house on Sturgis Avenue with money I got from—O miracle of miracles!—*The New Yorker* for a story, "Nearby Person Pleases Parents," which Roger Angell wrote me a letter about on creamy stationery saying, "We would like to publish it as soon as possible with only a few nit-pick changes. It is fresh and funny and stylish in every way and we feel fortunate to have it and hope you will write more—much more—for us in the future." And I sat down with tears in my eyes and thought, Well, thank you, God, now my life is not utterly wasted. If I should die when I'm thirty of stab wounds in a fracas in a county jail while I'm doing ninety days for public urination, nevertheless the obituary will say that I wrote for *The New Yorker.* I won't be just another vagrant who blew through town; my name will be associated with Literary Quality.

〰〰〰

I had loved *The New Yorker* since I was 13 and rode my Schwinn bike to the Minneapolis Public Library and perched on a high stool in the periodicals room and pored over old issues. Some boys hurl rolls of toilet paper into trees and recite the limerick about the curate from Buckingham, and other boys find pleasure in reading snappy fiction.

A. J. Liebling I loved with a childlike love—"The Wayward Press," *The Sweet Science,* his stuff about France—the man was a natural. I adored all of them, Cheever, Thurber, Calisher, Salinger, McNulty, White, Mitchell, Perelman, all of them Greek gods to me. And the minor deities: Audax Minor, Winthrop Sergeant, Whitney Balliett, Edith Oliver, Andy Logan. The very type font was sacred. I submitted my first story when I was at the U. They rejected it, but so gracefully ("Your story, 'MOBY WHO?' came very close indeed but in the end seemed to us to lack the sureness and inevitability that we feel certain you're capable of and though there was much to admire in it, there was also a faint sense of strain to the writing. Probably we are all wrong about this, and please do not let this disappointment slow you up for an instant. We look forward to having you in our pages.") that I kept trying and trying and then one night—sheer blind luck—I took an antihistamine and two aspirin and some zinc tablets and four hundred milligrams of vitamin E and for about forty minutes everything I wrote was easy and powerful. I got in a groove and every sentence fit and was balanced and yet pushed the next sentence and a sort of force field ran through it. It was 1,500 words long: a kid who learns to make $50 bills on a hectograph and is able to pay a band to march past the house every Monday playing "Rampart Street Parade."

I told Iris and she said, "Whoop-de-doo. Yippee for you."

"This is a big deal," I said. I tried to get her to go to Murray's Restaurant and celebrate with the Silver Butterknife Steak for Two, but she said, "Why throw the money away when we need to buy a house?"

"Why be tightwads? Let's be happy."

"Nothing wrong with a little common sense," she said.

Dear Mr. Blue,
I've been dating a wonderful woman and last night I invited her up to my apartment and opened a bottle of wine and we were sitting on the sofa which is also a fold-out bed and she asked me if I minded if she said a prayer. I said, "No, not if that's what you want, Evelyn." She prayed for God to show us the path He was planning for us and to teach us to honor each other and she prayed to be fruitful and bring forth a large family and teach them to love the Lord. Amen. I said, "But we aren't even married, Evelyn." And she said, "As soon as my papa knows I'm pregnant, he'll take care of that." Then I noticed her black bonnet. I honestly never realized until then that she is Amish. Anyway, I felt that even if God's plan is for me to be the daddy of twelve, it's not my plan, so I put away the bottle of Kama Sutra scented oil and I drank the wine myself and today I am feeling rotten. I really want to make love with her. How can I introduce her to contraceptives?

—Secular Humanist

Dear Secular, You two aren't singing from the same hymnal. Tell her good-bye. And thank goodness you discovered her Amishness now and not after several years of marriage, as happens more often than one might think. You turn to your loyal, meek, industrious wife, and say, "How about we go tie on the feed bag in some swell eatery, Snuggums?" and she says, "Thee shouldst spend thy increase on a domicile, Ezekiel, not on licentious living." And suddenly you're living in the 18th century, dealing with smallpox and ague and dropsy, horrible roads, the fear of witch trials, and your life expectancy drops to about 38. And you're 36 at the time.

~~~~

The check for $3,000 arrived and I took it to the Farmers & Mechanics Bank, and the teller looked at the name *The New Yorker*, and looked up at me, and asked for three forms of identification. "I'm sorry," she said. "You don't look like a writer."

The house we bought was stucco, three bedrooms, screened porch, garage, rock garden, dry basement, two blocks from West 7th Street, in a rundown neighborhood of bungalows and old frame houses, a few duplexes, with ratty yards, some wrecked cars up on blocks, dogs running free, and up above us, like El Dorado, the ridge where the fancy lived, the Summit Avenue swells. "Someday," I said, "we'll make it up the hill." "What's wrong with this?" she said.

When the alarm went off at 6 A.M., I arose from bed and went to work in the back bedroom, my studio, at a Selectric typewriter with Webster's *Second Unabridged* and *The Desktop Thesaurus of Ideas* and *Chapman's 77 Basic Plots* and I turned out publishable stuff. Iris walked to her job at Lutheran Social Services and then, she and her do-gooder friends started up a nonprofit called Minnesota Advocates for Moral Action, which specialized in programs for crazy old people and drug addict moms, with St. Iris at the helm.

~~~~

We celebrated with a garden party. Jug wine and burgers on the grill and ice cream. Our pal from the U (her pal more than mine) Frank

Frisbie, who we hadn't seen in years, came and he said, "I hear you're writing for *The New Yorker*."

"Oh, now and then," I said, as if it were something I did when I had a spare moment.

"I used to read that magazine," he said, "and then—I don't know—"

I used to think you were an ordinary decent person, I thought, and now I see you're a shit.

"I've been busy writing a book," he said. "I should send you a copy." He let those words hang in the air for a long minute, during which I did not say, "You? Write a book? You couldn't write enough to fill a book of matches!"

"Who's publishing it?" I said, expecting to hear The Wisteria Press or Gerbil Books or The Fund for the Verbally Handicapped.

"Random House," he said.

He said this the way you'd say, "Four-fifteen," if someone asked you what time it is.

I hadn't seen the guy in years. I wanted to choke him. I wanted to give him a swift kick where the sun don't shine. "That's great," I said. I wanted him to die a natural death but someplace where I could watch. "When?" I said. "In the fall," he said. "Terrific." He sent me a copy, of course. Signed, "To Larry, my friend and comrade."

I wanted him to choke on a bratwurst and fall down and hit his head so that he'd be in a wheelchair, steering it with a pencil between his teeth, and I could do a benefit for him, to raise money to pay for his colostomy, and he'd come up on stage to thank me, and sort of gurgle deep in his throat, and we'd be photographed together for the newspaper.

## FAMOUS WRITER HELPS OUT CRIPPLED PAL

Nationally recognized author Larry Wyler, whose work appears regularly in the legendary *New Yorker* magazine, is a guy whose success hasn't gone to his head. The two thousand St. Paulites who packed O'Shaughnessy last night to hear Wyler's unique blend of breathtaking story-telling and gut-wrenching hilarity can testify to that. The performance raised more than $100,000 to pay for an operation for Frank Frisbie, 29, of Summit Hill Care Center, who needs a new rectum. Frisbie, who suffered brain spasms in a bratwurst-related incident and lost his power of speech, as well of control of his colon, beamed in rapture from a front-row seat as Wyler held the crowd spellbound. Often compared to such *New Yorker* notables as James Thurber and S. J. Perelman, Wyler got a standing ovation from the audience when he announced that he is working on a book.

Frank is a pleasant guy, basically a suck-up and a loser but not evil or anything, just one more dust bunny under the bed of life, and here he had gone and written a novel. This was a shock. Like seeing Ray Charles sink nine out of ten free throws.

*Fair Henry.* A novel of 135 pages about an amnesiac deaf-mute who is beaten by drunken cowboys in a Wyoming tank town and befriended by Basques and hired to herd sheep, which he does over a winter and then the rancher's black-haired daughter falls in love with him and he with her, but he knows he would only ruin her life, so he rides away one night and never returns and is assumed to have drowned himself in the river.

That was it. End of story.

Two months later, the rave reviews started coming. "Look at this," Iris said and waved the newspaper at me—"has a lyrical luminosity that takes the breath away," she read. Frank was interviewed in *The Pioneer Press* about the importance of storytelling in building a sense of community. They compared him to Wallace Stegner. *Wallace Stegner! You mean Wally Ballou!*

This slack-jawed opportunist had parlayed his taste for pretentious crapola into a raging success—his little steaming turd of a book won the Mary L. Quimby Award of $50,000, a major pile of lettuce. It went into a third and a fourth printing. Frank bought a house on Summit Avenue. I could see his carriage house from our backyard. He was pictured in the Sunday rotogravure looking winsome and modest and thoughtful, a pipe clenched in his teeth, seated at an antique desk, pretending to write on a pad of paper, a shelf of leatherbound tomes behind him. I wished it would fall and squash the bastard like a June bug. I wanted to throw a dead raccoon in his yard. The thought that a pea brain could write a successful book was, to me, the handwriting on the wall and it said: GET BUSY.

So I set out to write your basic Great Midwestern Novel, an epic tale of sinewy people wrestling with the land, and enduring privation and blizzards. A guy who comes from silent people, as I do—my ancestors were fishermen who spoke rarely so as not to alarm the walleyes—is not going to write social comedy. I have no ear for dialogue.

"So how's it going then?" they would say.

"Oh, not so bad, I guess. How's it with you then?" they would reply.

I went at the GMN and accumulated a pile of yellow paper containing thousands of words about the Petersons, a heroic family descended from ship captains, their odyssey to Minnesota, their struggles and privations.

"We'll keep going," said Olaf. He did not look at Solveig. He could not bear to see the emptiness in her large blue eyes. "Why?" she said softly. She touched his arm as if to restrain him from walking out the door and through the howling blizzard to the barn where the horses stood, waiting to pull the sleigh to Fargo to meet the train bringing the union organizer from Minneapolis. "Because it is who we are," he said. "Can't you see? You and I can never realize our dreams without a strong Farmer Labor Party. If I die, you lose your Olaf, but if the party dies, then we lose each other, all of us."

Sometimes late at night I walked out the back door and looked at the flashing **1** and thought, "O, St. Paul, Maker of Scotch Tape, Mail Handler, Insurance Underwriter, Player with the Nation's Commercial Cleaning Compounds, City of the Swollen Ankles, let this boy write a novel that earns millions of dollars and is made into a movie and I'll never ask another favor as long as I live, I promise you.

I told my old classmate Katherine that I prayed to the First National Bank and she wrote a poem:

The man
In his
Garden
Worships the
One
In the
Sky
Of the Bank
Of Our First
Nation.

She was one of the literati of our university crowd, a little wisp of a thing, like Laura in *The Glass Menagerie*, her mouth in a perpetual 0. She stood up at Frank's thirty-fifth birthday party and everyone hushed and she recited in her tiny breathless voice

Isometric circus
Of the mailbox.
My
Friend
Is 35.
Audacious Apennines!
We rise to
An Acropolis
of sensuous
Forces.
Two eggs,
Refractory embryos
Of the
Future.

And then everyone was obliged to clap.

I thought: God, if I have to be a nobody in St. Paul, at least let me be smarter than Katherine.

The party was at the University Club, around the pool. A big band, waiters with traps of champagne, a sit-down dinner for fifty, fricasseed squab and lobster, very fancy. The big hot dog.

"I hear you had a story in *The New Yorker*, Larry," she said to me, not admitting to having read the thing, just that she'd heard about it, but she trembled as she said it: to Minnesota writers, getting published in *The New Yorker* was like dating Natalie Wood. It definitely set you apart.

"Frank is working on another novel," Iris said. "Good for him," I said. "He has such a gift," said Katherine. "There's something almost mythic about it."

One night I sat bolt upright, jolted awake. A premonition. The house was still. The light on the cathedral dome was not burning.

Why? Why dark? A car door closed. Voices. A woman and a man. Iris slept, curled like a cat, snoring gently, her headphones beside her on the pillow, a tinny metallic voice talking about the death of God. I picked it up. The BBC World Service. A shortage of cod. Off Newfoundland. Speculation by codologists about sun spots, radio waves.

I went to the window. A cop car cruised by. Next door, Mr. Ziegler sat at his kitchen table, a glass of whiskey in his hairy fist. He was one of those men who should never ever go around without a shirt, and there he sat, doughy, big-breasted, weeping. According to Iris, who visited him from time to time, he had retired from Woolworth and now whiled away his hours clipping newspaper articles, marching in Civil War reenactments, and caring for his dog, Susie, crippled by a stroke. His wife had left him, for fairly obvious reasons. Hopelessness, for one. People were afoot in other houses on the block, moving around in kitchens, thinking their 3 A.M. thoughts. Do I smell gas? Is there really a Trinity or are there trillions of them? Is my marriage an empty shell, obvious to everyone but me? And am I on the verge of a nervous collapse and don't know it? Could I suddenly go berserk later today and whack off my ear with a butcher knife? Is there someone just like me in Australia thinking the exact same thoughts, and if so, what time is it there?

All the 3 A.M. regrets, for the stupid things you said, for not calling up your mother, for not giving money to cerebral palsy.

And a clear thought that *something terrible is happening.*

In the morning, the big orange school bus swung up the street past the blossoming crab apples and the mommies stood on the porches and waved good-bye to the kiddos. And then the phone rang. It was Frank Frisbie. Our friend Corinne had killed herself in Seneca Falls, New York. A cheerful, hardworking, witty, loyal woman, a college teacher, an inspiration to students, and yet late the night before she had paddled a canoe out onto Cayuga lake with her jacket pockets full of rocks and tipped the canoe and sank into the cold water, fists clenched, and vanished from this world, leaving behind a crazy and tearful diary of her last thoughts, so desperate and dark, so unlike the person we knew.

Frank could hardly get the words out, he was so distraught.

We knew her at the university, the star of our little gang of writers, the host of every party, the girl every boy wanted to make laugh, and now she was cold and dead on a marble slab, those fluttering fingers, that pearly smile, that girlish voice.

"I can't believe she would do it," said Frank.

~~~~

The day of Corinne's funeral, Iris decided we should have a baby. She announced this as we left the cemetery, having laid a good woman in the ground. It was the right thing to do, to restore our losses. Death and rebirth. We could name the child Corinne. Or not. Either way, it would be Corinne's spirit among us.

"If we have a baby, I want to start going to church again," she said.

So Iris and I went to work making love on days when her temperature chart indicated ovulation. She read the thermometer hourly and if she seemed to be eggy, she came home on her lunch hour for a Command Performance. Load, aim, and shoot. Every night she peed in a cup and dipped the blue paper tab to see if it turned pink. Months passed. No luck. We refused to contemplate parenthood for fear of jinxing it. No baby things, no books. Just week after week of indentured copulation passed and finally, after four months with no baby in the chute, she asked, "Are you sure you want to do this? Have a baby, I mean."

"Of course," I said.

What else could I say? Having a kid is up to the woman. Any dope knows that.

"We're both so busy all the time," she said. "I don't have time to have a kid."

That sentence hung in the air for a minute.

"But if I don't, I may regret it someday. You know?"

So we enrolled at Dr. Wuefer's fertility clinic in Minneapolis.

Iris was planning two babies, Hilmer and Corinne. Sometimes Hilmer was named Charles, sometimes Frederick. Sometimes there was a farm in the scenario: a log cabin in the woods with a garden of corn and squash and tomatoes, a golden retriever named Fritz, a horse whinnying in the paddock on clear fall mornings, an enormous woodpile, stacked beside the dirt road.

We trotted off to the fertility clinic thinking life-affirming thoughts, and the nurse Brianna told us about the ovaries and sent us home with powerful drugs to stimulate egg production. Every day for a month, I jabbed a hypodermic in Iris's haunch and shot her up with chemicals, and then came the fertilization part. We went to the clinic for Iris to be seeded. I sat in the waiting room with ten other men conversing about the weather, the Twins, as I thought: I hope my sperm is clearly labeled, I do not want to raise the child of this moron next to me poring over the sports page. A challenge to a man's sense of dignity to sit next to a guy who knows that you—and you know that he—will soon be spilling his seed in a cold office with a copy of *Playboy* open to the "Women of the Big Ten" pictorial in the other hand, attempting to beget offspring.

Brianna was smart and quite stunning in her jeans and big cable-knit sweaters and running shoes and her voice was pure Minnesota, the elongated *o* in *So how are we doing today?* as she led me down the long hall to the jerk-off suite. She turned on a desk lamp and pulled the blinds and set the cup on the desk. "So you know what to do," she said. "Wash your hands and leave your deposit in the plastic cup and bring it to me at the desk. And there are magazines in the lower shelf if you need them. Okay? See you in a minute." And smiled and left, closing the door behind her with a *click*, and I un-zipped my pants and removed my tiny member and glanced at the magazines with their generic plastic blondes, and I tried to focus on Iris, and then I imagined Brianna whispering, "Oh my gosh, Mr. Wyler. Are you sure we should be doing this? What if your wife should come in? Oh God. Oh God. Oh my God." And then it was 1-2-3, go-team-go, and the Gopher winger sailed over the blue line, faked left and sent the goalie sprawling, and shot into the open net, *Goal! The crowd on its feet. Rah rah rah for Ski-u-mah. V-I-C-T-O-R-Y,* and I zipped up and frowned at myself in the mirror and got the idiot glaze off my face and strolled up the hall and handed Brianna my deposit and she said, "Good," and she took it into the next room to impregnate my wife. Driving home in the car we discussed whether she should go home and lie down or go to that meeting about the drop-in center for chemically dependent single moms, and of course she went to the meeting. People depended on her. "It's no big deal," she said. "If it happens, it happens." And then her friend Sandy got pregnant and entered the twilight world of daily nausea, bone-aching exhaustion, raw emotions, and weird urges, most of them unmaternal. Sandy was a woman who shared the smallest de-tails of her life with others. She just had a childlike faith that she was an interesting person. She told Iris about every episode of retching into the toilet, every thought of infanticide, every urge to eat raw oysters and inhale bus exhaust. For Iris, this took away some of the wonder of creating new life.

"I wish Sandy would tell more to Bob and less to me," she said. "He's the one who did it to her, after all."

~~~~

It was dumb for me to get involved with Brianna.

Oh my gosh. Tell me about it.

Take *that* to a therapist and put it in his pipe and let him smoke it.

Having an affair with the nurse from the fertility clinic who squirted my sperm into my wife's vagina.

I could say in my defense that I was doggedly pursuing a novel about political organizing among Norwegian farmers in the thirties that was hopeless tripe and this makes a man desperate. And jerking off in a doctor's office was truly weird and a sane man craves honest passion. And Iris could go for a month or two without sex. She seemed content in the service of the Lord, rescuing elderly wackos and druggy moms. So there I was with my thoughts of Brianna inspiring my specimen collection, and one day I handed her the cup and she said, "Great job."

Huh?

She said, "This is twice what you usually get. I'm impressed." She grinned. "Whose picture were you looking at?"

So there was some provocation on her part.

I said, "I was thinking about you, dear." Which was the literal truth.

"Oh, go on. Get out of here. You big liar." And she blushed. And there was so much in that blush, and the way she headed toward the basting room and turned and looked back at me and shook her head. *Men.* I stood smiling like an idiot. "You're a one-man sperm bank is what you are." And then she held up my specimen cup to the light and inspected it and said, "And they're strong swimmers, too. You've got enough for fifty ladies in here." Don't tell me that wasn't provocative behavior on her part.

And it was pure blind fate that I ran into her at the U of M choir concert at Northrop. I'd told Brianna that I met Iris in choir and perhaps I had mentioned the concert to her, but to run into her there in a crowd of four thousand people—I'd gone alone, Iris was at a meeting—and they did the Fauré *Requiem* with the melting *Sanctus* and *Pie Jesu* and the *Agnus Dei* that tears your heart out, the rousing finish and afterward, standing alone, stunned, near tears in the lobby, the beautiful Brianna, dabbing at her eyes, looking as if her life had been changed forever. She said, "I don't know where to go or what to do."

"Come with me," I said.

She said she had never felt this way before. She couldn't explain it. She just needed to be with another human being right now. People were scurrying past us toward the parking ramp, and I said, "Be with me."

"What does this mean?" she said.

"We'll find out together."

"I don't want to hurt anyone."

"Neither do I. So we won't."

And we walked to the Gopher Motel and there in room 206 we stripped off our clothes, with Fauré's mighty requiem for the dead in our heads, and we made love like angels, slowly and with great enthusiasm and kindness, and then rested, shared a bag of corn chips, talked about life, her life, my life, life in general, and she said, "It's inspiring being in the business of making people happy." We did it again and kissed good-bye, and I went home, thinking, How could you? But I had. And it was pretty miraculous.

~ ~ ~

**Dear Mr. Blue:**

I am a former novelist whose stories were published in *The New Yorker* and who taught creative writing at Rutherford for many years and then, in the midst of a mood swing caused by a blood-sugar imbalance, I said to a lovely student of mine, "I wish I could snuggle with you sometime"—my exact words, "snuggle sometime," no urgency, no overt sexual intent, simply a wistful desire for closeness—but the young woman labeled me a "sexual predator" and within 24 hours I was suspended by the dean, who hated my guts because my novel depicted Italians in (he thought) a negative light (he is

Italian) and he became my Kenneth Starr. He devoted himself to prosecuting my case. In his obsessive zeal, he dredged up a romantic fling of ten years ago and maneuvered me into the humiliation of lying before a faculty committee and kept the spotlight on me, and exposed my lies, whereupon my wife, LeAnn, divorced me and took the kids to Minnesota to reunite with her high school sweetheart, who my kids adore because he is a forest ranger and knows the name of every tree and bird and stone. He is their white knight and I am the Bad Daddy. I moved to Minneapolis so I could see them on weekends. No school will hire a sexual predator, so I became a night cashier at a parking ramp at the airport.

The stress of a major life change led me to find a personal relationship to Jesus Christ. I gained inner peace and set all bitterness aside. I no longer feel a need to write fiction. I simply take it to the Lord in prayer and He removes all my burdens that otherwise might have become novels cluttering up the world with useless irony. Through membership in the Joy Joy Joy Church, I met a wonderful Christian woman who guided me in my journey of faith. Her brother is the author of the best-selling Christian novels in the *Last Gathering* series, about a band of southern Baptists who are sent to take over a space ship during Armageddon to fight off Assyrians from another galaxy. It has been on the best-seller lists for the past four years and earned him gazillions and he now owns twenty thousand acres around Roswell, New Mexico, where the second coming is expected to occur in 2002. She and I were discussing marriage but she felt we must await a definite indwelling of the Holy Spirit—"I want to know that this is what God wants for both of us," she said. I felt that our intense loving feelings for each other should be evidence enough. But I was patient. She then decided it wasn't right for us to sit together in church on Sunday morning. That's when I sort of lost it. I said, "Myrna, I want to get between the sheets with you." It just came out of my mouth. I immediately apologized. She walked away and told her brother and he told the congregation and they threw me out of the church. For the second time in my life, I am an outcast. I am 55 and friendless in a world of sin and it's winter and I am depressed and praying for enlightenment, which does not come. My children are afraid of me because LeAnn told them I am liable to shoot them. What have I done wrong?

—Lonely Christian

Dear Lonely, There's a dark and a stormy side of life. There's a bright and a sunny side, too. Though we meet with the darkness and strife, the sunny side we also may view. And here you are on the frozen tundra, hounded by prosecutors, your lunch eaten by others, and you wonder, *Where is the beauty? Where is the grandeur?* You paid dearly for one tiny misstep and this sin brought you to Jesus, who (you thought) introduced you to Myrna, who turns out to be as unforgiving as any other woman. What can I say? There are women like her all over. And, Scripture says, "Whom the Lord loveth, He chasteneth." I happen to be married to a forgiving woman. I committed worse sins than yours but I did them when the prosecutors were at the ballgame. Go talk to a shrink about the depression and see what one of these snazzy new antidepressants can do. New ones are invented every day. The latest ones make you cheery *and* smart. If those don't work, there's always the Trappists. Plenty of work to do, no yakking, no Myrnas or LeAnns. Good Luck. Maybe I'll put you in my novel if I ever get around to writing it.

# 3 ✤ Best-Seller

Brianna was exquisite in a wholesome way. She was sleek and soft and carnally inclined, but she also knew all the Bible stories and knew about farming and fishing and church dinners. She wasn't a heathen. She wrapped herself around me like a C-clamp and though it bothered me that she said "axe" instead of *ask,* and "pitcher" for *picture,* I forgot about that when we made love, which we did three more times, unabashed whole-hearted aerobic Minnesota sex, and then she broke it off because she felt too guilty. "I wouldn't know how to explain this to my mother," she said. "Shacking up with a married man. I adore you and everything but it's not who I am, you know?" We kissed and she got in her car and waved and drove down University Avenue.

I didn't see how I could go back to the clinic after that and shoot into a cup, and I told Iris I needed to take a vacation from fertility, and she said, "Me, too. Let's give it a rest." A few times she mentioned adoption, in a vague way, as you might mention parasailing or hang gliding, not that you were planning to do it next week. And then thoughts of parenthood sort of vanished. Her mother inquired about it once at the cabin over beverages and Iris said, "I have no time to raise a child. And I don't want to hire somebody else to do it for me. The world is full of neglected children and adults suffering from their childhoods and maybe God put me here to try to make up the deficit." And that was that. We never discussed it. The door closed. I got a vasectomy in the spring.

≈≈≈

**Dear Mr. Blue,**
I have written a novel about an affair I had with Michelle, with whom I spent some memorable nights at the Paul Bunyan Motel here in Bemidji (don't print that). Oh my gosh, the fun we had in that Jacuzzi. (I never had any idea what those pulsating jets were for until she showed me.) Anyway, Michelle went back to her husband and I've written this novel (my first) and it's SO GOOD but I'm afraid it might offend my wife, Marilyn, with whom I have three children. What to do?

—**Leery**

Dear Leery, A romp in the hay lingers in your memory like the first line of a song but your true love is the one you make a life with and write more than one line about, you write a whole book. I'm sure that the Paul Bunyan experience was wonderful, your sensations were heightened, your skin tingled, your orifices pulsated, but please change it to the Joe Foss Motel in Yankton and change the description of the young honey to match your wife's. Make sure you get the color of the hair and eyes right. Tonight when your wife is asleep, pry open one eyelid and check the color. Give that color to the heroine. Then you'll be okay.

My Great Midwestern Novel was now called *The Land of Their Children,* and the Farmer-Labor party was gone, replaced by a cult of rune worshippers, but it was dull, dull, dull, nothing a person would actually want to read if you had a choice.

"How's it coming?" Iris asked.

"It's coming."

I kept rewriting the first paragraph:

The land lay quiet in the autumnal dawn, the yellowing sun burning through the ancient haze and throwing long accusing shadows across the miles of fence line rectangles along the silty river of the Rum that meandered through the fertile corn country, greening the groves and hillocks, gullying the pastures under the brooding cottonwoods of the sprawling Peterson farm, the shafts of glittering sunlight piercing the torn window shade in the upstairs bedroom where Svend lay, his blue eyes closed under a bramble of eyebrows, dreaming of mountains of harvested corn, the richly dazzling splendor of it.

And then one bright summer day I threw it in the garbage.

I read a book called *How to Write Your Novel in Thirty Days* and one paragraph jumped up and kicked me in the butt:

> The most visceral and vital writing is about bad people and allows the reader to see that "We Are Them." For reasons having mostly to do with arrogance and stupidity, young writers waste years attempting to impersonate goodness and inner peace. Bad move. What you really want to write about is greed, anger, pillage, thievery, corruption, eye gouging, meanness, shameless groveling, that sort of thing. And lust. Always lust. *He couldn't help himself, once he looked into those dark eyes. He kissed her again and again. They fell to the floor in an embrace. "Oh my God," she said.* Forget about goodness. Kahlil Gibran did that already. The world doesn't need more Bill Moyers. Think dark. Unbutton that shirt. Unzip those pants.

This was one month post-Brianna. It made sense. So I threw out the passages about the beauty of the prairie and the courage of the people yes the people, and I began a book in which four Petersons, Cindy and Stewart and little Carrie and Hugh, head for Duluth in a Chevy and stop near Hinckley to read an historic roadside plaque and a hitchhiker with a suitcase that says "Winnipeg" jumps out and pulls a pistol and shoves into the front seat next to Cindy and tells Stewart, "Drive, you sonofabitch, or the lady gets a slug in the chest and if you don't think I mean it, go ahead and press your luck." He is Canadian but he is rotten to the core. A few miles farther on, he says to Stewart, "You remind me of my daddy, who beat me to a pulp all those years. I could kill you with one blow to your windpipe and shoot the others and dump your bodies in the trunk and drive to a junkyard and put the car through the compactor and buy myself a porterhouse steak with the dough from your wallet and enjoy every bite of it, mister. I've hated your guts since I was eight years old. My daddy's dead, so there's no satisfaction to be had there. But somebody else ought to die for his sins, I say. And fate seems to have selected you. Do you believe in fate? I do. God gave me to my daddy and now God's given you to me. Killing is too good for you." And Stewart pleads with him. *Please please please.* "We're good people. We've never harassed anybody. Why not join the marines and go kill foreign people?" And the hitchhiker says, "I *am* a foreign people." And he laughs his brutal psychopathic laugh. And Cindy begs him to spare the children. And the hitchhiker says, "Ma'am, with all due respect, adulthood is no great prize for anybody and they'd be all messed up if they seen you get killed. They'd prob'ly go on a killing rampage of their own. More merciful to let 'em die innocent and happy." And he stuffs them in the trunk, tied and gagged and doped up, and the car is second in line to be compacted, and a little old deputy sheriff named Jerry Sandoval sees a shirttail poking out from under the trunk lid and sashays over and saves the day. He gets the Petersons out and he chases the hitchhiker in a stolen roadster at high speeds on gravel roads through peaceful farm country and the hitchhiker rolls the car and is thrown clear and runs to a nearby cottage where a family of potters lives and holds them hostage until the dad conks him with an earthenware platter and the criminal is sent straight to prison. "You ain't heard the last of me," he snarls as he climbs into the prison van, thus setting up a sequel.

I called it *Spacious Skies.* I sent it to an agent. Iris was busy raising money for a hotline for chemically dependent transgender people. Something like that. My father was sending me neoconservative books, pounds of them. The IRS was after me for $3,000 in back taxes. My Dodge Dart died. Jehovah's Witnesses kept dropping by to talk about prophecy. Katherine published a tiny collection of prose poems called *The River Whose Name Is God,* and when I sent her a note of congratulations, she sent me a letter complaining of loneliness.

I was lonely, too. Lonely and longing for a little fame. A line in the St. Paul paper gave me exquisite pain:

> Local writer Larry Wyler will read from his work at the St. Anthony Park branch library Tuesday at 3:30 P.M. Admission is free.

*Local writer.*

I clipped it out and taped it to my studio wall. *Local writer.* Not how I envision myself: *the guy who lives up the block and has written some stuff.* Please, dear Lord, do not let me die a local writer. Bury me out on the lone prairie in an unmarked grave rather than in Calvary Cemetery on Front Street under a tombstone that reads:

> Larry Wyler
> 1942–1985
> A guy from
> Around here,
> He did
> About as much
> As he could
> With what
> He had.

I patterned the Petersons after Iris's friends from the U, Bob and Sandy, and I patterned the murderous hitchhiker after their son, Eirdhru. Only six years old at the time, but I could easily imagine him putting people in a metal compactor.

They live in Frogtown so Eirdhru can grow up with people of other races, who Eirdhru is learning to beat up on. Eirdhru is Gaelic for "he who comes in the night with loud singing." Sandy, a good liberal, is dedicated to fighting the good fight against cruelty and ignorance and deep in her heart she knows that her child is both of them. A racist skinhead is exactly who Eirdhru will become—the signs are so clear. Sandy and Bob may someday be the Parents of a Famous Mass Killer and believe me, they think about this often themselves. A reasonable fear, given Eirdhru's temperament. He is rotten to the core, like that Canadian hitchhiker.

Two weeks after I sent the book off, the agent called, breathless, to say, "Guess what?"

"Really?" I said.

"Yes," she said. "I am so happy for you."

Two minutes later, Bob and Sandy walk in and he and I hug a caring male hug (required) and she gives me a sideways look as if I've just been acquitted of child molestation on a technicality, and she says, "Iris says you're working hard on your book."

"All done. Sent it off. And it was just bought by a publisher," I said.

"Oh," she says. "Cool." As if this sort of thing happened regularly in St. Paul, Minnesota.

Bob: "What sort of book is it?"

Me: "A novel."

Sandy: "Well, I hope it's not just about sex."

Me: "It's almost entirely about sex, Sandy. Except for some oak trees and two late model cars, it's entirely about sex. Upstairs, downstairs, in the yard, in the car, under the car."

"Oh, you're just being stupid—" and we go to the kitchen where Iris is throwing supper together.

"They are going to publish my book," I announce to Iris.

"Great," she says. She kisses me. I hold on to her and whisper in her ear, "They're giving me $75,000 for it." She stiffens. Delight or fear—hard to tell which. "I get the check in two weeks."

"That must be tough, writing a book," Bob says. "God. I don't know how you do it. Making up all that stuff."

"I don't make up a thing, Bob," I say. "You're in the book. Hair and all." He gives me a queasy smile. But he's not sure I'm joking. "I've got you in there, except I made you mulatto." He runs this line past a focus group he keeps in his head—Gloria Steinem, Mister Rogers, Al Gore, Maya Angelou—he asks them, "Is this funny?" And they shake their heads. So it's not funny. Sandy doesn't think so, either. Iris is thinking about the $75,000.

Sandy is in a snit over something she heard on the news and moaning about that—some fearful injustice or other, take your pick—as Iris serves up the beans and Bob pops open a beer. We sit down to eat and the conversation drifts along the familiar lines—*I don't know how people can live in the suburbs, I honestly don't, it's so sterile, I visit my sister in Eden Prairie and there's no place to walk, no downtown, no black people—I don't know why people send their kids to private schools, we're losing all sense of community in this town—I don't know what people see in television nowadays, all that violence and ogling of women*—and an alarm sounds in my head: *Old Liberal Talk. Get Away. Get Away. Grave Risk of Contagion.* Sandy's cold disapproving glance lands on me like a horsefly and Bob goes on complaining about the dreariness of mass media and how much more enlightened the Danes are, and I push back my chair and excuse myself. "I'm going for a walk." "Where?" says Iris.

She wants to come with me, but she doesn't know how to rid us of these two wounded woodchucks. "Anywhere. Just need some fresh air." This gets Sandy going on the subject of air quality standards.

∨∨∨

*Spacious Skies* came out in the fall and was immediately a hit. I climbed on that old toboggan of fame and fortune and over the edge I went and the hill went on forever and forever and forever. The world took my little book to its bosom, I was the blue-eyed boy, Mr. Touchdown, fortune's favorite, king of the hill, the blue-light special. Better men who had labored decades to produce novels of real substance were tossed aside like driftwood in favor of Mr. Wonderful— the world loves success and despises failure! If you're one of Iris's demented geezers, you can't get the time of day, but if you're a big winner and have everything you could ever want, America can't do enough for you! People strive to pile more and more crowns on your head.

I flew to Chicago, and Los Angeles, and Houston, and gave readings, and book editors took me to lunch and asked my opinion on publishing matters. My success conferred absolute authority on me—in regard to politics, personal relationships, the brotherhood of man, the search for world peace, I was a voice to be heeded. I stayed in small luxury hotels on quiet side streets, hotels with small brass nameplates and protective doormen. Big bouquets of flowers on the coffee table and bottles of Puligny-Montrachet on ice and Italian sheets on the beds and oil paintings of Paris boulevards and towels as big as sleigh robes on heated towel racks. A green marble bathroom with a basketful of amenities (shampoo and conditioner, but also Q-tips, bath salts, three flavors of mouthwash, aspirin, Vaseline, benzocaine, iodine, oxacillin, digitalis, laxative, and six kinds of soap, milled, castile, pumice, glycerin, liquid, and brown) and every step I took was cushioned, every door opened, every need attended to, the manager on the phone—"Everything okay there, Mr. Wyler?" The editor to say "The book is in its sixth printing." And I hopped in the limo and was whisked away to more interviews, where people fawned over me with a vengeance and I walked through a stage door and onstage and eight hundred people burst out clapping and I smiled and nodded and put my book on the lectern and read to them—read to them from my own writing! Stuff I wrote on Sturgis Avenue in St. Paul! People in Chicago and St. Louis and Dallas liked it, too!—and afterward they pumped my hand and I signed books and a lovely brunette murmured, "You're so much younger than I expected you'd be." The book shot to number 1 on the best-seller list. "That's great," said Iris. I flew home for a day. She was at the new drop-in center for single mothers in recovery.

It was a madhouse. Screeching kids and stoned daddies and the daddies' new girlfriends and the bipolar mommies riding out the backwash of the Thorazine and some of the mommies had bad new boyfriends or girlfriends and a pretty little girl whose name tag said "LaTeisha" was being pushed on a swing by two ladies, one behind, one in front, who chatted with her and ignored each other. The one behind was the daddy's ex-girlfriend in neon pink stretch pants and a V-neck T-shirt in which breasts the size of cantaloupes bounced around, and the one in front, his new squeeze, was skinny as a fence post. And LaTeisha's mommy was lying on the floor, dazed from the methadone. And through the chaos strode my good wife, the goddess Iris of the Streets, Protector of the Fallen, spreading light and succor, giving hugs, blowing noses, tying shoelaces, doing good, nothing but good, in this sinful world that is rewarding her wayward husband so handsomely.

"I'm going to LA," I said.

"Good-bye!" she cried, merrily.

"For three weeks."

"See you in three weeks!"

"Aren't you going to kiss me?" I said.

"I thought you'd never ask!" she said.

I told her that our ship had come in. We would be rich. When I returned in three weeks, I wanted to look for a new home.

"Don't get a big head," she said and turned away to see how LaTeisha's mommy was doing.

# 4 🙞 An American Guy

I came home after LA and the house looked so drab, so small.

Sturgis Avenue seemed junkier, meaner than ever, as if years of hard winters had knocked everything loose. Homes atilt, walks bowed, sidewalks cracked, trees bent, and a depressing clutter and mishmash—as if everyone were too busy managing their alcoholism to ever pick up a shovel or rake—Damn, this is ugly, I thought. Why not run a herd of buffalo through, hold a Black Sabbath concert? I left my suitcase on the porch and hiked up to the cathedral and walked along Summit, past the old Humphries mansion, where I will live someday though I don't know it yet, and past Mrs. Porterfield's rooming house porch where the young Scott Fitzgerald sat and smoked and thought about the fame that would soon descend on him, though he didn't know it yet, and past the stone house that Frank Frisbie bought with the money from his crappy novel and the University Club and the old apartment house where Katherine lives—

Russet brick
And ravaged
Shades and
Who could look
Up and guess the
Unutterable cravings
Contained behind that
Third-story window,
O mon coeur?

And in the little park with Nathan Hale on a pedestal, hands bound behind his back, I stopped and thought about the child Iris and I never had, who gave up his life before he was born. My little bumblebee. My little gumdrop.

I am a happy man. I have a duty to be.

Americans are meant to live, love, laugh, and be happy. The quintessential American philosophy: work it out—make the best of it—lighten up. We're optimists. Leave agonized introspection to the Swedes and cynicism to the French and *Weltschmerz* to the Berliners and *Ich bin nicht ein Berliner*. Problems can be solved. Don't sweat it. Play it for laughs. Where there is love, there's comedy. Don't hang out with unhappy people; don't go into a profession full of the humorless. Be happy.

All through my younger days, I had morbid fears of drowning inside a car or suffocating in a coffin, or having my skull fractured by a giant vise operated by evil apes, or riding a train that derails on a high trestle over a rocky gorge, or going to the electric chair at Sing Sing, or skidding off the South Rim of the Grand Canyon to the horror of thousands of Japanese tourists.

And then I learned that music can postpone dread. And so can sex. The *St. Matthew* or the passionate nakedness of two happy adults.

A beef sirloin is good, too, slightly charred on the outside and reddish pink in the middle, nicely peppered, with mustard aioli.

And sleep. A good solid eight hours of Z's in a room with a window open and a salt breeze blowing in.

Fresh melon from a roadside stand. An endive and pear and blue cheese salad. A rousing Broadway musical with some classy comic turns and a winsome leading lady and a terrific tap routine in Act 2 and a grand finale with the whole ensemble dancing with faces aglow and hands in the air. A good medicinal martini with a fellow martinist. Louis Armstrong and His Hot Five. The Beatles' *White Album*. A September day in St. Paul. A fine Episcopal mass in a sunny sanctuary and the organist plays quietly and the choir hangs together on the anthem and the homily is concise and your sins are lifted from your back and you come away from the Lord's Table filled with grace and walk out into the sunny world with a fresh chance at life. And the snooze during the Scripture readings is good, too.

Many things have the power to make us happy. A good ball game, score tied, bases loaded, two out, bottom of the ninth, and the local hero punches a double into the right-field corner—but no! the first baseman leaps and spears the ball for the third out!—No! The ball caroms off his glove and into the box seats and knocks the commissioner of baseball's rug off his head! The crowd rises, yelling, ecstatic. Walking around New York City on a summer night. Walking around the Minnesota State Fair. The Bach *Mass in B Minor* or *St. Matthew's* or Handel's *Messiah* and a big choir leaning into it like sled dogs on the tundra.

Moving can make you happy. America is a big country. If you're unhappy in Minnesota, you should try Iowa, or Wyoming, Oregon. Any state with an *O* in it. California, or Washington, or Montana, or North Dakota. Illinois. Vermont. Colorado. The list goes on and on. Don't accept grim fate. Dance on out of town, hop a freight train, ride the dog, borrow your mom's car, and make a fresh start.

I walked around Ramsey Hill thinking about New York.

My agent had gotten me a cool $200,000 advance for the sequel to *Spacious Skies*, to be called *Amber Waves of Grain*. I had written to Mr. William Shawn, the editor of *The New Yorker*, and asked if I could come to the magazine as a staff writer. He wrote back:

Dear Mr. Wyler,
Delighted to hear you're considering moving to New York and of course we'd be tickled pink to have you here on the premises. Roger Angell says you're quite the gent. Let us know your arrival

date and we'll order the flowers and the chorus girls and have
West 43rd blocked off for the parade.

**William Shawn**

P.S. What brand of hooch do you prefer? My guess is bourbon.

And one night I walk out the door and up West 7th and I call a
Manhattan real estate agent on the pay phone in the Day By Day
and leave a message on her machine saying, "Yes, I'm interested in
purchasing apartment 12A at the Bel Noir for one million dollars."

That night Iris and I lay in bed and I told her my New York
dream—to work at *The New Yorker* and run into John Updike in the
hall and say, "Hi, John," and he'd say, "Hey, Larry, how's it going?
Liked your last story." And I'd go to lunch at the Algonquin with Mr.
Shawn and in would come Mr. Perelman and Mr. White and Mr.
Trillin and we'd sit and yak about writerly things and I'd head home
to the fashionable Bel Noir on Central Park West and there would be
Iris in a silk pantsuit on the terrace, ready to go off to the Met for
*Der Rosenkavalier* and a late supper at the Café des Artistes—

"What's wrong with St. Paul?" she said.

"I want to live a bigger life. I want to be in the midst of things, not
out on the fringe."

"Maybe I don't. What's New York got that St. Paul doesn't?"

"That's what I intend to find out."

"We've got theater here. Music. Museums. It's good enough for
me. How come you're all het up about New York?"

I put my arms around her and lay my head between her neck and
shoulder and kiss her and say, "Do you remember the first time we
made love, that summer night? We sat on the grass listening to the
jazz band knowing something wonderful was about to happen? New
York makes me feel that way."

"I don't really feel like moving," she says.

"I'll help you feel like it."

She sighs. *Who is this man and what does he want, anyway?*

I talk about New York and the harbor, Wall Street, Trinity Church, Bryant Park, Soho, meanwhile my finger traces around her wings and down her spine and she leans back against me, and I unbutton her blouse, and she smiles, and I am kissing her—

"I am so fat, look at this," she says, pinching a little flab at her waist.

"You have the breasts of a goddess—I wish I had a painting of you nude. I'd hang it on the dining room wall and look at it as I eat dessert."

She glances down at her breasts as if she can't remember where she got them.

"You don't have as good a view of them as I do," I point out, grasping them gently, my little friends.

"Remember back in the seventies, those people in south Minneapolis? We went to their house for dinner. They had photos on the wall of a woman's belly and nipples and crotch as big as movie posters, and I tried not to look stare but then it dawned on me that these were the nipples and crotch of the hostess, who was tossing the salad. Remember them?"

"I don't remember that at all."

"Of course you do."

"What is it with men and breasts? It's so infantile."

I adore her and she keeps arguing with me. I cry, "Woman, don't you know you make me crazy when you take your clothes off?" She says, "Haven't you ever seen a naked woman before?" I say, "I love when you lie on your back, your arms behind your head, your little bush standing up so proud and delicate." She says, "It's not that different from anybody else's." I say, "Let's get a picture of you nude to hang in the dining room." She says, "I don't want the plumber looking at me."

"I'll do your plumbing!" I cry and I kiss her breasts.

I kiss her Aphrodite breasts and caress her thighs and turn her toward me so we lie face to face, chest to breasts, belly to belly, sword to sheath, peak to valley, peninsula to inlet, and we kiss long and sweet and I put my hand between her thighs and stroke her slowly, and she sighs, she murmurs, she gives off heat, and we move through the Seven Stations of Foreplay from the Anointing of the Nipples to St. Cunnilingus and head toward the finale—and as she mounts me, I imagine that maybe a few swimmers will penetrate the harbor defenses and paddle upstream through the marshes to the royal egg and dive into it head-first—and she swings her hips forward and back a few times and she groans with pleasure! Oh my God! Yes! Yes! Yes! But even in her bliss, she thinks about leaving St. Paul and feels bad and sits down on me, dreading New York, not realizing that sitting on Mr. Penis turns him into Mr. Penis, Jr. The guy is not a weight lifter.

"I don't know why we can't be happy right where we are," she cries.

I tell her, "You are a fabulous lover," and try to raise her up with my knees so we can resume the lovely thing we were doing.

She sighs. Words of praise don't rest easily on my Minnesota wife: she brushes compliments away like deerflies. She says, "How many other women have you said that to?"

I wish she'd get off the poor guy and let him breathe. A moment ago he was James Joyce and now she is turning him into a *local writer*.

She looks down and sees him, shriven, hanging his head. "What's the matter?" she says. "You lose interest?"

How to tell her? Praise inflates Mr. Penis, and a critical review is deflating. One more reason to go to New York. There's more hype. Hype works. Minnesotans don't think so but it does. The surest way to give a guy a powerful hard-on is to gasp in amazement and say, "My gosh, I haven't seen anything that big since the circus came to town! That is the Beethoven Ninth of all erections. What on earth has gotten into you? You been taking kryptonite or what? That is the *Giants in the Earth* and the *Woody Herman Big Band* and the *Peterbilt Tractor* of penises." This is how you turn a cocktail weenie to a foot-long bratwurst. *Advertising.* In Minnesota, they sit down on you hard and you deflate and they say, "Oh, well. Some other time."

It violates Iris's principles to tell a lie. So she slips off me and disappears into the bathroom, and Mr. Penis is all done for today.

We met as two kids in choir, locked in the majesty of the *St. Matthew Passion,* and I fell in love with her slender neck and sang the low note in the chord and she turned and smiled and that launched a marriage. If she hadn't smiled, we'd be nothing. It was a case of sympathetic vibration. Like two birds, we mated by ear, we asked no questions. We got married with less discussion than most people devote to choosing a restaurant. We married in the blink of an eye and walked down the primrose path and into the deep woods like everybody else.

One day I was a guy typing in an upstairs bedroom and the next day I was interviewed on *The CBS Evening News* ("What do you say to those who claim that the novel has become irrelevant to the fast-paced life that most of us lead today, Mr. Wyler?") and I came home in a daze and walked into the kitchen and Iris says, "I'm going over to Target if you want to come with. They've got cloth napkins marked down fifty percent. And wine glasses for ninety-five cents apiece."

"Did you see me on TV?" I say.

She shakes her head.

I slosh some Scotch in a glass with ice cubes.

"Your husband just spoke to twenty million on TV, and I come home and you ask me if I want to go to Target?"

"Well, if you don't want to go, just say so. Don't get your undies in a bunch over it."

And she goes off to Target and buys napkins on sale. My novel is bursting in the sky like fireworks, the gates are swinging open. The apartment at the Bel Noir awaits.

I am not going to live in a stucco house on the flats, on Sturgis Avenue behind the Burger King, and wait for the cloth napkins to go on sale. I want to go to New York and find the most expensive linens in town and buy those.

I went to the liquor store and when I came home Iris was in the backyard chopping weeds out of the flowerbeds. I had a bottle of Dom Pérignon. She crinkled up her face. "Sheesh. What's the big deal?"

"Our ship has come in, Iris. Time to start living the good life."

"I have a good life, thank you very much."

"I'm trying to tell you something. Work with me on this. Our ship came in. Our prayers were answered. We won the lottery, Iris. The Lord has blessed us. Mightily. Rained down blessings. Don't turn your back on a gift. Don't leave the harvest sitting on the dock. Why live like this if we don't have to?"

"I *like* this house. What's wrong with it?"

"Plenty."

"Then let's work together and make it what we want it to be."

"I did. I worked and wrote a book—"

"If you're thinking about moving up there—" she cocked her head at Ramsey Hill and Summit Avenue—"forget it. I am not going to spend *my* life putting on dinner parties and sucking up to a bunch of people from hoity-toi schools and their Junior League wingdings, no thank you. I am not a clotheshorse. I want no part of that. You want that, go marry somebody who looks good in black."

My wife. A good woman. Some women if they were held hostage in a dank dungeon for three months and fed swill in buckets and you rescued them and brought them to the Ritz and a lovely lunch awaited and new clothes from Saks, they would say, "*This* coffee isn't Starbucks! And I *despise* scallops. And whatever made you think I would wear *that shade of gray?*" Iris is a believer in Good Enough. I respect that. I happen to want something better.

She said, "I spent the past eight years trying to make this a neighborhood that anybody can be proud to live in and why would I want to walk out on it now?"

"Think of us as Ma and Pa Joad, heading for the orange groves. Think children of Israel in bondage in Egypt."

"I don't know where you get your ideas. You've got money? Fine. Put it in the bank. Don't throw it away on stuff we don't need. That kind of stuff will come back to bite you in the ass real quick." And she went back to cleaning out rocks and glass shards so she could put in flowers.

I opened the garage door. Full of grocery carts she was storing for crazy people locked up in nursing homes. Crazy people have the same right as anyone else to own worthless junk, so Iris offers free parking. Thirty-seven of them with garbage bags full of little treasures moldering away. She knew each one by name: Harry, John, Wally, Evelyn, Maxine, Luverne, Don, Agnes, Sheila, like a herd of dairy cows. I offered her sunny afternoons on the terrace and she preferred to be the custodian of lost minds. I was proud of her. And at the same time I wanted to shake her. I have never wanted to shake somebody so much as right then.

She said, "I'm going to clean that garage out. It's on my list of things to do."

"I'll call a garbage hauler to come clean it for you. Let's go out to dinner."

"I've got supper already started. Bob and Sandy are coming over. I made my bean dish."

Iris is not a gourmet person. I knew this when I married her. Any recipe with the words *marinate* or *tie up spices in cheesecloth*—forget it. Fry up some bacon, brown the ground meat and the onions, pour in some ketchup and Worcestershire, add brown sugar and mustard and vinegar, dump in a few cans of beans—kidney, lima, butter, navy, brown beans—and bake for forty minutes and you've got your dinner. Iris's Not So Bad Beans. After all these years, I know my beans. Maybe my problem is an allergic reaction to legumes.

I tried putting it to her directly. "I am a successful author, babes. I have a number one best-selling book and a quarter million in hand, and I wish to celebrate. Is this wrong? Why can't you call Sandy and Bob and tell them it's off tonight? You knew I was coming home tonight. Let's go out to dinner. You and me. I thought you'd be glad to see me."

"I am," she said. "I just don't see why I'm supposed to put on a big whoop-de-doo just because you come home."

I explained that I need rewards. I suggested that we keep the house and buy a New York apartment and live in both places. She shook her head.

"Have two homes? Why would we do that? Some people don't even have one." She looked at her watch. "They'll be here in fifteen minutes."

# 5 🐾 Lover

The sirens were calling from the shore. The Prodigal Son was dreaming of the Far Country. Iris was in San Francisco, at a conference on aging. I dropped by Macalester College for Katherine's poetry reading. Five of us sat in a room for sixty. Painful. We all felt miserable for her, especially when she said, "It's okay. It's two more than Emily Dickinson had." Katherine is no Emily. Afterward, she kissed me lightly on the cheek as if I were cracked porcelain and said, "I've been worried about you. You're so busy. I hear your novel is doing well, though."

In fact, *Spacious Skies* had gotten a nice review in the *Times* ("a dark and witty midwestern homage to Flannery O'Connor by way of Raymond Chandler") and was selling with gay abandon, but it's bad luck to discuss success, especially with another writer.

"It's doing okay," I said. "Your new book looks terrific." The cover art was one of those lush tropical leaves meant to look vaginal, spattered with dew. "Is that semen on the leaf?" I said.

She laughed. "It's been ages since I've seen you," she said. "Why don't we get together?"

She opened her book—"I wrote this one with you in mind"—

Everything
That is
Of
Importance
Begins with
One dog

Crossing
The lawn
To sniff
Another

A lady whose hair smelled of Lysol stepped in to talk to Katherine and Frank Frisbie cornered me and asked how my book was doing ("Fine") and referred to it as The Big Sky and said he'd heard good things about it. I escaped and headed down Grand Avenue toward my car and there was Katherine in the doorway of a bookstore, smoking, her foot up on the windowsill.

"Waiting for somebody?" I said.

"Yes. For you."

"What's up?"

"There's a lot you don't know about me," she said. "For one thing, you've always felt sorry for me, Larry, and you've got no business doing that, so stop it."

She took a tremendous hard drag and said, "I'm not a charity case. I'm a writer. You should never be sorry for another writer. Today, you're up and I'm not, tomorrow it could be the other way around."

She touched my arm. "If you can't recognize a fellow human being, Larry, then you're in the wrong line of work."

She moved over close to me. "It all goes by so fast, doesn't it. I think of Corinne every day. I keep wanting her to come back, and then I realize that what I really want is to step outside of my own boundaries and live my life as she must have wanted to live hers. Oh, I don't know what I'm saying—Kiss me." She put her skinny arms around my neck and I kissed her and she held on.

"It's so simple. We're writers. Writers open themselves up to experience. We're not here to win awards for good citizenship. Why should we give a shit what people think?"

She took a deep breath.

"I wish I were in bed with you right now," she said. "I just feel bad that you and I never were lovers."

I took her hand and felt a sharp twinge in my left glute, like an ice pick. Too many hours sitting on planes. I groaned and she said, "Kiss me again." So I did.

She said that the thought of being naked with me was making her wet.

It occurred to me that Iris was gone and that our house, a mile away, was empty. It also occurred to me that this was a dumb thing to do. I felt guilty for not being attracted to her. She wanted to sleep with me. An old friend . . . an old friend who's been darned lucky himself and could afford to be kind. I heard myself say, "What are we waiting for?" It was my voice.

There was a swelling in the shorts that accompanied this, and she noticed. "I'll bet you're good in bed," she said.

"Nobody's complained yet," I said.

It was remarkable to come into the old familiar kitchen with my old classmate who had spent evenings there with Iris and me and even brought a boyfriend once, and now I was the boyfriend. We kissed in the dark and I felt her hand in my pants. *Why am I doing this?* Because it is an experience. *Jumping off a cliff is also an experience.* This is not the same thing. It'll be okay. Settle down. She needs to seduce you, it's her way of showing she's your equal.

We went upstairs and undressed and she lit the candles on the dresser—I stuffed a stack of Iris's underwear into a drawer—and she put a James Taylor CD on. She had lovely breasts, small, with button nipples, and a rose tattoo just above her pubic hair, and she clenched me to her and whispered, "I'm going to make love with you until the sun comes up." This struck me as bad luck, to make a prediction like that. It also struck me that I wasn't hard anymore.

We lay on the bed and did some stuff and rolled around and she was breathing hard and I was trying to do the right thing, as if it were a project and I was going for the merit badge in adultery, and then she reached down for my member and found it in a diminished state.

She gave me a brave smile. Woman, the Bringer of Hardness. And she got to work on it and meanwhile the candles are blazing and James Taylor is crooning. And my back hurts. Stabbing pains when I roll over. *Ahhhhhhhhhhhhh.*

*Ohhhhhhhhhhhhhhhhh.*

She interprets this as a moan of delight and goes to work even harder, her curls shaking, panting, grunting, Woman at Work, and I twist the wrong way and feel a knife in my back. "Oh, Jesus!"

"I'm dying for a cigarette," she says.

She sticks her head and shoulders out the window and lights a cigarette. She asks if I have any wine. "I do, but I can't move. My back went out." She tells me to relax. She disappears and comes back with a bottle of rosé from the fridge and two cups. My member is now the size of a salted peanut.

It is so clear to me why adultery should always take place at a hotel: easier to make an exit if things don't work out. Never commit adultery in your own home. This is a rule never to be broken.

She reads me a poem:

The big raccoon
With diaphanous hands
And utilitarian businessman
Eyes
Drinks from the sky
Reflected
In the
Puddle

> On the
> Promontory
> Of my
> Insomnia.

I wanted her to vanish. "Could I give you a massage?" she said. I shook my head. "There is so much I want to tell you," she cried. She pulled out another poem.

"I wrote this on a camping trip," she said. "To the Boundary Waters."

> What is the body?
> It is billows
> Of masked fish
> Speaking lucently
> Of
> God, which is
> The power
> Of
> Kindness (Eros)
> Like a moon
> Pulling
> The sepulchral sea
> To shore.

"What do you think?" she said.

I said, "I like the way that under the surface of the poems so much is happening." I say I feel that her poetry is in transition, trying to find its own course, like a river—

"Someone told me that I eroticize everything in my poems. That everything, especially the animals, is sexual."

"I don't know about that," I said.

The phone rang. I didn't pick it up. It was Iris, unable to sleep in San Francisco, wanting to tell about her exciting day—something about schizophrenia, she had done some good deed for schizophrenics and she was happy and she missed me and she couldn't sleep, she was sorry it was so late, she wanted me to know how much she loved me—we listened to her voice and Katherine said, "She sounds tired."

"I'm exhausted myself," I said.

"I'm too drunk to drive home," she said. "Can't I sleep for a few hours?" I told her no. Drive slowly. But go home. Please.

"That's not a kind thing to say."

"I'm not kind. I'm a cruel novelist."

I managed to stand up, sort of, and I held on to the dresser and handed her her clothes and nodded toward the door. She wanted to meet for lunch. Fine, I said. Call me. She walked out the front door, naked, clutching her clothes and stood on the walk and sang something that sounded like Rodgers and Hammerstein in German, and staggered to her car, bright in the street lamp. She turned and faced my house and held out her arms, dropping her clothes, and shouted, "Mon ami! Mon amour!" And climbed in. And her car wouldn't start. A naked woman came to the house while you were away, dear—she said her car wouldn't start—so I had to start it for her. It needed the gas pedal pumped. And then it started. She honked twice and waved and drove away. I found a heating pad and fell into bed. I wondered why I was behaving so badly but before I could think about it, I was asleep.

# 6 ❧ Gone

When Iris came home, she found out about the whole thing from the neighbors and suggested that I leave.

*They said they saw this naked woman leaning out of our bedroom window. The one who you say stopped because her car wouldn't start.*

*Oh?*

*She was smoking a cigarette, they said.*

*Well, I was home the whole time. I don't know how they could have seen that.*

*You didn't have guests while I was gone?*

*I don't know where they got that.*

*Three people said they saw it.*

And then she held up the underpants. They were pale blue, and the embroidery said "Tuesday."

"Not mine," she said. "Did you win them at the coin toss or what?"

"I don't know whose those are."

"Well, I do. Whatever woman you had over here while I was gone left her undies. What kinda deal is this, Larry? I mean, to have your girlfriend over to the house while I'm out of town? You've got the brains of a boxful of hammers to pull a trick like that."

"It's not what you think. We were drunk, it was a silly thing, we got undressed, we kissed and stuff, nothing happened—"

"Don't lie to me. What about the nurse from the fertility clinic?"

A right hook to the jaw. I'm on the canvas looking up at the sky. Bells ringing. Knockout.

"I don't go for you messing around with other women," she said. "I'm not naïve but I'm not going to sit back quietly and watch it happen either. I donno. A deal is a deal. Keep your end of the bargain. Simple as that. Either you do or you don't. And you didn't. And that's the last word on the subject."

I promised that nothing of this sort would ever happen again.

"That's no good."

I started to say something and she held up her hand. *Don't. Don't even start.*

I spent a restless remorseful night in the guest room. And the next morning I took off on the next leg of my book tour. She'd left the house early and written a note.

I think we have a good life together but you feel otherwise. You've gone off the deep end. I just don't get what you're up to and I suppose you can't tell me. So maybe you better go to New York and get it out of your system and if you want to come back and be married again, then we'll see. I hope you know I love you.

—xoxo Iris

I went to church that Sunday, and the minister, whose voice sounded like a coffee grinder, preached on the subject of honesty. "Then have done with falsehood and speak the truth to each other, for we belong to one another as parts of one body. If you are angry, do not be led into sin; do not let sunset find you nursing your anger; and give no foothold to the devil" (Ephesians 4:25–27). So I spoke the truth to myself: I'm going to New York because I want to go, and let her do as she pleases. I love her and my home is here and when it's time to die, I'll come back. I'll lie in a green-tiled room with tubes in my arm and wires in my chest, catheterized and sedated, tended by plump nurses from Granite Falls, and I will get up out of my body and find a choir and slip into the bass section like a walleye released into Lake Winnibigosh and we shall sing the perfect *St. Matthew Passion* at last, but meanwhile I am going to New York.

"Well, I can't stop you," said Iris. "I can't keep you from running around with other women or going to New York or anything else. You're going to do what you want to do, so you may as well do it and get it out of your system."

"You could come with me."

"And do what? Sit and polish my nails and wait for Mrs. Rockefeller to invite me to tea?"

I could have gone into therapy, or read a book about happiness or filled my pockets with rocks and waded into the Mississippi, but I'm an American, so I left town and went to New York. That's how we do it. We move on.

## 7 ❧ The Bel Noir

There was no farewell party for me. Iris kissed me good-bye when she left for work. "Take it easy," she said. At 9 A.M., the taxi pulled up and honked and I threw my suitcases in the trunk and got in and rode away. Mr. Ziegler watched me from his front porch, a large sad man in yellow shorts. And I went to New York.

There is a restless strain in the Wyler family going back to the Welsh side and our ancestor David Powell, who started out in Pennsylvania, married, moved to Ohio, then Indiana, then to De Kalb, Illinois, and then to Charles City, Iowa, and Missouri. He was a farmer but he had the Powell in him and every few years he had to load his household in the wagon and head west. His children left the nest as the nest moved west and they stayed put in Illinois and Iowa and his wife put her foot down in Missouri. David, after a side trip to the Colorado gold fields, pushed south and joined the Oklahoma land rush of 1889 and put his marker on a claim and sat down under a cottonwood tree with a blanket over him and died there in the heat and the dust. A good death. His long pilgrimage had kept his heart fresh and eager, and he was taken up on angel wing to the alabaster city and set down at the Lord's Table without an ounce of regret, unlike his bourgeois children, who loved their homes and yards and furniture and cars and took their leave of this earth with great reluctance and fussing with medicine and entertaining false hope, but to David, Ohio, Illinois, Colorado, Oklahoma were only stations on the way to Glory.

And so, in the Powell spirit, I being in good health and of sound mind, walked away from my good life and the plane took off over the magnificent Mississippi and Fort Snelling on the bluff and ascended over Hastings, Red Wing, Wabasha, La Crescent in the summer twilight, the cows resting in their green meadows, chewing and dreaming, grain barges heading downstream, the diligent farmers tilling loam—I headed into the clouds and gallivanted off to New York City.

Life presents us with certain gifts. The fog lifts, the coast is clear, time to be venturesome. You've spent fifteen years in the potato fields: try the jazz life for awhile. Some odd experience is available now that might not be later. Put on your walking shoes, put $100 in your pocket, bring an umbrella.

Adventure. It saves us from smugness, the sin of the Midwest: that extra topspin you put on the truth when you know they know you're right; the vanity of the modest, their reflexive remorsefulness, their humorlessness—a little glorious stupidity can be a tonic.

We are good people and we are mean sons of bitches: we're fractious, susceptible to envy, suspicious, cruel. We did not fall to earth from a distant galaxy; we arrived via mortal beings with splendid faults, many of which we inherited. Mine is restlessness. I hate boredom. It terrifies me. Good-bye, Minnesota.

I flew into New York LaGuardia and a Lincoln Town Car picked me up and drove me across the Triborough, the towers of Manhattan shining softly in the distance, and through Spanish Harlem into Central Park, crowded with walkers, joggers, skaters, bikers, and I told the driver to let me out at the corner. I got out at 96th and Central Park West and fell in with the crowd flowing south past the ball fields, the Delacorte Theater and Belvedere Castle, around the lake of lovers in green rowboats, the Sheep Meadow, a thousand courtly loafers in the Monet sunshine, and an asphalt rink where roller skaters glided slowly round and round in celestial formations, and up ahead the great wall of hotels and apartment edifices shines along Central Park South. It shone for my countryman Scott Fitzgerald in 1920. It shines for me.

It was 76 degrees in the park at 3:08 P.M., said the sign at Columbus Circle. I half-expected some New Yorker to yell, "Hey! You with the hair! You're from Minnesota!" as if I were Blimpy the Human Pincushion or Koko the Dog-Faced Boy, but nobody did.

The Bel Noir on Central Park West is twelve stories high with twin towers atop that. The key to 12A was in an envelope at the front desk. The doorman pointed me toward the elevator beside a mural of a procession of pilgrims crossing a long arched bridge to the Golden City. I rode up with a nervous man and a young woman in dark glasses holding a Bonwit Teller bag and a mournful dog. He looked chastened, as if he'd been caught trying to escape and was waiting for his next chance.

The apartment had a sizable terrace looking out over the rooftops, what the agent referred to as a "Parisian view." The former owner, a guy gone off to Washington to help the Reagan administration stick it to working people, had left his junk out there: busted chairs, boxes of flotsam, curtain rods, crockery—but when I opened the door from the big sun-filled living room and stepped out onto the terrace, a high plateau in the canyons, I felt happy. Enlarged. Ennobled. I don't need a divorce, just enlargement. To know I could put on a clean shirt and go to a show, and then not go. To have the Statue of Liberty nearby and never see it. To hear the crowd not far away and join it or not join it. This is what I always wanted. The big city life. Home of fabulous restaurants and their proximity makes it all the more luxurious to order shrimp in garlic sauce to be delivered and eat it on the terrace and look at New York.

The apartment was disgusting. No attempt to clean your filth for the next person. Typical of Republicans. But there was a sweet little kitchen like a Pullman galley with stainless steel cupboards and a stainless steel fridge with double glass doors—which thrilled me, echoes of the Silver Zephyr train to Chicago—and a tiny bedroom off the kitchen and a pantry. A long dining room with a hanging lamp at one end and a wall of solid bookshelves. (What would Republicans do with bookshelves? Display their golf trophies?) A southwest-facing living room with fireplace. A guest room, small, dim, facing the airshaft (realtors call it the courtyard). No sense encouraging your guests to put down roots. The master bedroom with bath attached, a green-tiled shower stall and six shower heads to douse you on all sides. And the terrace.

I loved my terrace through sickness and health, in riches and poverty. A magnificent terrace with a windbreak of spruce trees and birches in big cedar planters, and boxes of tall swamp grass, and even on winter days it smelled of the North Woods. Planes flew high overhead, following the Hudson south, descending to make the turn over Staten Island and come in across Brooklyn on their approach into LaGuardia. Every time I flew back to the city, I tried to sit on the left side so I could look down from the sky and see my terrace. On calm sunny days, it felt like Palm Beach. At night, the Pleiades hung overhead and the moon, and the terrace seemed suspended from the heavens. When storms struck, you felt the full force of the wind; the trees bent, the awning flapped. At night when I led my guests out to the terrace, no matter who they were, Minnesota tourists or old West Siders, jaded rich or impressionable youth, they always stopped and took a deep breath. It was like stepping out on the deck of a ship anchored in a harbor of high promontories of lighted facades, the apartments of other cliff dwellers all around, a tableau of domesticity: a man typing in his bedroom, a Hopper woman brushing her hair, a TV set flickering and pajama-clad children running in and out of the room, a long lithe Latin woman reclining naked on a couch, the binoculars trembling in my hands. The leafy darkness of Central Park lay to the east and to the south the lights of midtown glowed like a smeltery, and rising up from the street, the heat and hum of the city, so erotic, an old slow music. I stood and gazed and sat down to supper under the awning, at a glass-topped table with Manhattan for a backdrop, and everyone who ever sat at my table seemed to shine with fresh purpose and gaiety, people wilted and brownish at the close of day sprang to life and clinked glasses and leaned forward, light-hearted and lucid, and gave of the best of themselves. Good lighting goes a long way toward bringing out the best in us, and New York is a grand movie set open to anybody. On summer nights we sat at the table under the awning and ate our salads and were finer people that you could be in St. Paul. Not better. Just finer.

I slept on the terrace that first night, on a busted chaise longue, awoke at 7, showered, dressed, and left, briefcase in hand, and took the C train from 86th Street to Columbus Circle and changed to the B and got out at 42nd and was too wrought up to go directly to the *New Yorker* office so I walked over to Bryant Park behind the Public Library. A green sward in a bright box canyon of glass and steel. I strolled beside the tulips and irises and found a vacant chair and sat down. The shady side of the park was deserted and this side, the sunny side, was well populated with suits and a few blue collars, punks, old coots, a smattering of tourists, and two or three disheveled people slumped on benches and grumbling to themselves, and all of us soaking up sun amid the grandeur of New York. Broadway ran a block to the west and on Sixth Avenue and 44th stood the old RCA studio where Elvis recorded and Leonard Bernstein and Chet Atkins, and I thought, "Dear Lord, don't make me go back home."

I presented myself at 25 West 43rd Street, a brick edifice with NA-
TIONAL ASSOCIATION OF FEDERATIONS over the arched entrance, and
walked into the long marble lobby that led straight through to 44th,
and waited for the elevator. A man sat behind a desk nearby and I
half expected him to ask me to show proof of writerhood, copies of
published stories, maybe take a quiz. I got off the elevator on the
seventeenth floor and saw the sign, THE NEW YORKER—STAFF ONLY
BEYOND THIS POINT, NO SOLICITORS. LEAVE SUBMISSIONS IN BASKET.
FOR SUBSCRIPTIONS, GO TO 12TH FLOOR. QUIET—PEOPLE AT WORK.
MESSENGERS SHOW I.D. (SIGNED) WILLIAM SHAWN, EDITOR. I told the
receptionist I was here to begin work. "What work?" she said. I told
her I was a writer. "What do you write?" "Fiction. All sorts of stuff.
Wyler's the name. Larry Wyler." She was a doll. She gave me one of
those Who are you looking at, numb nuts? looks that New York
women do so well. "Have a seat," she said. I felt a shudder of delight
at having made it so far and sat down in the waiting area and waited.

*TWENTY-FIVE WEST FORTY-THIRD STREET!!!!* An address
emblazoned in the brain of every ambitious young English major in
America. We wrote the address on an envelope, in big neat block letters, on the odd chance that the editors might pay attention to neat
handwriting, and carefully folded our neatly typed manuscript of
"Hollyhocks," and sealed it, and put it in the mailbox that we believed was the lucky mailbox for that day—maybe the downtown
one, maybe the one on the corner by the school where children
danced around waiting for their bus—and went home and day-

dreamed about the new life that would be ours when *The New Yorker* put its large hand on our little head and said, "You, my son, are worthy. Enter into the gates of literature."

1. Untold wealth
2. Admiration of women
3. Opportunities to travel
4. Personal friendships with other writers
5. Discounts on trips, automobiles, jewelry

What we did not enclose with the story was our cover letter. We debated whether to, and then nixed it.

To the editors:

I suffer from chronic pain syndrome and can't eat and am all skin and bones and the lone bright spot in my life is when I sit down with a tablet and ballpoint pen and write my stories. I enclose one that I worked on for almost three years. If you publish it, I will be the happiest boy in the U.S.A. If you reject it, I will kill myself. Maybe in the oven, or else in the car with the engine running and the tailpipe plugged. In my pocket will be your rejection slip. Think about it.

Larry Wyler

We watched the calendar from the day that "Hollyhocks" was mailed, and three days later, we imagined a *New Yorker* minion opening the envelope—some smart young bunhead lady with horn-rim glasses reading the first sentence—

She took the lettuce from the crisper drawer and as she washed it she suddenly wished that spring would come, and Jack would leave.

And her Vassar heart pounded *pum–pum–pum–pum* and she read on, and on, and on, with mounting delight—*Yes! Yes! O yes! This is it, the real thing! Call Mr. Shawn! Call typesetting! Get me a layout man! Let's get this baby into type!* And word spreads up and down the august hallways—New Writer on Board, A Good One—and the serene figures of literary dons in their tweedy gowns flit from one dim marbly den to another, passing the word that a Soul has entered Valhalla.

After a week, we watched the mail daily for the acceptance letter. Ernie the mailman came around 1 P.M. and we peered out the window, expecting to see the dude come at a dead trot, waving the envelope aloft, hollering, "It's here, young 'un! Fer you! From that magazine!"

But it was not to be. Two weeks later Ernie brought an envelope from *The New Yorker* with "Hollyhocks" inside and a rejection slip, a discouragement, and yet we felt exalted that someone in the sacred wood had actually read our story. It had been there. It had lain on a table and E. B. White had looked down in passing and caught the first sentence and thought, Nifty. And now here I am.

I'm here! What every English major dreamed of, I have attained. I stepped out of the chorus line and into a starring role and married the leading lady. I shot the puck in the net and the Golden Gophers won the Stanley Cup.

Mr. Calvin Trillin came out to the waiting room and ushered me into the august corridors—"This way," he said—the very floors that Ross once trod! Benchley! Liebling! Lois Long! The Long Winded Lady! Our Man Stanley! George Booth! Charles Addams! Alabaster walls and green tile floors and heaps of old magazines and old glass-front bookcases full of books by faded *New Yorker* writers and big yellow nautical charts marking water depths in New York harbor and a library table stacked with newspapers, the *Post* and the *Daily News* and the *Observer* and the *Times*, and there, around a couple bends, was my office.

"We call this hallway Deadwood Gulch," he said. "I'll let you figure out why."

The office was small, 6 x 8, and dusty. The Thurber drawing was on the wall over a scratched and pitted desk. There was an old oak swivel chair and a bare bookshelf and a typing table with a Smith-Corona on it and a note: "Doesn't work!"

"I can't tell you how thrilled I am," I said. I glanced around to gather impressions of this moment in case I should someday write a memoir (*Me and The New Yorker*) but my one impression was a feeling of sheer abject gratitude.

"Mr. Trillin," I said. "I don't know what part you played in securing this office for me, but please know that I will repay you if it takes the rest of my life."

"Good," he said. "You do that." He handed me a key. "Don't leave your office unlocked. There's a gun in the desk, top right hand drawer. Don't shoot yourself in the foot. If you need paper, dial O for office boy. If you need advice, call your uncle. They serve drinks downstairs in the library at five o'clock. If you consider yourself a poker player, feel free to join in but don't sit at Shawn's table. If he wants you there, he'll nod at you. If you want to bring him a little gift, I recommend a box of Jose Cañu cigars. Or a bottle of Jim Beam. And one more thing—try not to stare. Be cool. If Jeanne Moreau should walk down the hall, or Catherine Deneuve, don't let your mouth hang open and your eyeballs pop, okay? Shawn has a thing about actresses. And if Jerry Salinger asks you to coauthor something with him, say no and be firm about it. That guy thinks up some new project every morning and gets people all excited and by five o'clock it's deader than Mrs. Hurley's dog."

He left and within five minutes Salinger stuck his head in and said, "Hi. Like your stuff. I've been thinking about doing a Holden Caulfield cookbook. What do you think? There weren't recipes as such in the book but a guy's got to eat, right? How'd you like to work on it with me?" And ten minutes later there was Updike, all gray and distinguished, a bag of golf clubs on his shoulder, inviting me to join him at the driving range.

"A driving range in New York?"

"On the navigation deck of the Staten Island ferry," he said. "I went to Harvard with Captain Tibbetts. I tee up right behind the pilot house. Not to toot my own horn, but I once stroked one that caught a gust of wind and landed in the torch of the Statue of Liberty. No shit. Ball had my name on it and a park ranger sent it to me. That baby must've sailed 300 yards."

The magazine was a club, liked the U.S. Senate, and once you got in, you hobnobbed with everybody. There was no high-hatting, no stiff-arming the junior members, only a pleasant pool of amiability. E. B. White took me bird-watching and E. M. Frimbo took me on the Bangor Night Mail, and Pauline Kael took me to movies. She always brought her own popcorn because theaters didn't use real butter. I played Ping-Pong with S. J. Perelman ("Stand up there and I'll whip the bejiggers out of you, you sullen peasant. The S. J. stands for San Juan, baby—are you familiar with the word *muerte?*" ) And after he whipped me, he adjusted his chapeau and loped away, natty, cool, keen as a wolfhound, off to lunch with some lissome starlet and lure her back to his pied–à–terre at the St. Moritz. J. F. Powers took me to his barber, Joe, around the corner from St. Ignatius. Salinger gave me his memoirs, a cardboard carton that weighed about thirty pounds. Shawn dropped in. He was short, muscular, bald, with big hands. He said, "You sail?" I said, "I have." He said, "You're on."

I wrote to Iris.

Darling Iris,

I am writing this on New Yorker stationery as you can see. I have a whole stack of it here. I am sitting in my office on the 17th floor and just down the hallway is J. D. Salinger, author of *Catcher in the Rye* which I read four times in three days when I was 17. Is that a coincidence or what? From my window I can see Times Square and the Paramount Building where my hero A. J. Liebling once interviewed Pola Negri as she reclined in her white peignoir on a white chaise longue like a crumpled gardenia petal and said, of Rudolph Valentino, "He was the only man I evair lawved. But I am fated always to be unhappy in lawv. Because I expect so mawch." And I can see the Hotel Carter which used to be the Hotel Dixie where Jimmie Rodgers the Singing Brakeman died of TB after finishing a recording session. It was the home of Liebling's friend, Colonel Stingo, the horse-racing columnist for the National Enquirer. Colonel Stingo said, "I sit up there in my room at the Dixie, working away on my column. I finish, and it is perhaps one o'clock. Up there in my retreat, I feel the city calling to me. It winks at me with its myriad eyes, and I go out and get stiff as a board. I seek out companionship, and if I do not find friends, I make them. A wonderful, grand old Babylon." And that is exactly how I feel being here at the New Yorker. A wonderful grand old magazine that winks at me and invites me to write. I think I will go out and get stiff and tomorrow I'll write something. I miss you, honeybunch.

xoxox,

Larry

What to write?

I roamed around Manhattan, looking for little vignettes of life, and found them, and sat and wrote and rewrote and agonized over details, writing sentences on Post-its and sticking them to the wall like paragraphs and they stuck there until the glue dried and they fell like autumn leaves.

*A water main breaks and police cordon off the block, lights flashing, traffic barriers, people stand in little groups talking about it.*

*If the Algonquian Manhattan Indians had invested the $24 they got from the Dutch back in the 17th century, they'd have $13 billion right now.*

*Enormous corporate buildings including a black-marble tower with* THE WALL STREET JOURNAL *over the door and not far away are cheap walk-up hotels that probably don't offer room service and hole-in-the-wall shops where you can get passport photos or have something copied or get your nails done or cash a check or purchase incense or maybe all five.*

*A* NO PARKING *sign is like an eye chart. The big letters at the top "No Parking Anytime" and then in smaller letters "No Standing, 8 A.M.–4 P.M." and under that "Alternate Side Parking Tuesdays and Thursdays" and under that "Wednesdays and Fridays, 8 P.M. to 6 A.M." and under that "25 cents per hour" and under that "Except Between No Parking Signs." That's why most New Yorkers don't own a car.*

*The ads on the subway aren't for BMWs or ski resorts, they're for hemorrhoid treatments and what to do about sore feet, bunions, bad skin, bad teeth, drug addiction. One for Tide* detergente, *with the phrase* blanquier tan blanco *("whiter than white"), not such a useful phrase to know in New York.*

*Where Broadway slices across 44th and Seventh Avenue, you can look into six different canyons of glass and stone hundreds of feet tall and covered with brilliant flashing signs, news banners, rivers of people moving along, it's the most amazing sight in America. It's okay to be gay here. It's okay to be a dancer or a writer. Okay to wear black. Black jeans, T-shirt, sandals, black toenails. It's okay to be a billionaire. In the Midwest we despise the rich but New Yorkers don't. And it's okay to be alone. You can sit in a café and eat alone and not feel weird, or go to the movies and buy one ticket. Delis sell half a sandwich, one small brownie. Lots of studio apartments. Women go around alone, day or night, and as a defense they develop an expression that is the facial equivalent of a wall. If you come from Minnesota where you expect people to smile at you, this can be a jolt. And it's meant to be.*

*In other cities, when the president comes to town, people feel sort of happy and honored and wonder if they'll get to see him. In New York, people feel a sense of dread, especially on the East Side where the UN is and the Waldorf and there is only one subway line. The arrival of the president is, for hundreds of thousands of New Yorkers, a natural disaster, a sort of blizzard.*

*The word* minority *comes from the word* menorah, *it means stock up on candles, you may need them, those people are likely to come after you at any time.*

I kept putting notes on the wall and nothing added up. *The New Yorker* certainly wasn't in the market for starry-eyed tourist postcards by a Minnesota guy dazzled by Times Square. I got a fortune cookie at a Chinese restaurant that said, "There is yet time for you to take a different path." I began a piece about old Indian trails in Manhattan and the dirt road called Broad Way and the herds of milk cows grazing among the apple orchards on the farm of Daniel Horsmanden which, in 1776, lay where 43rd Street is now, and the city of New York was a few church spires on the horizon.

I worked on a memoir ("A Boyhood on the Mississippi") and wrote a few thousand words about fishing and rafts and camping on islands and then decided that Mark Twain had done this much better.

I tried writing a piece about 44th Street when it rains and the taxis glisten as they race through the puddles and the hotel doormen hold their big umbrellas over the elderly couple looking anxiously up the street, late for their flight home to Cleveland, and decided that E. B. White did that sort of thing to perfection and why should I do a poor imitation?

I began a profile of Arthur Godfrey ("The man in the tan raincoat and the gray homburg who entered the Columbus Circle subway station was undistinguishable from any other straphanger until he asked the woman in the ticket booth if the uptown B train was still skipping its 81st Street stop on account of the construction project that has been going on there for most of the fall and she recognized one of the most familiar voices in the history of radio and said, 'You'll want to take the C train to 72nd and walk, Mr. Godfrey. It's quicker, and it's a nice day for a stroll.'") only to realize that he'd been dead since 1983.

I thought about writing a profile of Robert E. Lee. Then I thought about Peggy Lee, and Lee Radziwill, Will Rogers, Rodgers and Hart, Huntington Hartford, Ford Madox Ford, Betty Ford, Earl Battey, Katherine Lee Bates, Kate Smith, Howard K. Smith, Maggie Smith, Sal Maglie, Sol Hoopii and His Royal Hawaiians, Jane Wyman, the YMCA. Jack Dempsey. Dumpsters. Teamsters. Hamsters. Hamilton Jordan. Jergens Lotion. The Locomotion. Perry Como. Barium. Syngman Rhee. Ralph Stanley. Stan Musial. The musical *Oklahoma*. Hummus. And so on.

I looked in the box that Salinger left, and it was not so different from any other *New Yorker* memoir. Tales of gloomy mild-mannered eccentrics and their tiny feuds and Ross loping down the hall and yelling, "God bless you, damn it!" and Thurber's noontime assignations at the Hotel Seymour and White's agonies of revision and the tragedy of Liebling, who needed a big windfall success and never got one and worked himself to death. I couldn't let Salinger ruin his reputation with this crap. I lifted the box up to the open window and let the pages waft out and flutter toward 44th Street. One line caught my eye as the page flew away—"Mr. Shawn threw Hemingway to the floor and got him in a leg scissors before calmer heads—" and then it was gone.

**Dear Mr. Blue,**

**I have been a voracious reader since childhood, devouring fiction, history, science, philosophy, like a vacuum cleaner. I'm the only person I know who's read everything by Sartre, Simeon, Dickens, Trollope, Patrick O'Brien, and Jean M. Auel. I've read the Koran, the Buddhist canon, the C. H. Mackintosh commentaries on the Bible, Beowulf, the Icelandic sagas. And now, at the age of 48, I seem to have crashed. I have not opened a book in the past two years. It doesn't interest me. I look at the books on my coffee table and they're like bricks to me. Any ideas?**

**—Scorched**

Dear Scorched, No sin to be aliterate. There's a whole world out there that writers write about that you can discover for yourself. Cooking, travel, clinical depression, exile, self-destructive behavior, the accumulation of vast wealth, inappropriate romance, just to name seven. I'm on the other side of the canyon from you, a writer who is staring at a blank page and trying to figure out how to make a brick out of it. Someday, somebody should bring nonwriters together with nonreaders to see what they have to say to each other.

I was okay. My candle still had two good ends left and I flapped around town like a fruit bat, hanging out with socialites and starlets and literati, feasting off publishers' parties, hobnobbing, charming the pants off people, and was never in bed before 3 A.M.

Like any famous, or semifamous, author, I had loads of offers.

I was invited to guest on *Jeopardy*, to do the voice of Skeezix in a film adaptation of *Gasoline Alley*, to write 5,000 words about families for *Good Housekeeping*, to write 2,000 words about "My Most Unforgettable Parent" for *Reader's Digest*, to write about Madagascar for *National Geographic*, to serve as honorary chairman of the White House Council on Storytelling, to narrate a documentary about Robert Scott's race to the South Pole, to appear on the cover of *Newsweek* with children of different races, to tour Europe for the U.S. Information Agency and present lectures on the American Literary Heartland, to host a PBS show about "trends in culture" or "really, anything you want to do," to write the text for a book of photographs of *Childhood Homes of American Writers*, to do commentary at the Winter Olympics, to appear on various TV shows, to host a salute to Phil and Don Everly at Carnegie Hall, to chair the Right to Read Music committee of the American Choral Association, to appear at benefits and to serve here and lecture there and write and host and spread the substance of my being like a grease stain across the breadth of America.

All I wanted to do was write something good for *The New Yorker* magazine.

One day, I wrote on a piece of paper: WHY DO I WRITE?

1. The big bucks. It might happen again. You never know.
2. The adulation of readers. People coming up in restaurants and saying, "Your stuff cheered me up once during chemo."
3. A cool thing to do. *What do you do?* I'm a writer. *Oh. Cool.*

4. Am otherwise unemployable. As a nonwriter, I'd need to work as a parking lot attendant or clerk in a convenience store or else be institutionalized for a period of time.

5. The inscription on the façade of Northrop Auditorium at the U of M, about the search for truth.

6. How many people get the chance to write for *The New Yorker* magazine? Not many. There are Phi Beta Kappas from Princeton happy to work in the mail room and sharpen pencils and deliver galley proofs. The receptionist is a former Rhodes scholar who is at work on an article about the spine. If I listen closely, I can hear the *ptptptptptptppptpt* of her computer keys.

7. Want to please my old English teacher, Mr. Hochstetter, who thought I had talent though in retrospect this doesn't say much for his judgment.

8. Want to impress women. Shakespeare was out to impress the dark lady, and Keats wrote for Fanny, Wordsworth for his sister Dorothy, and Balzac and Dickens and Hemingway and all those rascals. All of them out to impress the ladies.

9. A chance to speak to the youth of tomorrow.

10. Big bucks tend to lead to bigger bucks—TV, movies, soft goods. Look at A. A. Milne. He was a hardworking hack, cranking out stuff about the Boer War and motoring and country houses and Bright Young Things, and then he hit on Talking Animals and discovered the importance of subsidiary rights, product, marketing tie-ins.

Mr. Shawn sent me a note:

Dear Mr. Wyler,
Whenever you have a piece you want me to look
at, please come right up to the 19th floor and

> knock on my door and come in. And let's get
> together one of these evenings and sail.
>> Bill Shawn

Every day I awoke early and stood under the shower listening to WQXR and saying, "This is the day I run up two flights of stairs to Mr. Shawn's office, with a piece of writing in my hand, and he reads it, jumps up, and gives me a big hug." And I dressed in my black suit and white shirt and drank my coffee out on the terrace with a glance at the *Times*—no Iris to lecture me about the Palestinians—and headed out the door and hiked briskly south to 86th Street and caught the C train and stood at the front of the front car, watching the track ahead as we careened between the rows of pilings and at 59th I switched to the B and hopped out at 42nd and strode briskly past the hot-dog vendors and the steel-drum guy playing "New York, New York" and went to 25 West 43rd and into the marble lobby and stood at the bank of elevators, thinking, I am from St. Paul, Minnesota, and I am going to work at my office at *The New Yorker*. Me. The little guy they used to call Weasel. My golfer parents in Palm Beach consider me a big fat loser, but I'm not. No, I'm not! Today is my big day! Today I am going to get a big hug.

# 9 ✒ What Do You Know?

Write about what you know. Somebody told me that back in college, I forget who.

So what do I know?

Today? Not much.

"You know more than you think you do," said Dr. Spock.

Oh? Really? Maybe I'll write about unaware knowledge then.

Write about danger. Sudden death in the afternoon.—A crowd lines up in front of Radio City Music Hall to purchase tickets to see Barry Manilow, and a bike messenger races the wrong way on a one-way street, and a nice man in a blue turtleneck steps backward off the curb to get a snapshot of his wife and her sister and *wham!!!!* It's the last picture on this guy's roll, he's out of here, his body is shipped back to Sioux Falls, and who cares? You think about this often in Manhattan. *What if I fall down in the street with a nasty heart attack, will anyone notice, or what?*

Write about beautiful women.

Women like Shahtoosh, a fact checker at *The New Yorker*, who wore ragged jeans and a T-shirt and a silk wrap shift lined with feathers from snowy owls sewn together with tinsel. It weighed fourteen ounces and cost $16,000. That's what she said. I don't know. Very soft to the touch. She put her head on my shoulder and told me I was the only man who understood her. She was from Buffalo, her birth name was Ethelyn Garber, she was doing coke big-time. I'd take her out to dinner, she'd lay her little mirror and sprinkle on the table and sprinkle the joy dust on it and stick the rolled-up dollar in her nose and snort. "You need to eat more than just breadsticks," I said. But she was a fact checker and knew exactly what she needed.

Women like Fiona, with her shock of strawberry hair and green eyes and long sure stride, who I followed one Sunday morning for sixteen blocks down Fifth Avenue, mesmerized by her style and gait. Followed her into St. Thomas, a big gloomy church of rampant Gothicness and Anglitude on a Disneyean scale, the boy choir in their starched collars tootling in the stalls among the enervated clerical faces and the desiccated ladies with breadboard chests, the camphor mothball aroma, the whole raging Anglophilia of the place—the sermon that morning was "The Coat of Many Colours"—but I threaded my way through the crowd in pursuit of her, and then lost her and wandered off to the side, by a big yellow banner, JOYFULLY ENTER INTO HIS GATES, while the choir sang a *Benedictus* that struck me as highly erotic and then my elbow was touched and it was her. "Weren't you following me?" she said. "Weren't you wanting to start a conversation?" I nodded. "Then why did you give up? Is something wrong?"

"Do you come here often?" I said. She shook her head. "I came in here because I thought this was where you were headed."

I'd never been stalked by a woman who was in front of me at the time, but that's how they do it in New York.

~~~~

Her body was all tan, no white zones. She lay face down on the bed and I dripped oil on her back and massaged her neck and shoulders and along her spine and down her legs, the soles of her little brown feet.

"I can't believe I'm actually doing this," I said. "I never do this sort of thing. I'm married, after all."

"I don't want to hurt anybody," I added.

I study her fine backbone and shoulder blades and firm butt, with the tufted darkness below.

"Okay, let's not hurt anybody," she said. She sat up. "Let's each stay home and pull the shades and read Flaubert and not hurt anybody. Let's abstain from meat, and not wear nonunion clothing, and be sure our coffee beans come from growers who have signed the Golden Rule, and while we're at it, let's keep silent, and above all, let's be celibate because, mister, you can't have children and not hurt somebody." She stood up and grabbed her clothes.

"No," I said. "Don't go. Lie down. I'll lie beside you. If we hurt them, we hurt them."

Such a cheerful lover. No shame or reluctance. She was enthusiastic and talked a blue streak and then as her pleasure mounted, she emitted a series of ululations, like yodeling in slow motion, and climaxed and cried, "Oh, what you do to me!" and shuddered to a stop. Afterward, we lay wrapped in white robes on the terrace and she said she was a psychiatrist. ("Is that a problem?" I saw no problem there at all. None.) She'd never been to Minnesota in her life, nor even to Chicago. She didn't know the Lord's Prayer, or *The Great Gatsby*, or *The Music Man*. She was the child of academics who summered every year in the Hebrides. I sang " 'Til There Was You" and she was quite touched.

She asked what I did, and I said I was a writer, and she said, "What do you write?" and of course, she'd never heard of *Spacious Skies*. She didn't read novels, she said. She found them too porous. She loved my terrace, though. And she thought I was a good lover. Better than expected. B-plus.

"So you had this in mind when you saw me walking down Fifth Avenue?" I asked.

"Of course."

"Will I see you again?"

She thought about that.

"I have to tell you the truth," she said.

I nodded.

"I would like to see you again but I'm afraid I might become attached."

I pointed out that I was married.

She looked off in the distance for a long moment, weighing her words.

"It's so easy for love to become habit, and before you know it you're taking trips together and arguing about politics."

"Politics doesn't do much for me, erotically," I said. "I'm a Democrat."

"And then familiarity leads to the discovery of unsavory details. Beauty by its very nature is rare, and this beautiful afternoon would only be cheapened by repetition."

So we parted. I wrote my phone number on her palm. She said she would think of me as she washed her hands.

One morning I was eating breakfast on the terrace with a young woman whose name I could not for the life of me recall. She was talking about how she hated auditions so evidently she was an actress or a musician. She mentioned us maybe flying to Antigua for a week so perhaps I'd mentioned something about that the night before. Then the phone rang and the doorman downstairs said, "Mr. Wyler, your wife is on her way up." I said, "My wife? You mean Iris?" He said, "I didn't get her name. She's wearing a Gopher hockey sweatshirt." I said, "Try to slow her down."

Sixty seconds to clear the decks.

I said to the girl, who was in a baby-blue bathrobe, "Grab your clothes and go down on the service elevator and I'll call you later. My wife is on her way up."

She wanted to discuss this, unfortunately—she wanted me to look at this from her perspective, starting with her assumptions when she met me the night before at the Piebald Pony or P.J.'s or that little bistro off Sheridan Square with the snail appetizers—and I had to steer her vigorously to the bedroom and scoop her stuff into a Fairway sack and head her out the back door and wait an agonizing half-minute for Pepe to bring up the service elevator while Miss Dallas or whoever she was said, "I feel ridiculous about this—did you mention to me that you were married?"

"The subject never came up," I said. I caressed the elevator door and thought positive thoughts.

"I don't want you to think that I'm that sort of person."

"None of us is that sort of person," I said. "Think of it as an accident. A wonderful accident."

I almost asked her name but that would've seemed so crass—and then the elevator door opened, Pepe smiling, and off she went, and seconds later, I was at the front door, smiling, horrified, to let Iris in, and we embraced. "What a lovely surprise," I said. Then she sniffed perfume.

"I just put it on," I said. "A gift from someone. I forget."

We stepped out onto the sunny terrace. "What a glorious day," I said. "Let's go for a walk until the cleaning lady is done."

"Why two coffee cups and two plates?" she said.

"A guy from the magazine was here to talk about a piece I'm writing."

"What piece is that?"

"It's about Denmark. That's why we had the cheese Danish."

"What do you know about Denmark?" I ignored that. "I'm so surprised to see you, my love." I said.

"Should I have told you I was coming?"

"No, no, no, no. Heavens, no."

I cleared the table and brought her a Danish from the kitchen and a cup of coffee.

"I don't see how people can live here," she said. "All the extrava-
gance. The Mercedeses and doormen and little kids in designer
clothes. Who pays for all this? And two blocks away there are homeless people sleeping in the park. People in sleeping bags in cardboard
cartons." She walked over to the railing and peered down to see if
she couldn't spot some poor people on 90th Street. And found a little golden earring right there on the rail.

"I meant to tell you," I said. "I've decided to get my ear pierced."

Iris and I sat on the terrace and talked. New York has this effect on
Minnesotans, it opens up the vocal canal. People who don't ever talk
back home come to Manhattan and suddenly the chains loosen, the
gates clang open, and big secrets come flapping out like storks.

"I shouldn't have come," she said. "Everybody I know thinks I
ought to have my head examined. But I had to come out and see how
you were doing."

I am doing fine, I said. I am very happy here. Working hard. Eating sensibly. Walking. Getting my sleep.

"Are you coming back for the fair?"

"I've been busy," I said, apropos of nothing. "I can't seem to finish
anything for the magazine. I keep trying and nothing works out."

"Well, I'm sure you'll be just fine." She paused a couple beats.
"I'm not sure whether to order season hockey tickets for next season or not," she said.

"Well, of course, you should. You can find somebody to go with."

"Wouldn't be the same without you."

She drank her wine. The sun went down and the moon came out.
A summer night and the stars in the sky and the lights of airliners
on the approach to Newark and a helicopter chugging up the Hudson valley, the city humming along. "You like it here, don't you," I

said. "It's all right," she said. "Say *I love New York*," I said. "Let me hear you say it. *I love New York*." "It's all right," she said.

"How're you getting along with all your girlfriends?" she said.

"Well, it's a scheduling problem, but so far, okay. Can't complain. Could be worse."

Iris laughed. She said, "It's our anniversary tomorrow, you know."

*Omigod. Yikes.*

"Yes," I said. "I know. I was thinking of coming home."

She said she thought we should make love. New York has that effect on Minnesotans, I guess. You go through the harrowing landing at LaGuardia, skimming over the rooftops of Brooklyn and thinking about the short runway ahead and the one slight miscalculation that sends the plane skittering off the end of the tarmac into Long Island Sound and you'd have to push and kick and punch your way through the panic-stricken mass of passengers to get to the exit row and step on small children to propel yourself out the little window and onto the wing and into the water and paddle to shore, using your seat cushion as a flotation device, and blue lights flashing, the screams of the burned, the drowning, the pounding of helicopters—and then the plane lands and you collect your luggage and ride into the city and by George you're in the mood to take off your clothes and hop into bed.

I said, "I thought we were separated."

She said, "I'll let you know when we're separated." We got into bed. She said she wished I'd come home for the fair. She held my cock and talked about how beautiful the midway is at night, the cotton candy and Tilt-a-Whirl and the doughnuts, and the double Ferris going up, up, up above the trees and then we fell upon each other like cougars and made love and good Lord the astonishment and delight, the sheer fervor, tall trees fell in the forest, boulders rolled, lightning crashed, and in the aftermath, the sense of accomplishment—two old married people, estranged but nonetheless able to put on a show—I wanted to say, "Of the three women I've slept with this month, you were by far the best!" She kissed me and we went to sleep together, me and Iris, entwined, like in the old days, her hand on my leg, her breath on the back of my neck.

# 10 🦫 Me and Bill

William Shawn took a shine to me right off the bat, and I was intimidated and couldn't imagine writing anything good enough for him to read. Every time I ran into him in the halls, I became a kid in junior high and he was Mr. Big, the Hercules who edited every sentence in the magazine. I saw him at a party at Roger Angell's when he'd just returned from Alaska, where he and an actress named Delilah Van Kaar had climbed Mount Young and shot a caribou from a whitewater raft, and in his excitement he spilled whiskey on me and as a gesture of comradeship he poured whiskey on himself and we sort of bonded.

"Did you and Delilah do any fishing, Mr. Shawn?" I asked.

"Fuck you if you think I'm going to tell you about that," he replied.

I threw back my head and laughed hard.

"Glad you're not creepy and obsessive like some of these introspective sons of bitches around here," he said. "I've had a bellyful of neurotics. White and Thurber drove me nuts and all those affected Harvard snots. What a bunch of phonies. Pretending to be sophisticated when they'd never been west of the Poconos. You look like a midwesterner. Me, too. Chicago. Call me Bill."

"What does caribou taste like?"

"Like snake. Bull snake. Not bad if you fry it with onions and chase it with whiskey. It's gamy but that goes with the territory."

I walked him home to the apartment of the starlet Theresa Montouth (he and Delilah had split up three days before—she was bitter about some little thing or other) and we stopped to shoot billiards at a little smoke-filled joint called Patsy's and at the jukebox we discovered we shared a fondness for old Chicago bands like the Jazz Equestrians and the Skippers of Rhythm and the bass saxophonist Adrian Rollini. We both knew the rules for a poker variant called footsie. He was an excellent bowler and arm wrestler and could toss cards into a top hat with accuracy at up to thirty-five feet, farther if he was drunk. He knew everything by Irving Berlin and also, oddly enough, Schopenhauer. His eagle eye could detect a great deal about a man from the soles of his shoes and his pocket linings. He could tell if you'd recently been to church or Zabar's or taken an unmarried woman to the movies. He knew every species of bird and he could open any lock with a paper clip and a smidgen of gum. He and I were the only Rolling Stones fans in an office full of Beatlephiles. He knew all the words to "Tumbling Dice" and "Brown Sugar." He could disassemble a typewriter and put it back together in two minutes flat. One night when he and Shochine Deligny and I went bowling (this was two weeks later, the thing with Theresa hadn't worked out), he told me his life story: it just flowed out. All about his mama and how she prayed every night that *The New Yorker* would be free of typographical errors. His childhood in Chitown. His Irish dad, Sean Hanratty, a button man for the Bugs Moran gang, killed in the Arbor Day Massacre. Young William changed his name and hitchhiked to Vegas to deal blackjack for Bugsy Siegel and then was called to New York as Harold Rossi's stickman, back when the magazine was a hotbed of steady tipplers and wisecracking women with hinges on their heels.

"Did you say Rossi?"

"I meant to say Harold Ross," he said.

"But you said Rossi."

"It was a nickname." I could tell he was lying, but I didn't want to push him.

"And Bugsy Siegel? You worked for him?" I asked.

"Did I say Bugsy Siegel? I meant Martin Segal." Another lie. Mr. Shawn got a flush in the cheeks when he told an untruth.

"You're so different from the William Shawn I always imagined," I said. "James Thurber portrayed you as a flustered guy who spoke in a whisper and obsessed over commas and ate dry cornflakes for lunch and dreaded elevators and other motor vehicles."

He had his arm around Shochine there in the lounge of the West Side Bowl, drinking a boilermaker, and he said, "Thurber was blind, you know. The phone rang and he'd pick up the steam iron. He needed a lot of supervision. Him and White both. He struggled to operate an ordinary stapler. A coffeemaker was beyond him. *The Years with Ross* was about as true to life as *Rebecca of Sunnybrook Farm*.

"Sometimes I feign fluster—it's a useful stratagem with women," he said.

"I liked hanging out with Dorothy Parker because she could talk louder than anybody else. Glamorous woman, if you like the sweet smell of gin. She had a voice that could crack ice. Most guys were scared shitless and of course her pal Benchley was completely in the bag, so Dotty needed a man to stand up to her. We were having lunch at the Algonquin and Kaufman was there and Marc Connelly and Harpo Marx and Joe Kennedy and Dietrich and that whole crowd, and I said to Dietrich in kraut, 'I got a sausage for your bun, *mein Schatz*,' and that got Dotty all jealous and she was running her toe up and down my calf. So I took off her shoe and pissed in it without anybody noticing and handed it to her and said, 'Hey, you're in luck,' and she jumped up and yelled, 'He pissed in my shoe!' and they all said, 'Aw, shuddup, you're drunk.' All except Dietrich. She saw the whole thing. She saw that the great thing about being a quiet little bald guy is that you can piss in a lady's shoe at lunch and nobody will ever believe you did it. She leaned over and said, 'I have a sentence I'd like you to invert for me.' And we went upstairs to her suite and we steamed up the windows for a while. Hemingway was passed out on the couch. I put a ladyfinger in his shirt pocket. She was crazy about me, and so were some others, but who's counting? Now I've got Shochine and I've never been happier."

This was before he broke up with Shochine and took up with Louise Twelve Trees.

He gave me the nickname Prairie Dog and he'd ring me up around 5:30 on a Friday afternoon and yip into the phone, "Come on, Skip, let's go get our pants-legs wet," and off we'd go to the 79th Street Boat Basin with a bag of groceries and board the *Shawnee* and cast off the lines and motor down the Hudson. "Ain't this the life!" he said. He got out of his suit and into shorts and a sleeveless black T-shirt. He just felt so much freer out on the water, seeing midtown slide past on the port side, the cross streets like corn rows, and when 43rd passed, we yelled, "Boogers!" and hooked little fingers. Around Canal Street I hoisted the mainsail and we caught fresh wind at the Battery and flew around Governors Island and out under the Verrazano Bridge to sea and he sang out, "The sun's over the yardarm, Prairie Dog!" and I broke out the bourbon and poured two china cups full and he drew a chestful of salt air and started talking.

"I'm a hunted man. Crazy magazine's got me jumping like a rat on a hot plate. Some fool stuck his head in my office today and asked what's the difference between a solecism and a solipsism. Go spend a week with a dictionary, I tell him. A writer is supposed to know the English language, dang it."

I asked him about the perils of success and how fame and fortune seem to dig a deeper hole for a guy and throw up roadblocks you never dreamed of . . . like with me and *Spacious Skies*—it felt like I'd crossed the Red Sea and was headed for Canaan after years of bondage and suddenly I had enough money to afford good wines and good times and whammo, I wind up with a case of the cold shakes. Can't write. Nothing works anymore. Sitting there on the seventeenth floor writing notes and throwing them out.

"An old story. You're swinging too hard. Trying to aim the ball." He spat. "Listen, kid. Every writer I know is on a winding mountain road in the fog. Some try to deaden their fear with bourbon and wind up confused about their capabilities, like a sumo wrestler trying to run the 440 low hurdles. Or they wind up as preachers pandering to high-minded dipshits. The Betterment of Man is the worst motive for writing. It's the worst. Better to write out of sheer cussedness and heave a cherry bomb into the ladies' latrine and make them all jump out of their camisoles than climb into the pulpit and pontificate about the meaning of it all.

"John O'Hara had it about right. The purest motivation for a writer is to earn a pile of money. Which of course makes you the target of envy and you wind up with gobs of spit on your shoes and you don't win the Pulitzer and critics lowball you for the rest of your life. But what the hell."

Mr. Shawn walked to the rail and looked at the houses of Brooklyn as it slipped past in the twilight. "That's Bay Ridge," he said, pointing to a low rise. "I was in love with a girl who lived there. Bright red nail polish and curlicue hair and some of the nicest epidermis you ever saw. Met her at a party at Norman Mailer's. What an arrogant blowhole he was before I slapped him around a little. He was coming on to the Brooklyn girl at that party and I had to take him outside and give him a nosebleed. Now the guy can almost write sometimes. My gosh, she was an angel. I'd be sailing along and she'd come swimming out from Coney Island with her clothes tied on top of her head. Not that the woman needed clothes. My gosh.

"White was a fine writer. And then he wrote that crazy *Elements of Style* and inflicted writer's block on millions of college kids. If I were teaching college composition, my first assignment would be:

write something that would horrify E. B. White. Write a scene in which a man backs his pickup to the edge of Yosemite National Park and dumps a load of empties into a stand of Ansel Adams birch trees. Write a scene in which a guy picks up his grandma and throws her over the sofa. Write a scene in which Grandma takes lighter fluid and torches his rare Pete Townshend guitar that he paid $400,000 for at Sotheby's. The challenge for a writer is to get outside yourself. I'm an editor. That's my job. But when I'm on my boat, I'm somebody else. Who is also me. Comprende? Damn, I'm drunk. Pour me another." I refilled his cup.

"You're the greatest editor of the twentieth century," I said with a certain degree of sincerity. "You're my main man, Mr. Shawn."

"I never wanted to edit," he said. "All I ever wanted was to fish."

We got through the Verrazano Narrows and tossed out a line and pulled in some sea bass and grouper and I cleaned them and grilled them on a hibachi in the cockpit as Mr. Shawn sat down at the spinet piano in the main salon and played Gershwin and Kern and Porter and then I hollered, "Eats is ready, Mr. Shawn baby!" and he and I sat on the deck and ate the fish with raw onions doused in gin between slices of pumpernickel and got good and tight.

Mr. Shawn took me golfing at the Westchester Country Club. He had a beautiful swing. To correct for some bursitis in his left shoulder, he adjusted his stance about 18 degrees clockwise and turned his right foot in and pinned a lead sinker to the bill of his cap, which hung down like a plumb bob, helping him to keep his shoulders level.

"Some people only know me as an editor, a spooky little recluse who obsesses over commas and semicolons," he said, "but my big love is golf and what I obsess over is my swing."

It took him a minute to set himself up for the shot. He picked up some grass and tossed it to test the wind, got his feet dug in, adjusted the plumb bob, and waggled the club a few times. "I whipped Updike's ass but good. Many times. He's a yakker, you know. Likes to stand behind you on the tee and just as you get your feet planted, he'll say something like 'That sand trap sure reminds me of the crotch of a woman I knew once' and try to throw you mentally off your game, but here's what you do to shut a guy up—" And Mr. Shawn hit a beautiful drive that flew straight and long and dropped and rolled and rolled, a huge shot, and he marched down the fairway and hit a five-iron to the green, and then a long putt that curved and caught the corner of the cup and fell in for a birdie, meanwhile I had topped my tee shot and sent it dribbling twenty yards and then laced it into the neighboring fairway and wound up with an 8.

He turned to me as he shoved the putter in his bag. "Writers like to think that writing is like Arctic exploration or flying the Atlantic solo but actually it's more like golf. You've got to go out and do it every day and live by the results. You can brood over it but in the end you've got to take the club out of the bag and take your swing. You hit the ball to where it wants to go, a series of eighteen small steel cups recessed in turf, on a course that others have traversed before you. You are not the first. You accomplish this by practicing an elegant economy you learned from others and thereby overcoming your damn self-consciousness which trips you up every time."

He teed up and tied the lead weight to his cap and turned 18 degrees and set the back foot and waggled the club and hit a 200-yard beauty straight down the fairway.

"I can tell that you're of the self-consciousness school," he said.

"Oh?" I replied.

"Guys who spend a lifetime lining up a four-foot putt, reading the bent of the grass, the wind, the planets, checking out the geologic formations below, and then they tap the ball and it rolls eighteen feet into a mud puddle."

I wasn't sure what he meant, I said.

"Talking about your writing, Mr. Wyler. You've got the problem so many English majors have. You're terribly self-conscious. Your writing is mannered. It's all fussy and girlish."

"Girlish?" I was shocked.

"You write sometimes like an old poof. Using words like ensconced and blandishment and peripatetic and perambulated. Showing off for the other poofs."

"Girlish?"

It was the ninth hole. Par three, 215 yards. He had a piece of mine right there in his pocket: "*We were peregrinating along Lexington one afternoon last week with confreres and found ourself near the old Sneden's, the dark and dazzling nitery where back in the Age of Bon Temps one squeezed into a banquette with one's near and dear, and worshipped Mabel Mercer as she held forth on frosty winter nights, ensconced in a swatch of silk of lapis and bronze and other chinoiserie, offering up with terrifying beauty the brightest baubles of Cole Porter and Irving Berlin to torrents of applause from the jaded young, and we could not help but recall a very particular loose-knit soiree of hers, when, at her most magisterial, she delivered the definitive reading of 'All Alone' and brought us all to our feet, figuratively speaking, for there was hardly room in Sneden's to think one's thoughts, let alone do any leaping, and how often now do one's thoughts perambulate back to that Little Eden of merriment and manners that lay where now, alas, a very different hostelry, a coffeemonger known as Starbucks, squats toadlike in paradise vending overpriced java to jittery poseurs.*" I read it as Mr. Shawn took a three-iron and hit a monster drive that held up, pin high, twenty yards to the right of the green, and took an old wedge and popped the ball over the bunker and onto the green, rolling, rolling, and in the hole. *Click.* Eagle.

"See what I mean?" he said. "You let the piece get away from you before it even started. There's nothing there except some twitches and lipstick.

Girlish.

I slunk back to my office, stung, humiliated. I had worked two whole days on the Sneden's piece.

Girlish.

I couldn't help but remember the day I sat down on the C train opposite a young black woman reading a book that—*sacré bleu*—it was my very own novel, *Spacious Skies*. She was reading my words! I wanted to tap her on her little black knee and say, "Hey. It's me. Look at the photograph on the back. See? I'm him. The guy who wrote that." And then I noticed that she wasn't smiling. A slim well-dressed black lady, 29, heading downtown to her job at a brokerage firm, scowling and flipping pages, looking for something of redeeming value and she shook her head and closed the book and put it down on the seat beside her—O my dear African-American lady of 29, let me show you a passage or two that are sure to bring a smile to your lips—and the train pulled in at the 34th Street station and she got off and left my book behind. I almost broke down and cried. Felt devastated for days.

That was my most painful authorial experience until now. *Girlish.*

I didn't write much for a long time after that. I'd finished my second novel and was ready to start a third, but couldn't. Words wouldn't come. I sat in my office and thought about writing but nothing happened. I went to the doctor and he told me that for a man my age and in my condition, I was, for the most part, okay. There was a metabolic vasodilation in the intracerebral hemisphere, a certain vasoactive deanimation, and the peptides in my nerve endings were slightly hematized, but otherwise, not bad. I left his office feeling puny, shriveled, disease ridden.

On my way back to the office, I saw men sitting in doorways on cardboard scraps, begging, jiggling change in paper cups, and one faded old-timer with a sign against his chest, PLEASE HELP FORMER NEW YORKER WRITER DOWN ON LUCK. WILLING TO REMINISCE FOR FOOD. I gave him a five-dollar bill. "For twenty bucks you can have my sign," he sneered. "You may need it someday. Once I was just like you and then, take it from one who knows, a person can fall a great distance in a short time. It happens all the time in America. There are former stars of stage and screen hustling their next cup of java. Nothing fades faster than reputation, boy. Tempus goes fugiting along and your chins drop, your rave reviews yellow and your name becomes a trivia question. I've written a book on this. *Avoiding Downfall.*" He handed me a little pamphlet, mimeographed, about fourteen pages, with several gold stars pasted to the cover. "For you, ten bucks. Two for fifteen. This could save your life."

I opened the book. There was something about being kind to your minions because someday they'll be on top. Nothing new here. I handed the book back.

"You wait and see," he sneered. "I give you three weeks."

His curse followed me the rest of the day. I went home to my terrace and shook up a shakerful of gin and drank it, and the curse sat like a bad guest and wouldn't go away.

# 11 ❧ I Become Mr. Blue

Three weeks after Mr. Shawn said my writing had gotten girlish, I took a train up to Halifax to write about Canada. I thought Canada would be good for me. A change of scene. But it rained for three days and the hotel room smelled of beer and I sprained my ankle getting out of bed in the middle of the night and I wound up sitting in a bar and drinking Rusty Nails with a Canadian with a huge grudge against the United States. I fell into bed like a boxful of hammers and woke up at noon with a great idea, and got on the train to go back to New York and sat in my compartment and wrote a beautiful broadside against Our Neighbors to the North and said what every American has wanted to say for the past hundred years about Canadian independence—*Oh, get off it*—and in Portland, Maine, the train stopped and I disembarked and walked around the station and bought some magazines and used the men's room in the depot and there I forgot the yellow legal pad with my anti-Canadian harangue—left it on a ledge next to the urinal—and walked to the train and the conductor said, "How's that piece of writing coming along, young fella?" and I let out a yelp and dashed back to the men's room and the legal pad was gone. I emptied the wastebaskets. Nothing. I hustled around the waiting room looking in trash barrels. No luck. Finally the whistle blew and I climbed on the train, distraught, and went to the club car and had a whiskey and soda.

"Something wrong? You look terrible," the bartender said. So I told him. "It was the first good thing I wrote in a year and it's gone," I said.

"Well, that's a shame," he said, as if I'd lost an embroidered hankie instead of a literary creation. A woman with red hair was sitting at the bar. She said, "Just sit down and write the story again. That's what Fitzgerald did when Zelda left the manuscript of *The Great Gatsby* on a train in Zurich. He sat down in a hotel room and wrote it again—and it turned out even better! And he got the idea of Nick Carraway as the narrator instead of Gatsby's cleaning lady, Jean."

I hate people who give you inspirational advice like that. I loathe them.

A man in a wrinkled brown corduroy suit said, "I heard that Faulkner's *As I Lay Dying* was pitched into the fireplace by an illiterate field hand, and Faulkner proceeded to get drunk and write the whole thing from memory in two days straight."

"Easier said than done," I said.

"The power of memory," said the woman. "T. S. Eliot's *The Waste Land* fell into a hot bath and the ink washed off and he had to rewrite it and he made April the cruelest month, instead of the 'coolest' which it had been. Robert Frost once wrote a poem that was eaten by a dog who ran off into the woods, chased by the poet, and only then did he decide to change the poem to 'Stopping by Woods on a Snowy Evening' instead of 'Stopping at the Dew Drop Inn on a Wednesday Night in January,' which is what it was when the dog ate it."

We were bumping along through New Hampshire, bound for Boston, and the bartender gave me a double whiskey and soda, on the house, and the corduroy suit said, "Did you know that Philip Roth's *A Boy's Life* was sent to the cleaners with a box of sweaters and eaten by solvents and he rewrote it as *Portnoy's Complaint*. In the original, the guy's name was Porter."

"You see?" said the woman. "All is not lost."

Mr. Corduroy continued: "And John Updike's *Rabbit Relaxes* was sent by mistake to Tehran in a brown Samsonite suitcase, then New Delhi, Sydney, and Lima, Peru, and only after it returned did he decide that Rabbit maybe shouldn't retire and get involved in volunteer work. He decided to kill him off and spare the reader."

"Okay," I said. "I get the point."

"Walt Whitman's original manuscript, which he lost, was *Leaves and Grass*. William Carlos Williams lost his poem about the two beers left in the icebox and realized they should be plums."

The bartender chimed in: "Adversity is an opportunity for innovation! That's the American spirit. You lose your manuscript, you write a better one!"

"But you should've done it right away and not come in here and had two big glasses of Scotch," said the woman. "That's what Emily Dickinson did when she lost her poem 'Because I could not stop for Lunch.' She was at the tennis court with Lavinia. The poem was written on a scrap of paper folded and tied with string. She didn't sit around getting pie-eyed, she sat right down with a towel around her neck and rewrote it better."

I returned to my compartment and got out a sheet of paper and looked at it and everything I could think of about Canada was nothing but ashes, a pale shadow of the original. I got to New York in a grievous mood and I never wrote much after that that was any good.

It was soon after that, I became Mr. Blue.

~~~~

*Amber Waves of Grain* came out in September—though I'd told my editor, "It's not done yet! The buns need to bake!"—and the reviews were all torpedoes. ("What a dumb book!" said the *Times*.) Sales were lousy. Pitiful. Two weeks after publication, big stacks of it were on sale at Barnes & Noble for $1.89 and the security tags had been removed so as not to hinder shoplifters.

A dumb dumb dumb dumb book. Why did I write all that stuff about soybeans in the first chapter? And then in chapter 2 the agronomist, Danny Montalban, suddenly is no longer in Fargo, he's in Fresno, and we're at a lesbian commitment ceremony at a pimento ranch with ladies in denim caftans whanging on little drums and chanting sapphic things and Cathy and Denise affirming their love for each other and riding away on a piebald pony and then there's that whole thing about the transcontinental railroad and the driving of the golden spike—and then George Eastman and the Kodak—where did all *that* come from?

The answer is: I tried too hard. I tightened up at the plate and swung too hard and tried to aim the ball. Just as Mr. Shawn warned me not to do.

Suddenly I was a joke. I walked down 43rd Street and heard the word *soybeans* whispered and people tittering.

What suffering can fall on us out of the blue! I was on 7th Avenue in the thirties, walking fast to make a lunch date with the fact checker named Shahtoosh, and a construction guy passed me pushing a handcart piled high with lumber and the cart tipped and a half ton of lumber brushed against my pants leg and crashed to the sidewalk. Had it fallen six inches north it would have snapped my left leg in two. And then Shahtoosh wasn't at the restaurant. She left a message: "Sorry. Something came up."

*Soybeans.* That's what came up. The word was out: *Wyler Laid an Egg. Wyler Pissed His Pants.*

I was on the B train and a young woman said, "You wrote a book. Right?" I nodded. She said, "I remember your picture from the dust jacket."

"Oh," I said. "Sure."

She said, "You probably get people coming up to you all the time saying they recognize you from your picture."

I said, "No, not that often."

She said, "Really? I would think it would happen a lot."

I said, "Not as often as you might think."

She said, "Well. You learn something new every day."

And we rode on together in silence all the way to 42nd Street without her ever saying, "I loved that book of yours. You're so talented." Nothing of the sort.

My agent, Leona, who had gotten me an advance of one half million dollars for *Amber Waves of Grain*, said that the publisher wasn't ready to discuss an advance for a third book, *Purple Mountain Majesties*, quite yet. They were reexamining their options at this point.

Oh, go suck a rock, I thought. But it hurt.

And then out of left field came a letter from a woman named Lorna at the Minneapolis *Star Journal* asking me to write an advice column.

I'm sure you must be extremely busy these days, what with novels and all, but I've admired your work for so long and I thought, What harm can it do to ask? So I'm asking. And I just feel from reading your work that you have so much insight to offer people who are going through difficult times, bad romances, career struggles, et cetera.

She wanted two columns per week. The readers would send me their letters by e-mail and I'd edit them and write my responses and e-mail the column to Lorna and it'd go into the newspaper.

"I know it's a long shot and you're probably much too busy," she wrote, "and we can't pay much. Six hundred per column."

Actually I wasn't busy at all. I was writing nothing. I couldn't. *The New Yorker* was paying me nothing. So $1,200 a week looked good.

I called up Lorna in Minneapolis. She was thrilled.

I said, "Don't you already have an advice columnist? A Miss Becky? The one who always advises readers to seek professional help?"

"We had her for twenty years and then she took a cruise on the Aegean and had a romance with an Albanian waiter and it didn't work out and she came home and stuck her head in the oven."

"I might be able to do it for six hundred," I said.

"It's a deal," she said.

So I became Mr. Blue.

The name came from the hit song by the Make Rites, "Mr. Blue," their one and only hit before they died in a plane crash south of Reno on their way to accept a crummy prize (Best Liner Notes, Male Vocal Group) at the Grammys in LA. They are not with Buddy Holly, Otis Redding, Patsy Cline, Ricky Nelson, and others in the Plane Crash Hall of Fame in Mason City, Iowa, because, frankly, they weren't big enough stars. Their song, "Mr. Blue," was about longing for something that you know will turn out to be exquisitely painful, but you want it anyway.

You're no good for me, baby,
You're strychnine in my stew.
Someday you're going to kill me.
Still I'm in love with you.
Don't know why I come here.
I shouldn't but I do.
My life's a mess but I love you, yes,
I'm your faithful Mr. Blue.

The thought of seeing my own words in print appealed to me, after my long drought. I was back in business. The *Star Journal* printed a quarter-page ad for "Ask Mr. Blue." **Lonely? Confused? Angry? Tell your story to Mr. Blue. Offering commonsense answers to life's persistent questions, twice weekly in the *Star Journal***—and fifty e-mails arrived immediately. **Lonely** was lonely and **Angry** was disappointed in love and **Disappointed** had a wonderful husband

who was crippled by jealousy and **Brokenhearted** was missing her
boyfriend who was happily dating other people and when I retrieved
the e-mail, a message flashed on my screen.

HOTNHEAVY: hi Mr Blue :)

MRBLUE: hi

HOTNHEAVY: are u married?

MRBLUE: yes

HOTNHEAVY: cool :-( i'm 34 bi swf vgl 5'2 132 br/br lve soccer
cooking pets (2 dogs) movies lkng for LTR or?????

MRBLUE: Great

HOTNHEAVY: email me

MRBLUE: k

HOTNHEAVY: bi

# 12 🌸 Crossandotti

A picture of Harold Ross, the founder of *The New Yorker*, hung in the men's room off the lobby of the Algonquin Hotel, and when standing at the urinal, waiting for the water to fall, I looked up and saw the inscription: *"To Fingers, a great guy, yr pal Rossi."* And I wondered who Fingers was and who Rossi was before he became Mr. Ross.

And then Mr. Tony Crossandotti appeared in my office one day. He was a big guy, solid, about the size of a Harley, with eyebrows like cockroaches, gray-black hair swept back, helmet-shaped, every strand in place. Manicured nails, and gleaming shoes, and a magnificent gold tooth lit up his smile. He wore a bright purple shirt and orange tie and a green pin-striped suit with red silk pocket hankie folded in the shape of a horse's head. And yellow-tinted glasses. A lot of colors going on there but somehow it all worked.

"Please come in," I said, though he was already in.

He walked over to the window. "Hey," he said. "Still there. Look." There were deep scratch marks on the windowsill. "That's from Mr. Gill's fingernails," he said.

Brendan Gill was a sweet old guy at the magazine, very patrician, very Century Club, gray hair curling over the collar, horn-rim reading glasses, nappy sweater, vintage port, shelves of O'Casey and Yeats, summers on the Cape, the whole deal.

"Me and a couple of the boys had to hang him out the window coupla years ago. Wrote a profile that made a reference to Lucky Luciano that made my blood boil and about give me a coronary infraction and we came trundling up here and stuck a gun under his chin and heaved him out the window and let him hang by his fingernails for a few minutes and then we reeled him back in. He ain't given us no trouble ever since."

The marks on the sill were deep grooves. The man whose fingernails made them wanted very very much to go on living in this world.

Crossandotti sat down on my desk, on top of the papers. I heard a pencil crunch. "Some guys, you know, lose track of where they come from and you got to remind them. Gill got it in his head that he was a Harvard guy and we hadda bring him back to the real world. His name is Brentano Guillermo. Sicilian. His papa was a sanitation worker. Good friend of my papa's. That's why I got him the job. Brentano is a good boy. Knows about theater, about architecture, writes very good quality stuff. He just got out of hand a little and we hadda thump him.

"This is sort of what a publisher does: he brings you writers back into contact with the real world in which most of us live most of the time."

I said, "I'm Larry Wyler, Mr. Crossandotti. Forgive me, but I don't believe we've met." I was trying not to sound servile and yet I could see that the man was carrying a loaded revolver.

"I take it you work here in the building," I said.

"That's very funny," he said. It didn't sound as if funny was a good thing to be.

He put his right hand on my shoulder. It sat there, lightly, but a person got the message: if he wanted to, he could take that hand and rip your face off.

"I own the fucking building," he said. "I'm the fucking publisher of *The New Yorker*. Okay? And I know everything about you. Okay? Where you live and your wife's name is Iris and she's on Sturgis Avenue in St. Paul and you got a garage full of grocery carts and—hey, anything you want to know, just ask me, okay?"

I nodded. That was okay with me.

He took the hand away.

I said, "I like your shirt."

Mr. Crossandotti was pleased that I noticed his wearing apparel.

"I got it at Corso. Silk and poly and Egyptian linen. $300. Dean Martin wears these. You remember—in *Rick Mercato*? The scene where he's waiting in the café for Gina Lollobrigida and instead Mr. Big Pants walks in? He was wearing this shirt. It comes from Corsica. You've got to order them three months in advance."

He looked at my black suit and white shirt and decided not to express an opinion.

"So how the hell are you?" he said.

I said that I was having a good day, thank you, and hoped that he likewise was prospering.

"I was coming around looking for somebody to do a job for me," he said. "And then I remembered about Brentano and I came to see if his fingernail marks were still there."

"What sort of a job?"

"A good job. You busy?"

"Not right now."

I run this thing called DWI. The Distinguished Writers Institute, okay? It's located upstairs from the magazine. It's a service for young people who want to learn how to write"—as he told me this, I noticed a whitish flake on his upper lip. I wasn't sure if it was eggshell or oyster shell or what, but it was hanging there and it didn't fall off.

"Here, you probably seen this," he said, and he handed me an advertisement—"Earn $$$$ Writing Fiction, Poetry, Essays, Memoirs, Literary Journalism"—which offered a "critique" of your work by a "professional editor" for $195.49 and there was a picture of a happy guy reading a note from DWI ("Very effective use of language,

Brent, and with just a little more attention to form, you're sure to be appearing in *The New Yorker* in a few months.")

"Interesting," I said. I wished he'd wipe the eggshell off his lip. It was bothering me. "You want me to write critiques of people's writing? I could do that."

"Naw, we get that done in Malaysia. We got little kids who punch some keys on a computer and out comes your critique. Naw, I need somebody to write the computer program. You know anything about that?"

I asked him how many clients DWI had and he said, "Between twelve hundred and two thousand a week."

"A gold mine," I said. He nodded. Even with him nodding, the flake didn't fall off.

I told him he had something on his upper lip.

He peeled off the flake and examined it. "I had oysters for breakfast," he said. "That was four hours ago. I been walking around with a flake on my lip and nobody told me?"

"I guess they were too polite," I said.

He couldn't get over the fact that none of his lieutenants had dared to point out the flake of oyster shell.

"I'm the fuckin publisher of *The New Yorker* magazine and people can't point out a fuckin oyster flake on my upper lip for Christ's sake?"

"I take it you're not married," I said.

"I mean, here I am, fuckin walkin around with this piece of crap on my face and these assholes can't fuckin say, 'Hey, Tony, you got a flake or something on your face'? I don't get it. What the fuck is going on here?"

"It was a small flake," I said. "Maybe the light was poor."

"I been talking to that asshole Newhouse and he can't even do me the decency of pointing out a fuckin oyster flake on my lip? Jesus!"

And he brought his big fist down on the desk so hard that the telephone jumped a couple inches. "Somebody oughta yank that Newhouse's chain and get him off his high horse if you ask me. Guy thinks he's a mogul! He's nothing but an asshole!"

I was not there to disagree with him. On the other hand, I had no grudge against Mr. Newhouse, whoever he might be.

Mr. Crossandotti got up to leave. "Think about the offer, kid," he said. "And don't worry about me throwing you out the window. I give it up for Lent." He chuckled and slapped me on the back and I could feel a rib crack. "Oh, by the way—what's this I hear about your writing being girlish? That's what somebody told me. What's going on?"

"My writing isn't girlish in the least. Anyone who reads it knows that a man wrote it, I warrant you."

He poked a toothpick into his mouth. "You ever write a story in which somebody gets shot in the head?"

I shook my head.

"Why not?"

I explained that most of my stories are set in the Midwest, where gunfire is a rare occurrence, except during hunting season.

"The fact that it's rare oughta make it even more interesting. Sez me." He hiccupped and let out a long rich belch and reached into his mouth and dislodged a shred of meat from between two upper molars on the left side. "If you want to hear about how I snuffed that family in Kansas so Capote could write *In Cold Blood*, come over to the Algonquin, I'll buy you a drink."

"You murdered that whole Kansas farm family so that Truman Capote could write about it?"

"How else was he gonna do it? He couldn't shoot 'em himself."

"What about the guys who went to the gallows for it?"

"Couple of losers. No big loss to mankind, believe me." He examined the shred of meat and then chewed it. "Capote wrote girlish stuff, you know. But then I give him some murders to write about and he did a bang-up job. And then he came back to New York and he wrote girlishly again. Wrote gossipy stuff and moony stuff about fame and loneliness and futility. Magnolia blossoms. I don't know what. Then he kicked the bucket. If you're a man, don't write that stuff. That's all I got to say. Fuck futility. Just do your job. Right?"

# 13 ✎ Calvino

A flood of mail came in for Mr. Blue. Torrents. I had no idea that the readers of the Minneapolis *Star Journal* were so troubled. I thought of Minneapolitans as fundamentally sound, Scandinavian people given to low-fat diets, aerobic exercise, listening to public radio, but here was the grandfather of **Distressed** holed up in the attic, ogling naked nymphets on the Internet, hour after hour, tying up the phone line, an embarrassment to the family. The mother-in-law of **Astonished** goes into a grocery and eats the vegetables right off the produce counters, carrots, tomatoes, Brussels sprouts, even bananas—she stuffs the peels in behind canned goods—and when he protests, she says, "They figure it in when they set prices. I'm paying for it anyway." She is 62, a college professor, and she shoplifts food. **Horrified** wanted to know if she should attend a baby shower for a 17-year-old neighbor girl living in the basement of her unemployed boyfriend's parents' house and the two of them watching cartoons while awaiting the birth of their child. **Floundering** fell in love with a guy, and he with her, and then he went ahead with a three-week fishing trip to northern Ontario with his buddies—during which she looked through his desk and found the poems he wrote that suggest that he is Bob but is also "Blanche" who is not happy about sharing a body with Bob and wants it to be more her own—what should **Floundering** read into this? She's 34 and has no time to waste. **Headache** wonders if she is "too nice" to her boyfriend, who lives in a filthy apartment with mountains of dirty clothes and dust bunnies the size of ponies and says he can't marry her because he is depressed because he thinks he might be gay. He isn't sure. She pointed out to him that gay men have perfect hair and shiny skin and live in fussy apartments with little antique lamps and lacquered trays. She wonders whether to drop him. She has no time to waste either.

~~~~

Too bad I was Mr. Blue, otherwise I'd have written to him about my own situation.

~~~~

**Dear Mr. Blue**

1. I can't write.
2. I work at a magazine that appears to be under some type of criminal management.
3. My wife and I are separated and I still love her and yet have no particular urge to live with her.
4. I have a new gig as an advice columnist and am trying to respond confidently to people's alarming dilemmas and in the back of my mind I'm thinking, What if I tell this sad confused person to just take life one day at a time and instead she takes a canoe out on the lake and jumps in with rocks in her pockets because she is clinically depressed and any idiot would've known that from reading her letter, but I didn't see it, and I am responsible for her death as much as if I had choked her with a strand of barbed wire?

—Mr. Blue

~~~~

A person looks at *The New Yorker*'s cover, a painting of an old frame beach house aglow on a summer night, and you never imagine there's somebody like Tony Crossandotti running it and dangling somebody like dear old Mr. Gill out of the window to hang by his fingernails. I wanted to discuss this with Mr. Calvin Trillin but he was hard to reach. I left a dozen plaintive messages on his answering machine and once even passed by the fashionable Aeolian Hotel on West 22nd and looked up to see if his penthouse lights were on. They were not. He was in Los Angeles on *The Tonight Show.* His new novel, *No Parking,* was an enormous hit. Michiko Kakutani called him a genius in the *Times,* and Harold Bloom, writing in *The New York Review of Books,* called the book "essential" and said that all literate people should take notice, and Helen Vendler, in *The Times Literary Supplement,* referred to him as a "national reference point," and at the same time his handsome visage adorned the cover of *People.* Mr. Popularity!

It was hard not to draw comparisons between the blockbuster success of *No Parking* and the quiet demise of *Amber Waves of Grain,* though of course I admired Mr. Trillin and wished him well.

Nonetheless I felt he owed me some straight answers. I sent Mr. Shawn a note asking about Mr. Crossandotti and he wrote back—

```
Don't let that big woofer get you spooked.
His bark is worse than his bite. If he's
bothering you, tell me and I'll slip him a
Mickey Finn.
                     Bill
P.S. How's the Alaska piece coming?
```

Alaska piece? What Alaska piece? I never went to Alaska in my life. Had no desire to.

Mr. Trillin came by the office one day, and when I mentioned Tony Crossandotti he closed the door and told me to sit down.

"Forget what you learned in English composition," he said.

"You're not in Minnesota anymore. The magazine is a snake pit. Sorry I didn't warn you. Crossandotti is a shark. Cross him and you're dead. He's got a lot of pals with hair on their backs and if they decide to not like you, you could find yourself in Umberto's Clam-house face down in the linguini with your brains for white sauce. So keep your nose clean."

He walked to the window. "Those cigarette burns on the desk are the result of nervous guys sitting here waiting for the knock on the door. You got the gun?"

I nodded. "Top left-hand drawer."

"Loaded?" I nodded. "Good," he said. "Mr. Ross wished he had one, I'll bet."

I asked him why our founder, Harold Ross, was referred to as Rossi by certain people.

Mr. Trillin looked out the window for a long time. "I'll make this brief," he said. "My name is Calvino. Buddy Calvino. And I'm not from Kansas City, I'm from Palermo. My papa brought us here when I was thirteen years old and he paid for speech therapy to straighten out my accent. By the time I was sixteen, I spoke well enough to get into Yale, even though I had too many vowels in the old patronymic. The old Wasps looked down on my people as garbage men even though we produced Michelangelo and Dante and Vivaldi. Those blue-eyed thin-lipped patricians saw an Italian name and visualized a paper sack dripping with coffee grounds and orange rinds. They accepted the Irish after a hundred years, grudgingly, but we Italians couldn't get our foot in the door. So I kept my head down and made inroads where I could and met a guy named Lobrano and his aunt Pauline Coeli was a writer at *The New Yorker*. She was Brentano Guillermo's cousin. He was related to Gianni Chivera, who was Roger Angeli's cousin, and Roger is the stepson of the great E. B. Blanco."

"E. B. White is Italian?"

"The one and the same. The guy who wrote about Carlotta the pig and Stuart Piccolo."

And then I saw the bulge under Trillin's jacket. It looked like he was packing a toaster.

"Are you telling me that *The New Yorker* is owned by the Mafia?" I said.

He said, "I'm not telling you anything. I'm walking out that door and you and I never had this conversation. Ciao, baby."

# 14   Blocked

Let me tell you people,
Every morning is the dead of night.
I say, when it's 2 P.M. for you,
For me it's past midnight.
I've got the writer's block blues
Because I cannot write.

I am sitting in the darkness
And the page is blank.
It's like a hole six feet deep,
So dark and blank.
It's where my plane went down,
It's where my ferry sank.

All I ask is water,
Not a glass of wine.
Ordinary Minnesota tap water,
No need for sparkling wine.
But I have a crystal goblet
Filled with turpentine.

Baby, I miss you,
I want you back again.
My Muse. O little darling,
I need you back again.

But you walked away, Sugar,
In search of younger men.

I used to wake up hoping
Today the sun will shine.
I used to think tomorrow
Is the day that it will shine.
I feel the cold steel bars
Around this heart of mine.

I was forlorn. I was a man with a mysterious disease. Except for Mr. Blue, I couldn't write. Other writers avoided me in the halls, afraid of contagion. I tried antihistamine, aspirin, zinc, and vitamin E, varying the dosages. I tried ice cold showers. I went to a shrink on Madison Avenue who said that maybe I was blocked because I was terrified of rejection. She thought it could be related to toilet training and Mommy making her little boy stay on the potty until he produced. She prescribed a pill to lighten my mood but said I shouldn't use it if I needed to operate a motor vehicle or work with numerals.

One horrible night, thinking this might help, I took a tab of acid in an Oreo, and a few hours later, on my terrace, I saw green and orange neon lights, parrots, Roman candles, violet wallpaper, sopranos, rivers of taxicabs, I was talking to Baudelaire. My ears were ringing. And the next day, a doorman came up with the four notebooks I had thrown over the railing, which almost hit an old lady on the street. The notebooks were pure gibberish. A gibbon would have done as well.

Mine wasn't the longest-running writer's block at *The New Yorker*—far from it. The place was famous for sheltering the non-productive. Shawn, for all his bluster, had a soft heart, and there was a whole stable of writers who drew nice salaries to sit in their offices and brood, such as J. D. Salinger, whose most recent story was "Ira and Ellie" in 1972, about Seymour Glass's son Ira and his girlfriend and their weekend in Miami with Franny and Buddy and Zooey and Bessie and Woody and Jerry and Rodney. Joe Mitchell was another famous nonwriter and then there was J. F. Powers who had dreams in which he read his own new work and found it so substandard that he never wrote any.

I told Salinger that I was blocked and he gave me a white silk prayer scarf from the Rabindranath Janarandamahakrishnamurti Meditation Center. "It helped me," he said. Helped him do what? I wondered.

I felt claustrophobic in my little jail cell of an office. Once I had a panic attack and dashed to the end of the hall and threw open the EMERGENCY ONLY door and stood on the fire escape gasping. I was paralyzed. Locked into failure. I kept trying and trying, but you come up to bat with 156 consecutive strikeouts and the bleacher crowd is chanting, "Hey hey, Mister K!" and no matter how you try to steady yourself (*Visualize success. Accept good fortune. Open your arms to it. Swing from the hips.*) you feel that chill in your shorts and you no sooner get settled at the plate than ZOOM comes the ball and it's *steeeeee-rike ONE* and you think, Okay, here we go again. Hello, failure. *Steeeee-rike TWO, steeeeee-rike THREE.* And you turn and walk back to the dugout, feeling some sense of completion.

I found myself sitting and looking at three words on a screen, *It would appear,* and changing it to *It would seem* and then after lunch to *One might conclude.* I heard about a little club near Times Square, where mature women in sturdy foundation garments force naked men to speak in a foreign language and correct them without mercy. Strangely appealing, I had to admit.

I went to Siegfried's for a haircut ($85), the same place Trillin went and Updike and Tony Crossandotti, and there amid the stylish young hair designers in black jeans and T-shirts was an old guy named Earl and naturally I got him and his hands were shaky and before I knew it he'd mowed a big bald strip down the center of my scalp and I wound up having to go to a place called Domenico's House of Hair and buying a small unconvincing toupee.

I called Iris to beweep my outcast state and she was in a sour mood over a losing candidate for Congress. Some thoughtful fellow seeking to improve mass transit and reduce class size and clean up lakes and rivers and build affordable housing and he got his gonads cut off by a Republican rottweiler who wrapped the flag around himself and accused Mr. Bright Eyes of undermining national security and wanting to tax the jammies off people and confiscate guns, slingshots, and paring knives. The dog bit the man and the man ran away. No news there. But she was all torn up over it. She was thinking of selling the house and moving to Vermont. Our old stucco house with our old bedroom and the rickety garage full of grocery carts and covered with honeysuckle vines.

"Good," I said. "Sell it. The sooner the better."

"You're never here, and I don't want to be here, so why not sell?" she said.

"Sell it and come to New York. I need you."

"Ha. I doubt that very much." She said, "Somebody asked me what you were up to and I had to say I don't know."

"My life is falling apart. I can't write anymore. I'm no good without you."

"Well, if it isn't one thing, it's another," she said.

⌄⌄⌄⌄

I wrote her a letter telling her how much I loved her and needed her and then didn't mail it. It wasn't good enough. The tone wasn't right. I rewrote it. Still not right. Too stilted. Like a bad translation. Self-conscious. Girlish.

And then I ran into her online. I visited a chat room called Lib Blab and there she was, under the screen name LADY LIBERAL, in a discussion with some people about Where Liberalism Went Wrong, and I clicked on her name for a private chat.

MR. B: Hey. Whassup?

LL: Who's this?

MR. B: Bernie. Saw your comment about gays and couldn't agree more. The left keeps getting drawn into cavalier battles over equal rights for dancing dogs and hermaphrodites that bleed us white and divert us from the one battle that really means something and that is: where does the money go? The bread and butter stuff. Caring for the homeless and all these deinstitutionalized mental patients who've been left to fend for themselves here in New York. First things first.

Well, that got her interest. She told me that her husband lived in New York and I asked her why she didn't and she said, "I'm not his type anymore."

MR. B: What a jerk. I'm 45, single, tall and in good shape, U of M '66, and I enjoy conversation, good food, music, travel. Where would you like to go?

LL: Is this a pick-up attempt?

MR. B: <grin>

I jabbered along (ah, the childish pleasure of anonymity), winking and LOLing and ROFLing and I said I wanted to meet her for coffee.

MR. B: I'm looking for my dad. He's 72 and has a gear loose. He ran away.

LL: Really.

MR. B: Schizophrenic, or something.

LL: Call the police.

MR. B: I want to meet you.

LL: Why?

MR. B: I like talking to you. Tell me more about your husband.

LL: What about him?

MR. B: Do you love him?

LL: Of course.

MR. B: There's no "of course" in love.

LL: Oh?

MR. B: Let's meet. I like you. ((((hug)))) Want to call me? Say yes. 8-]

LL: No. Sorry.

MR. B: Oh. :-X

I was grateful for that *no*. Iris might be confused about us but she wasn't in the market for random liaisons with strangers.

One night, sailing around Staten Island, I told Mr. Shawn that I couldn't write and he said, "When was the last time you got laid?"

"It's been a while," I said.

"Maybe that's your problem."

I finished one story, "Our Far-flung Correspondents: Riding the Lift
Bridge in Duluth," and Mr. Shawn bought it, all 650 words, and it
never appeared in print. A mercy acceptance. But I was grateful.

**Dear Mr. Blue,**
**I've always wanted to be a writer but when I try, I sit and gaze out**
**the window and don't get any good ideas and after a while I go and**
**read a good book. What's wrong?**

**—Dazed**

My dear Dazed, You and me, too. We need motivation to write, just
as we would if we were driving to North Dakota in January. The
prestige of being there is not enough. You might go there to earn big
money or escape from the FBI or to find hot sex with a librarian in
Valley City but the thrill of writing a letter with a North Dakota
postmark would not be strong enough motivation. Not for me. Un-
less I were writing a letter about that librarian.

**Dear Mr. Blue,**
**I spend my days in a tiny cubicle writing meaningless drivel, sur-**
**rounded by brain-dead coworkers and Dracula managers, and all I can**
**think about is that long concrete ribbon that leads to Montana and a**
**life of freedom and adventure and honesty. Why haven't I left yet?**

**—Discouraged**

O **Discouraged,** I know exactly what you mean.
I was drinking hard. A big glass of Scotch or two when I got home

to the apartment and then a third and some red wine to induce sleep, but I'd pace the terrace late at night like the captain of the *Titanic* and worry about losing Iris, worry about my prostate, about money, my savings flying away like dry leaves in a hurricane—*Mr. Wyler, this is MasterCard. May we expect a payment from you this week?* I was becoming more familiar with daytime television than an adult of normal intelligence should ever be and one day I saw J. D. Salinger on *Hollywood Squares*, happy as a kid in a toy store. He answered all the questions correctly and sang "K-K-K-Katy," which I was amazed he knew, but he did, all the words. I switched the channel and a lantern-jawed actor murmured, "Kimberley, David can give you a house in Greenwich but he can never give you love. He can give you wonderful clothes, but not the spiritual peace of mind that you crave. This squalid struggle for money and publicity—let's leave it— you and me." I made myself a tequila sunrise. I thought, Shame on you, a graduate of the University of Minnesota, with a proud tradition to uphold, and here you are, a common lush.

My darling dear,

It's warm and bright in New York and this morning I walked to work through Central Park, where the drive was thronged with walkers and skaters, and then down Fifth Avenue, making a detour into St. Thomas for a little prayer time. Asked God to give me something to do with my life, and if He doesn't want me to be a writer, okay, fine, then what's my new assignment? I stopped at Scribner's bookstore and picked up *Great Expectations*. Thought maybe I'd steal some ideas from Dickens, who had so many of them. My afternoons are fairly empty. So are the mornings, for that matter. Dickens was one who never faltered. Writing came naturally to him. Chekhov, too. And Updike. I saw him today in the hallway outside Shawn's office, tall, graying, courtly. The model of a modern man of letters. I was a few feet away, pretending to study a wall map of New York harbor, checking the water depths in various places. Updike had an old black briefcase. If he got up and forgot it, I was going to steal it and hold it for ransom and the ransom would be that he writes a story for me to publish under my name. I've been struggling for a year to write one—he could do it in an afternoon. (And if it were under my name, it wouldn't have to be as good, right?)

He took the briefcase with him.

Then I thought of taking him out on Mr. Shawn's boat and dumping him overboard, the briefcase filled with bricks, chained to his ankle, and keeping the contents to publish at my leisure. Larry Wyler's thoughts on Cubism. Larry Wyler's dense new novel about mathematics. Larry Wyler's brilliant critique of Reinhold Niebuhr.

This is how desperate I am. Considering bumping off a beloved American author. Snuffing the Rabbit man.

But in my current state (frozen) I find Updike's flagrant success oppressive and vulgar. While I sit in this dingy cubicle on the 17th floor, whittling away at the same old stick, winding up with nothing but shavings.

Well, I must go now and think. Hope you are well. Write when you have time. Do you think you might move out here to be with me? That would be nice.

Love,

Larry

Dear Larry,

It was nice to hear from you. I'm sorry you're having a hard time. So are a lot of people. I went to clean out Mr. Hoffstadter's apartment today, having succeeded in putting the old booger into a nursing home. He's been working his shopping cart route along Rice Street for five years now, yelling at the streetlamps, trying to keep them in line, and living off cigarettes, coffee, and cashews from the Episcopalian food shelf. Anyway, the apartment was a horror show. Filth and trash and spores of fungi everywhere. A nephew was supposed to take care of it but one look and he decided to pass. Some alien life form occupied the refrigerator. Anyway, the potato salad was moving. I thought I might have to shoot it. Amid the debris were some lovely oil landscapes and antique furniture and rare editions, souvenirs of Mr. H's previous life in the upper middle class. He was the comptroller and vice president of Hyperion Mutual Life until dementia got hold of him. Unfortunately, he retained much of his executive personality even after he lost his other marbles and was able to intimidate people as he marched up and down the street, pushing his cart, shitting in his pants, screeching in an authoritative way, and people let him be. Poor old thing. I got him roped in and sedated and now the apartment is cleaned out and the nephew, who stands to inherit upward of two or three million, has sent a donation of $100 to MAMA along with a Hallmark thank-you card. You learn so much about people in this line of work. If you find New York unbearable, you should come home.

xxox,

Your Iris

I asked Shahtoosh, my fact checker honey, if she had any advice for a blocked writer, and she just laughed and said, "Hey, lay back and enjoy it."

We were lounging around on my terrace. She couldn't believe that anybody who owned such a nice apartment could be in real trouble.

"I wonder how John Updike does it. My gosh, the man is indefatigable. Short stories, novels, literary criticism, art criticism, poetry, reporting—"

"You wouldn't think so if you knew what I know," she said. "He gets a lot of help from checkers. You knew that he can't spell, right? Words like *lien* and *lean*, and *here* and *hear*. *Indefatigable*. Can't spell it."

I wanted to cry. Another hero, kneecapped. The author of the Harry "Rabbit" Angstrom novels that I admire beyond words— *Rabbit Rent, Rabbit in Rehab, Rabbit Is Raunchy, Rabbit Relaxes*— a bad speller.

**Dear Mr. Blue,**

My wife used to be a federal judge and we were all terribly proud of her, and then, after ten years on the bench, she took a sabbatical to "explore her identity," and now she is a serious roller blader. She is 51. She has resigned her judgeship so she can go off to senior women's amateur tournaments all over the country and compete. She has never won anything above a bronze medal. She used to have opinions on literature and politics and culture, but now she is totally dedicated to leaps and figure 8s and the double axel. She is not a slender little thing, and I hate to see her embarrass herself skating around in a skimpy little skirt and blouse like a circus bear, but deep down, I am losing respect for her. Why is she doing this?

—**Exasperated**

Dear Exasperated, Your wife got tired of people being proud of her and decided she doesn't care if anybody stands up at her memorial service and talks about her legacy or not, she would rather have some fun. She likes to roller blade. So she decided to spend her time doing it. What don't you understand about this? I have devoted most of my adult life to writing stories and now, in late middle age, I've washed up on a reef and can't write for shit. I must say that roller blading strikes me as entirely honorable and useful compared to what I'm doing now. Maybe you should blade on your wife's rollers before you get down on her like this.

~~~~

Dear Mr. Blue,

Is it mere coincidence that the word therapist also makes the words "the rapist"? My psychiatrist Jekyll is giving me the creeps, milking prurient details out of me about my love affairs with older men with big eyebrows. I got to talking about my latest lover and Jekyll got all giddy, whereas he shows not a glimmer of interest in the fact that I am a compulsive hand washer and have a thing about chickens. I am a successful career woman (a county prosecutor, but don't print that in the paper), but I have forty-three sets of bed sheets and pillowcases with chickens on them. Sixteen chicken tablecloths. A recorded rooster awakens me every morning. I have a Leghorn chicken night-light. If I don't wash my hands at least three times an hour, I begin to sweat and shake. Jekyll couldn't care less. All he's interested in is my sex life. I'd walk away but my self-esteem can't take another shot in the chops.

I'm a good person. I tutor inner-city kids, I take public transportation. But in addition to chickens and hand-washing, I have this other compulsion to say cruel things to fat people. For example:

What do you keep in those creases?

Need me to get something out of your back pocket?

Ever think about buying group insurance for yourself?

Where'd you get baptized? SeaWorld?

I asked Jekyll, "Why do I get my jollies from poking fun at these porkers?" and he shrugged and said, "Tell me more about Dale and your weekend in Duluth." The other morning, on the bus, I said to a black lady who was occupying two seats, "Who paints your toenails? The guy at the auto body shop?" I live in fear that I will be arrested and it'll get in the papers and my mother will disown me. Mom is the most important person in the world to me. She's a little hefty herself. In fact, the only way we can get her out of the house is to grease the doorframe and stand outside holding a Twinkie. I know it would break her heart if she knew that I was inflicting gratuitous pain on blimps and wide rides. Should I get a new therapist?

—Nice Lady

Dear Nice, Yes. Get a new therapist. And stop abusing the obese. It is protected by the First Amendment, but one day some fatty will fall on you in anger and you'll need back surgery and physical therapy every Tuesday and Thursday afternoon and you'll fall into deep depression and turn to baked goods for comfort and not just the occasional cheese Danish but whole crates of sugar donuts from Krispy Kreme that you sit in your full-size car and devour greedily until one day you see a porker in the mirror trying to avert her eyes, and you can say, "Hey, for a fat lady, you don't sweat that much."

Meanwhile, I was putting on the pounds myself—in days past, when I strolled onto the terrace in my Speedo, binoculars flashed in nearby buildings as women sought a glimpse of me, but no more, alas—I had left my old weight of 195 behind and passed 225 at a dead run and was lumbering within sight of 250. I did not set foot on a scale after 245, I just bought expandable pants. My old skinny clothes hung in the closet, and my Porky Pig outfits were getting tight now and soon I would need to purchase clothing by phone from Hootie's Pants Warehouse in Tupelo, Mississippi.

Dear Mr. Blue,

I am a radio announcer, fifty pounds overweight, bipolar, with an odd bulbous head. I'm hearing impaired due to the earphones being too loud, but I guess I sound sexy on my all-night jazz show because gals call on the request line and clamor to meet me, which is nice until they actually do meet me and their unmistakeable look of wan disappointment is followed by a few minutes of strained conversation and the inevitable "Well, I've got to be going." I can't bear this rejection anymore. Don't kid yourself: looks matter, they always will matter, and women will always prefer an imbecile with a nice chest to a mature guy like me.

—Confused

Dear Confused, Get out of jazz and find a job at one of those AM talk stations aimed at Angry Suburban Males who are pissed off at liberals for causing sunspots. Learn to rant and rave, fulminate and fume, and you will be a big hit on the Right where most people are overweight and have bulbous heads.

I was washed up, no doubt about it. Nothing I ever wrote would be of the slightest interest ten years from now. I was yesterday's fish wrap. If I died of a massive heart attack my body would lie undiscovered for days. And Iris wouldn't come to New York to retrieve it. It'd be drained and dried and boxed (XL) and flown in the bowels of a Northwest Airlines flight from LaGuardia, and a few feet above my pale and waxen form, passengers in First Class would sit savoring their bloody Marys and reading the *Times* Op-Ed page and looking forward to a weekend of canoeing the St. Croix with Maureen, and all I'd have to look forward to is a black hole in Lakewood Cemetery, a short hike from the beach at Lake Calhoun where in our salad days Iris and I once skinny-dipped at midnight and embraced, looking at the lights of downtown Minneapolis.

I had a dream in which my prostate was about to be removed by a tall surgeon in black riding boots who took the cheroot out of his mouth and said, "You won't be needing an anesthetic, will you? A big fellow like yourself?"

I'm okay, I kept telling myself. I am basically okay. Depending on what is meant by "basically." I still had some dough left and was in reasonably good shape, despite the booze, and fairly alert, and women were attracted to me, at least a couple of them were. I was not what you'd call a tragic figure. No. Not yet.

**Dear Mr. Blue,**
**My mother is married to the man who killed my father. He (Dad) went off to avenge my uncle, whose wife, Helen, had been stolen away by some Trojan people, and then this man fell in love with my mother. When my dad came back, this man killed him, and he and my mom married. Anyway, my brother, who lives far away from here, has vowed to kill our step dad and Mom. He is very upset. I am going nuts. Any suggestions?**

**—Electra**

Dear Electra, Speak to your family doctor or priest or oracle or maybe appeal to a goddess, like Athena, and tell her exactly what you told me. You may have to make some sacrifices. But there is help available.

# 15 ❧ Turkey Lurkey

Writing Mr. Blue was a comfort to me for sure. As rancid as my own situation was, there were Minnesotans who were suffering right along with me. **Still Hurting** was wanting to sue her uncle for leaving the bathroom door open and exposing himself to her when she was eight, a traumatic memory that she'd been dealing with for thirty years. **Bummed Out** was in love with her gay male friend and got angry and jealous when she spotted him with other guys. **Jaded** was tired of life, period. Ready to move on. **Curious** was in love with her doctor. **Angry** wanted to put sand in the gas tank of her cheating boyfriend. **Shocked** was engaged to a woman who (he found out) did not shave her underarms.

~~~~

**Dear Mr. Blue,**

I grew up in Midland, Texas, and went to Yale though I am no reader and married a fine woman who supported me through my Lost Weekend years when I goofed around in the oil business and got high as a kite on weekends and went around making a fool of myself. With the help of dear friends, I was able to sell my bankrupt company at a handsome profit and then obtain a major-league baseball franchise and get public financing for a ballpark, whereupon I sold the team for a fabulous profit. What a lucky duck. Now that I'm off the sauce, I am considering taking a stab at politics (my dad was a politician though not a very good one, IMHO,) but I hate hanging around with dull people who yak about the fine points of public finance or Whatever! And my wife says, "Why don't you try writing? You have so many good ideas." What do you think?

—Curious George

Dear George, Writing is not as easy as you might think. You're required to sit in a little room by yourself for periods of time and the English language can be darned frustrating sometimes. But there's no harm in trying. I'd recommend that you try writing a book for children. Not so many words and the story line can be pretty basic. How about the story of Pecos Bill? He was a Texan. Or an aviator story that doesn't involve bloodshed and gore. Perhaps a group of friends who get together and fly jet warplanes for the sheer fun of it. You're the author! You decide!

I told Salinger I was writing an advice column and he gave me what appeared to be a wry smile—Salinger sometimes wore a fake beard and dark glasses in public so it wasn't easy to read his facial expressions—and said, "That sounds like wisdom talking, Larry. Advice to the lovelorn. I envy you. You must learn a great deal from that." I do, I said. I do.

Dear Mr. Blue,
I'm a faded number from St. Paul, living high and dry in New York, a writer who had one big success and then a lot of little failures—yes, that old story—no pals to tell my troubles to, so I'm filled with dread. Pacing my terrace on the 12th floor, looking out over the rooftops, thinking dark thoughts about failure and disgrace—writing is what makes me happy. But I can't write. My wife is busy help-

ing crazy old people. I am fast becoming one myself. Is it all over for me? Is the arc of my life unalterably set? Where is the joy, where is the incandescent beauty?

—Big Fat Loser

Dear B.F.L., A gloomy guy can decide not to be and take the stone out of his shoe and walk straight. So do it. But don't expect to do it tonight and tomorrow. Impatience is the luxury of youth. The rest of us must take things in steps. If you don't know this, life itself will teach you. Life is a relentless instructor. Gloom and dread are dispelled by making slight progress; progress, even slight, leads to more progress; and gradually the glacier shifts, the ice jam breaks and things move in the direction of your dreams. Keep trying. PS The Mr. Blue cure for the blues is a good night's sleep. Anytime you feel bad and it isn't your fault, just curl up and go to sleep. It will be better in the morning, especially if you go to sleep expecting so.

It was the easiest writing I ever did. It just squeezed out like toothpaste out of a tube. It came winging out of the blue like a stork with a baby in a sling. Lorna at the *Star Journal* sent me an e-mail:

Everybody loves it. You've made me a heroine here at the paper. Nobody thought I could ever persuade the great Larry Wyler to write for us, and then I did, and now people are stopping me in the halls to say, Thank you. I hope that Mr. Blue isn't taking you away from your other work, though. I haven't seen anything by you in *The New Yorker* for a coon's age. Are you busy working on a new book? I didn't get a chance to read *Amber Waves of Grain* yet but understand that it's quite special.

O my dear lady, you don't distract me from my work. Mr. Blue *is* my work. I looked half my life for this work. The meaning of life is, first, to earn a living. You may be digging your own grave, but if you dig it straight and deep and they pay you, it's honest work. Work is redemptive. I was wasting time being lonely and drinking and making late night phone calls to friends and writing long weepy letters to my darling Iris and suffering gruesome hangovers and getting crushes on waitresses in coffee shops and enduring writerly paralysis and yet—I am still in the game. I am Mr. Blue. It is humble work, but one day, lo and behold, there was a note from my old friend Katherine seeking my help, and I don't mind saying: I was gratified.

~~~~

**Dear Mr. Blue,**

**How important are schmoozing and politicking in getting one's poetry published? I'm the author of two collections of poems, and when I show my work to people they say, Oh that's nice, but there's no real respect, as there would be if I had a major publisher instead of Thistle Blossom Chapbooks of Minneapolis. (Don't print that, please.) I've read most of the "major" poets and frankly I think I'm in that league. I have a very strong suspicion that if I went to New York and attended the right parties and stood around drinking Sauvignon Blanc with the right people, my stuff might get published pronto. No? Am I kidding myself?**

**—Moonflower**

~~~~

Dear Moonflower, Enjoy the craft of poetry and leave the art of sucking up and schmoozing to others. But if you want to suck up, don't apply suction to lower middle management, which is who drinks white wine. People with real power to get a book of poems into print are gin or bourbon drinkers. Don't kiss the wrong butt.

And two hours later, she wrote again:

~~~~

**Dear Mr. Blue,**
I am the poet who wrote you asking how to get published. Please destroy that letter. I don't want it to appear in the paper. Everybody I know will know it's me. Could you print the following instead—

~~~~

**Dear Mr. Blue,**
I am single, 45, attractive, fun to be with (according to friends), and well educated, and my life is going nowhere. I want to fall in love with the right man and settle down. I dated a Norwegian and he was so taciturn it took me six years to find out that he was married with children. I joined a church and got involved in community activities, and now I know a lot of other single women in their forties and fifties, but I want someone to come home to and snuggle with. Is that so impossible?

—Moonflower

~~~~

Dear Moonflower, The supply of available heterosexual men who are psychologically sound is small. You're hunting for mountain goats, basically, so you probably need a guide, someone who knows a goat personally. The truth is that men hate to be single. So they hang on to a mate until another comes along. They hate to be at sea, so they hug the coast, and a woman in search of one is forced to become a pirate, drifting through the knots of married couples, letting the men appreciate her charms, her openness, her lovely skin, her insouciance, her availability, and letting the women loathe and despise her. I don't recommend that, but it's been practiced successfully by many women who thereby became somebody's second or third wife, and there is an advantage to buying a horse that's already broken and accustomed to the traces. But never mind. You are not that sort of person, thank goodness. But just in case you should change your mind, be sure to pay attention to your physical person. "Attractive" isn't enough when you're 45. You need to be a knockout. A woman men look at and think, Wow. Don't waste your time on the subtleties—you have two powerful assets, located on your chest, and you'd be a fool not to use them. A little décolletage—or a lot, what the heck, Christmas is coming—can work for you. If you want to attract a man, unbutton your blouse. You can discuss books afterward. Boobs come first. I could lie about this, but why?

~~~~

**Dear Mr. Blue,**
For several years, I lived with a fascinating woman from a world very different from mine, a Zoroastrian from the Minor Rawalpindi archipelago who weaves white cotton garments on a small loom and lives on lentils and yoghurt and speaks very little English. Her name is Nhunu. I'm a civil engineer turned professional turkey caller and a major Vikings football fan and a barbecue guy and I love to grill a whole hog's hindquarters on my motorized rotisserie and toss back a double Scotch on the rocks and shoot down balloons with an air gun. For all of our differences, we were fairly happy together until one day she became fearful and agitated. Either that, or she was asking to take swimming lessons. (We communicate mainly through hand signals.) Then she upped and flew back to Rawalpindi, leaving me a note saying that she had shackles on her feet, twenty-nine links of chain, and on each link an initial of her name, and that she was not sick, she was just dissatisfied. She also said something about the water tasting like turpentine.

Should I follow her to Rawalpindi and make a life there? I could get a job driving a taxi, but the language is mostly vowels and it sounds like someone gargling with rutabagas. Is the gap between our backgrounds simply too wide? Should I stay or should I go? I really miss her a lot.

—Turkey Lurkey

Dear Turkey Lurkey, Hand signals leave so much room for misunderstanding, but we must go on what we know, and you should consider yourself lucky. Her feelings for you are in transition. You won't be happy in Rawalpindi, so put that out of your mind right now. Of course you miss her. But loneliness is a manageable problem. And instructive: your soul is chastened, shriven, uplifted by loneliness, you become kinder and more loving. Loneliness is only hunger: stave it off with crackers and baloney sandwiches and wait for dinner to arrive. If you have friends, you'll find romance; romance is only a juiced-up version of friendship. So quit moping. Get out of the house. Go wherever there are big crowds—the Boat Show, a Billy Graham crusade, a protest march, a Dixie Chicks concert—and mingle. Let your elbows brush other elbows. Inhale other people's exhalations. Get out of your gloomy introspection and back into the World We Live In. Someday you'll look back on Miss Lentils as a bump in the road you had to drive in order to get to the arms of Miss Peach, who loves and understands you and is fun to be with and shares your fondness for roast pork and football and marksmanship and turkey calling.

Dear Mr. Blue,
Thanks. You're right, of course, and after the loss of Nhunu, I try to go out and have fun, but I think of those summer nights with her when life seemed to twinkle and beckon to me. Now that she's gone

life is just one grim obligation after another: my job, my ailing mother, my ex-wife, my other ex-wife, my neighbor with the 30-foot chainsaw sculpture in his backyard (art, my ass) and I'm in court over that and then there's this other court case hanging over my head—oh boy—I got wrecked on whiskey sours and got it in my head to rob a bank so I parked across the street with a pistol in my pocket and waited for the lobby to clear out but by the time that happened I'd had a few more drinks and was three sheets to the wind and in no shape to rob a small child, let alone a bank. I got out of the car with my ski mask on but with the eyeholes in back and I walked into a parking meter and shook up the family jewels and fell down and the gun went off and it blew a big hole in my wind-shield and I thought to myself, If I'd been sitting there, I'd've been killed, which made sense to me, as drunk as I was, and I started bawling like a baby, and the cops came and arrested me for public drunkenness and possession of a deadly weapon with intent. My mom had to put up $50,000 bail. I feel sick.

Whatever happened to the beautiful life Nhunu and I had? Will I ever find it again?

—Turkey Lurkey

He attached a photo of himself in camo clothes, a slight potbelly, aviator glasses, poofy blond hair. And an audio file of his turkey calls (MALE CHALLENGE, FEMALE COURTSHIP, MATING-URGENT, TERRITORIAL), which sounded like pure male panic, a man with a pair of waxen wings about to leap from a cliff.

Dear Turkey Lurkey, You and Wordsworth and Keats and me and everyone else, we all mourn our lost youth and brood over the odd course that life took. You're beating your wings against the window, sir. This can eat up time and it makes you poor company, especially if alcohol is involved.

Avoid solitary tippling. Limit booze to when you're in the company of others who are drinking the same stuff you are and in similar amounts. Keep pace with them so you see in them what is happening to yourself and when they get stupid, you know that you are, too.

Every life has its parameters. Take mine, for example. I'm an aging white male of moderate intelligence and prickly personality and what's to be done about that? Not much. Get a good lawyer. Be glad you're not up for bank robbery. Plead guilty to drunkenness and throw yourself on the mercy of the court. Don't fight the neighbor. Deal with things one day at a time. Above all, GET OUT OF THE HOUSE.

**Dear Mr. Blue,**

Who do you think I am? I am not a pirate and I am not going to go prancing around at parties with my boobs hanging out. If that's what men want, then I'd rather be a nun. I'm sorry I ever wrote to you. What a pathetic creep you are.

—Moonflower

**Dear Mr. Blue,**

My brother is wildly in love and seeing him walk around gaga has relit a fire in me that I thought went out when Nhunu left. I've been guarding my heart, but now I want to find somebody. The truth is that when I meet a woman and she asks, What do you do? I tell her the truth, that I'm a professional wild turkey caller. She seems interested, but when I demonstrate turkey calling and strut and gobble and shake my wattles and shriek and snort and puff, just as I do

professionally at hunting shows around the country and get a standing ovation, she can't dump me fast enough. (Maybe that's why
Nhunu was attracted to me: she thought I was speaking Rawalpindi.)
Any advice? I believe in honesty as an absolute base standard, and
don't want to lie about myself, so maybe I should go back to civil en-
gineering.

Oh, and I forgot to say this before, but I have herpes.

—Turkey Lurkey

Dear TL, First impressions are everything, and gobbling and shrieking should not be the first thing a woman sees in you. Let her see the
more cultivated side of you first. Save the gobbling for farther down
the road and invite her to a hunting show so she can see the standing ovation, too.

# 16 🐾 Love

I told Mr. Shawn about Mr. Blue one evening aboard the *Shawnee* as
we sailed under the Verrazano, me at the wheel and him at the cocktail shaker. It was one of those golden October days when New York
is enchanted, electric, and a guy is almost able to forget that he can't
write worth shit.

I said, "Something wonderful has come along for me and I want
to share the news with you," but he was more interested in a flock of
cormorants swooping over our bow. He tossed them a handful of
croutons, which of course attracted a vast herd of birds and for some
reason he had invited a camera crew aboard from PBS—"They're
doing a documentary on *The New Yorker*," said Mr. Shawn, as if this
explained everything. I tried to be a good sport, but it was a pain in
the ass. I was busy being the helmsman and Earl the TV director was
telling me to talk about the ocean as a metaphor of freedom. I told
him I don't do metaphors for free.

"How do you feel about New York as a symbol of the American
promise, then?" he said. "The lady with the lamp and all."

"It's a good harbor," I said. "Better than Boston's, that's for sure.
But Baltimore has a good harbor, too. And Norfolk. You want to talk
harbors, talk about Norfolk. Hampton Roads. Maybe they should've
stuck the Statue of Liberty there. You got the U.S. Navy in Norfolk,
speaking of women and liberty."

"Say more."

"Don't have more to say."

The cameraman was right in my face with his lens, and I was trying to keep my eye on a garbage scow that was swinging across our bow to starboard.

"Talk about liberty and your feelings about it and New York in terms of your own writing or your memories of France."

Earl was one of those young guys who shave their heads to give themselves a hip menacing look, but the truth is, they have the brains of a beach ball. Like every other TV producer in the world, Earl was clueless about the real world, he had no sensibility, so he had to shoot thousands of miles of film because things only made sense to him when he saw them on a screen.

"You have a blankness about you that in my opinion would spell success as a TV host," Earl remarked, looking down at his video monitor. I told him to blow it out his ass. I said to Mr. Shawn, "Do we have to stand here and let this moron take pictures of us?"

Mr. Shawn is sitting on a coil of rope, in a black shirt, barefoot, mirror shades, a .22 across his lap, a brimming martini glass on his knee, studying the 14,000 terns and gulls and cormorants whom a handful of croutons can attract to a boat. He says, "What are you afraid of, Wyler?" Right away, the camera zooms in on my look of surprise.

"I object to being enlisted as an extra in somebody's stupid video," I say, knowing my words will be edited out.

"Afraid you might look foolish, Wyler?"

I am shocked at this, coming from a man whom I love and admire. Earl and his cameramen are tense with anticipation.

"That detached ironic tone, Mr. Wyler. The perpetual precocious adolescent flitting about, mothlike, creating trifles, feuilletons, elegant piffle. That's the root cause of writer's block! The source of all true art is simplicity! Stripping away! Making plain! Removing the ornamentation of the literary social climber. Getting a grip." And he slaps me on the back. Hard. "Stop feeling sorry for yourself," he says. To me! He says this to me, on camera! "If you don't have the goods, then give up the game. Don't hang your head. It's no shame to fail. Just do it and get it over with. Don't base your whole life on it."

I'm trying to steer the damn boat through an obstacle course of freighters pulling up anchor and ridiculous powerboats buzzing around and the Staten Island ferry plowing across our bow, so I've got plenty on my mind, thank you—But a videocam doesn't get the big picture, and what the folks at home will see is a worried guy (me) being told to Be Myself.

And then Mr. Shawn heaves another handful of croutons and five hundred large birds swoop down toward me and I flinch and duck and the camera gets a close-up of that. The *Shawnee* is streaked with bird feathers and bird shit and careening in the wake of the Staten Island ferry and Mr. Shawn looks up at the World Trade Center, all golden in the twilight, and raises his arms as if signaling a touchdown, and he cries, "It's not that complicated, Wyler!

"We walk around the house. We feed the dog. We sit in our father's chair. Life is remarkable for its kindness. But the seeds of kindness do not give us words. To the contrary. Writing is a passage through narrow straits and there is always bumping into rocks. So much important writing begins with bad dreams. What we call a bad dream is simply one that intends to teach us something—" and he throws more croutons in the air and another flotilla of gulls comes in low.

The TV guys are going nuts. One cameraman is lying on the deck, shooting Mr. Shawn through a flurry of white wings, and the other guy is climbing the rigging for a high angle, and the director is practically peeing in his shorts.

"Either one accepts this or one doesn't, and if you do, it's a clear gamble and of course you feel a profound sense of loss—of mysteries conspiring against you—and then you see it, Wyler!"

He climbs a few rungs up the mainmast and points toward Brooklyn.

"There is no poverty! There is no loss!"

Earl is trying to get his attention. The microphone has come unclipped from Mr. Shawn's collar.

"There is no reason for longing!"

"Can we do this again, with sound?" says Earl.

"Life has given gifts to the immortals and naturally you long to be one of them and you covet their gifts. But life has given you gifts, too. And the chief one is receptiveness."

"I'd like to shoot this again from the part about bad dreams," says Earl, reaching for the microphone which is tangled around Mr. Shawn's left ankle.

"Receptiveness! The little raindrop splashing on your hair—you feel it! The sweetness of gesture and manners! The rhythm of dailiness, you feel, and the lyrical energy of sex! Like a river current! A Mississippi of sex! Even a Housatonic isn't bad!"

Earl gets hold of the microphone and tugs it. "We need to go back to the bad dreams," he says. And Mr. Shawn looks down at the blank bald head of Earl and says, "Everyone makes his own hell, doesn't he." And he grabs the .22 and aims it at Earl's feet. "If you don't listen, I will have to find another language," he says, and fires at the deck, and Earl is over the rail and in the water, holding on to the microphone cable for dear life, planing over the waves.

"Why steal water when it's raining?" says Mr. Shawn. "This is basic to life. We live by a basic pigeon sense—a boy throws a rock and the pigeons rise in the air—and the impulse to write is the urge to fly on one's own. So fly. Raise your sail and let the wind fill it."

"I love you, Mr. Shawn," I said. "I don't say this easily or elegantly, coming from the Midwest, but I love your ass, Mr. Shawn. I'd die for you."

I wanted to throw my arms around him. I wanted to, and I did.

"I love you, Bill," I said. I kissed him on the cheek. He was somewhat impassive about this, but I believe he enjoyed it, in his own way. "I'll never give up trying to write something that will please you, Bill. I'll be writing for you the rest of my damn life. After you're gone, Mr. Shawn, you will still be my Number 1 reader."

The cameras were off. The cameramen were trying to reel Earl in toward the stern. So my big hug never got on film, but I didn't care. I said what I needed to say.

# 17 ❧ Turkey Cont'd.

**Dear Mr. Blue,**

I am the professional turkey caller, 34, who wrote about wanting to find someone. Well. I met a lady (she is a poet) and there was a definite attraction. We went to her place in St. Paul and we were talking about this, that, and the other thing, and pretty soon the lights were off and we were kissing, etc., and I decided to let out a little turkey gobble and this got her going like you wouldn't believe. We got naked pronto and were both clucking and puffing and strutting and went at it hammer and tongs for approximately an hour and that was pretty great, I must say, and then she hauled some poems out and asked me to look at them. I'm no critic but I think they're not good. Read this:

> Oh shine down
> Your primordial enthusiasms
> Goddess of Sky
> And take
> This disfigured asparagus
> From the turbid gelatins of
> My heart.

She has written hundreds of poems, all of them like that. I am all in favor of personal expression but I think I know crap when I see it. Should I tell her what I think?

—**Turkey Lurkey**

**PS My lawyer got the drunkenness charge reduced to Public Un-steadiness and so I'm going to AA. Should I tell my lady friend about this, too?**

~~~~

Dear Turkey, Do not be honest with a poet or she might slit your throat with a serrated steak knife. Poets do not accept criticism gladly. A sour word about their work makes them very very quiet. Turkey hunters are Sunday school teachers compared to poets, whose murderous impulses toward enemies real or imagined are not to be underestimated. Their feuds go on for decades, their vendettas rival the Venetians' for sheer malice. Tell the poet that her poems mystify you with their depth and resonance on many levels, and let it go at that.

PS Save the news about AA for the right moment when she's a little snappish with you and you need to make her feel guilty.

~~~~

**Dear Mr. Blue,**
**Please forget that angry letter I wrote. I am terribly sorry. I met a wonderful man at a reading of mine and he's one in a million. I wasn't wearing a low-cut blouse at the time, but then we came to my place and it disappeared entirely. Thank you, thank you, thank you.**
**—Moonflower**

**P.S. I wrote you a poem:**

Whoever you
Are
Who just smiled
And waved
Across the abyss
Of shrieking febrile blackness,
The tom-tom ostinato

Of your liquefied amplitude
Has Saved My
Life.

~ ~ ~

Dear Mr. Blue,

I am the turkey caller in love with the poet. Last week, I got a letter
from the Zoroastrian girl from Rawalpindi whom I used to live
with. She said she loves me and wishes to move back to the U.S. but
needs money for a passport, and—I made myself a big drink (I've
been on the wagon for three months since my gun-discharge inci-
dent) and I sold my house, sent the money to Nhunu, and moved in
with Mom. (Mom and I have always gotten along well.) I don't
know how to explain this to my poet friend, though. And then Mom
hired a private detective who found Nhunu in a commune run by a
voodoo cult. Lots of chicken slaughter and blood smeared on people
and candle wax and nakedness and so on.

Mom said, "That bitch has put a spell on you, Brian. That's why
you're mooning around like a teenager. You've been cursed. Let me
call Father Fred and have him put a stop to it." Mom is a devout
Catholic. Of course I feel bad about Nhunu and her voodooism but
more than that I'm worried about Katherine (she's the poet). I've
written to Nhunu and asked could she please return the $175,000 I
sent her when I was drunk. No response yet.

Meanwhile, Mom went into my computer and found naked pictures of Katherine, and boy did she give me a piece of her mind. She
said, "Now you got yourself another chippy in addition to the
voodoo gal in her black capes and plumes and leather lace-ups, mut-
tering incantations. You've got a bad poet with droopy little tits.
One's got her hooks into you for $175,000 and the other one has got
you drinking again."

Well, I reminded Mom how she bailed out my younger sister

when she got pregnant by that drippy piccolo player in the high school marching band whom she had sex with on the band bus because she "felt sorry" for him. (How you can have unprotected sex on a bus with someone you don't even like is beyond my comprehension.) "What could I do?" Mom said. "She's my daughter." She then called Father Fred to do an exorcism. He came over and gave me a brochure, "What to Do When Temptation Tiptoes to Your Window."

Now I find myself obsessed with Katherine, doing our chart (I've gotten into astrology, now that I've lost my turkey calling jobs due to my drinking) and the vectors and trajectories are pointing toward a Great Confluence. Should I ask her to marry me, even with all my problems?

I hate to worry Mom, who is nearing the end of her earthly sojourn, but when I told her I want to marry Katherine, she cried, "*Et tu*, Brian! Go! Betray the mother who brought you into this world! Go with your droopy-titted poet or your voodoo gal! But before you do—go get the butcher knife and plunge it into my heart! Because that's what you're doing. So do it!" It took a long time to get her calmed down, meanwhile the detective called to say that there's no trace of the $175,000. I want to do what's right. Love has no limits. Love is giving without reservation, giving joyfully. I am pretty sure I want to marry Katherine.

—Turkey Lurkey

Dear Brian, Let me call you Brian, okay? The $175,000 is gone. Kiss that good-bye. As for marrying Katherine, have you ever considered poverty and celibacy? There are groups of men who practice both and they live in handsome brick-and-stone enclosures in scenic rural areas and they seem content with their carpentry, bread baking, brandy distilling, or whatever they do. Do a Google search on the word *Trappist*. Send for a brochure.

**Dear Mr. Blue,**

My boyfriend Brian and I are very happy living together here in my place. He is drinking less and his mom doesn't call so often now that she's in the nursing home and he seems to have forgotten about turkey calling, which is a blessing. I'm sorry, but it was getting on my nerves. I've quit nagging him about neatness on the theory that we need to let housekeeping seek its own level while we sort out our feelings. I have this awful retroactive jealousy thing and find myself very upset about his ex-girlfriend Nhunu the voodoo queen and the $175,000 that she stole. As I wrote to him in a poem,

> I think of you
> And the unutterable
> Dented madness
> Of the testicular dialectic of snakehips
> Gyrating that hymns my solitude
> —O I have been a very very bad poet
> But why did you
> Let her take you
> To the
> Cleaners?

Am I just ridiculously petty and lacking perspective? I can't seem to let go of this.

—Moonflower

Dear Moonflower, Young love is replete with sweet pangs and retroactive jealousy is one of them. It's a sort of greediness born of happiness, trying to extend the romance back into the past and bump off all rivals. Be happy, move forward, live memorably and your romance will attain a rich history of its own and the distant past will fade. It might help if you'd stop writing poems for awhile, though.

~~~~

Dear Mr. Blue,

I am a woman cop, 32, in St. Paul (don't print that), single, trying to spread my wings after a long rough spell (cancer, drugs, grad school, a guitarist boyfriend), and I have a crush on a coworker with beautiful green eyes who even under standard fluorescent lighting looks terrific. I sure wouldn't mind if he hung his parka in my closet! Unfortunately, I'm in Vice, he's in Homicide—so we're strangers, and I've been thinking of making a Secret Admirer card and slipping it in his slot. I've written him a poem but I'm afraid I may have gone overboard and it would embarrass him: What do you think?

> Here in this dark world like an alley in a film noir
> And me the broad in the red dress smoking the cigarette,
> I look across the busy street and suddenly there you are.
> My dear, you thrill me, although we've barely met.
> And though it'll probably turn out wrong
> And lead us into a month of breakup hell,
> I want to dance with you to a Frank Sinatra song,
> And have a drink, and take you to a small hotel.
> We're no angels, we know what time it is—
> Me in Vice, and you my love in Homicide—
> We know how soon the champagne loses the fizz,
> How soon the audience gets glassy-eyed.
> And yet I want you. Tonight. Lying next to me.
> No matter what comes afterward. Linda. Ext. 1573.

As a backup, I wrote a limerick:

> There is a young man with green eyes
> Who makes my hair follicles rise.

I would unstrap my gun
And my clothes, one by one,
If I knew he'd remove his likewise.

Which one do you think would work the best? You can be frank.
I've been looking for someone ever since that shithead guitarist finally got out of my life. Everyone says, You'll find Mr. Right when
you stop looking for him, but maybe I have found him and he
doesn't know it. We talk sometimes around the coffee machine and
he never asks what I'm doing this weekend. Mostly we talk about
the Twins or Vikings or his mom's health problems. I just want him
to show some interest or something. Is that too much to ask? Am I
trying too hard? How can I avoid scaring him off?

—Smitten

Dear Smitten, Get out of Minnesota. This is not a state where men
can accept getting a poem from a woman, especially not one as frank
as yours. Try New York. There, a woman can sleep with anyone she
wants to sleep with and nobody says boo about it.

# 18 🌿 Copenhagen

In the midst of my long drought, I met a Danish woman named Lone ("Pronounced LOAN-uh," she said sweetly) and for a couple months she became the Glorious Woman who would rescue me from myself. The name was on her place card at the Max Henius Society dinner sponsored by the Danish consulate and her place card was next to mine. She had short red hair and a big grin and she led me out onto the dance floor and we gyrated vigorously to a Dixieland band and sat down and held hands through the speeches— Denmark is a nation of after-dinner speakers and there were fourteen of them that evening, each one proud of his ability to be funny in English. I was completely potted. Henius was a chemist who ran an institute of fermentology in Chicago in the 1890s, a far-sighted man who tried to persuade the beer industry to stave off Prohibition by cleaning up the American saloon and making it into a beer garden with good food and white tablecloths, but his advice went unheeded and soon public tippling was outlawed by the beady-eyed Baptists, and Henius returned to Denmark, where the finer things of life were still appreciated.

We all drank a toast to Henius, and to Queen Margrethe, and to the president, and to amity between nations, and in my alcoholic fog, I sat at our table and listened to an engineer discuss wastewater management, and then turn to the woman on his left and resume a conversation about the male superior versus the canine position in coitus. Danes are so free with each other!

Someone at the podium up front was yakking about trying to

make a difference in the world and not just earn a lot of money, and lo and behold, it was someone introducing me for my award. What was it for? I hadn't the faintest idea. Little did they know how drunk I was. I managed to rise to my feet and take a bow, but no. They wanted a speech. People were waving me toward the front, so up to the podium I went. Someone handed me a glass of something. A vodka sour or something. My fine motor skills failed me and I dropped it—on myself, unfortunately—as I grabbed the microphone and bent it toward me and it made an explosive rumble.

> ME: I thank you so much for this award. It means a lot. A person never really imagines that something of this sort will come to him. You just do your job the best you can and you never think that someday you'll be standing in front of a group as distinguished as this and receiving this tremendous honor from the Danish people. This is so neat. Of course I couldn't do it by myself and I want to thank a number of people, starting with my wife, Iris, who could not be here. She has been my inspiration for so long and—you know how it is: you never tell a person who is so close to you just how much they mean until—well, until you do, and that's what I'm doing right now.

I got teary-eyed about Iris and talked about my writer's block and living in New York and *The New Yorker* and the problem of girlish writing—the speech was going very well! People were enjoying it! I talked about Iris and her crazy people and old Gus at the open house and saying that to the TV cameras—and then Lone guided me back to my seat. I was grateful to her. People clapped.

I had an ugly tear-shaped Lucite trophy in my hand. I told Lone I hoped to visit Denmark someday.

She said, "Come over and stay with me in Copenhagen."

She meant it.

"I could stay in a hotel," I said. "Really. There's no need to put you to a lot of inconvenience."

"Nonsense. I live alone in the heart of Copenhagen. You'll stay in my apartment."

So I went. Flew SAS and landed at Kastrup Airport early in the morning, in the lovely rain, the air fragrant with green grass and coal smoke, and took a taxi past the green soccer fields and a stream of bicyclists in bright yellow and red and green rain gear biking to work, poker-faced Danes queued up for buses, streets of brick apartment houses with brown tile roofs, stone churches with green-and-gold steeples, the Royal Theatre in its sooty stone castle, over the train tracks, to a narrow street and a door with a golden 3 above it, and Lone's big, old, echoey apartment with fourteen-foot ceilings with plaster moldings of flowers and fruit—it looked as if they'd just finished drafting the Treaty of Ghent and gone out for breakfast—and Lone had made coffee. She poured us cups and I thought, How remarkable to fly across an ocean to be with a woman you don't even know. She wore a sort of rose-colored wrap over her pajamas and was quite happy to see me. She said that we'd have to go see Rosenborg Castle and the Marble Church and the walking street and Magasin and Tivoli and Karen Blixen's house, and then she said, "But first you must come to bed and sleep." Through the open window, the smell of the sea and the whoosh of express trains racing north toward Elsinore, and a police siren like in an old spy movie echoing off the gray stone buildings, and the telephone rang its musical Danish ring, and she didn't answer it, she closed the bedroom door, and then she and I were kissing, and then we descended into the soft white bed, under the down comforter, and embraced, our two coastlines gently washing against each other.

I stayed in Lone's apartment there on Trondhjemsgade for a whole week of starstruck pleasure. She was an unabashed sensualist.

She'd stroll into the living room naked from her shower, natural as could be, and we sunbathed in the nude with hundreds of others in the park in Frederiksberg. A glorious week. We dined on oysters and champagne in Kongens Nytorv and rode bicycles around the lakes and through the old star-shaped earthen fortress, Kastellet, the salt breezes blowing her close-cropped red hair as we pedaled up along the coast through the Royal Deer Park at Klampenborg and Taarbeck and Skovshoved to Hamlet's castle in Helsingborg and stood watching the car ferry cross the water to Sweden. Her family owned a chain of optical shops; she was an optician. She was also, so far as I could tell, a communist or the next thing to it. And yet she lived gloriously well. Good wine, good food, sex. I visited her mother, Elly, one day for lunch in an apartment complex in the suburbs. A tiny one-bedroom apartment full of dark furniture, with a tiny balcony. She had fixed steak and French fries and bought a California cabernet and baked an apple pie. A tall woman of noble bearing. Americans were friendlier than Danes, she told me, pouring Jim Beam into a glass full of ice. The Danes had collaborated with the Nazis, while the Americans drove the bastards out of Europe. She wept. "I cannot speak of the Occupation. To me, it is too painful. Thank God for America and the Marshall help." She looked at the floor coquettishly and twisted her hands. "I always wished that Lone would marry an American," she whispered.

"I almost married an American. In 1939. I used to go dancing at a club called Zigeunerhus, the Gypsy House, where Victor Borge played in a jazz combo. Once he jumped up from the piano and danced with me. He was wanting to move to America and escape the Nazis and get into the movies. I told him, Don't get a big head. He introduced me to a guy named Howe from the American embassy, and I fell in love with him. He was quiet and kind and he had money. I saw a lot of Mr. Howe. We biked along the coast and took the ferry to Sweden and went to jazz clubs, and in August, he took me on a vacation trip to Leningrad, and we had a marvelous time. We rode the train through Germany and Poland and into the Soviet Union in that beautiful green August, and we were so much in love, we never so much as glanced at the newspapers. All we thought about was love and marriage. We returned to Copenhagen on the train on the last day of August. On September 1st, the Nazis invaded Poland and World War II began. All the little villages we saw from the train, the children running in the streets, the people riding their bicycles, that world was pretty much destroyed in the next five years. And Mr. Howe went off to war and he never came back. We said good-bye in the train station and that was the end of it. He died in North Africa. Everything was changed after the war. I married Oscar and had Lone and Mette but I never forgot my American."

"You look so much like him," she said. "A pity you're thirty years younger. But I'm too independent to marry, anyway." She poured another round of whiskey.

"I like independent women," I said. I was drunk.

"You'd die of boredom in Denmark. All of us old Social Democrats, we'd bore you to tears. All our silly customs. And you'd try to learn Danish, but believe me, a language learned in middle age is a leaky boat. You're lucky if you can float, there's no such thing as navigation. And besides I'm far too independent to be tied to one person for the rest of my life."

She drained her glass. "God, you remind me of him. But we Danes are realists. We seldom lie, and never to ourselves.

"The Little Mermaid never married the prince, you know. Her feet hurt so bad, trying to walk on dry land, she cried all the time, and she missed her mermaid pals too much, so she shriveled up and turned into sea foam. Like so many women. She fell in love with the wrong guy. She should've looked for a nice dolphin."

I walked around Copenhagen, around Kastellet and along the waterfront, where the cruise ships dock, and down to the Gefion Fountain with the great bare-breasted goddess, her whip hand raised, lashing her oxen as water gushes up from the blade of her plow and sprays from their flared nostrils, and through the streets to Gråbrødretorv—the loveliest square in Copenhagen and impossible to pronounce, with four separate r's to swallow—and sat in a café there, a pint of Tuborg in front of me, and thought, I am already very well married to a suitable woman, I just need to find my way back. Which is like trying to retrace your 1939 journey across Europe in the spring of 1945. But I suppose it can be done.

# 19 ❧ Dear Mr. Blue

Lone was astonished that I gave advice to strangers in a newspaper column. "Don't you realize the harm you could do?" she said. "People are complex. It's no joke. You can't just read someone's letter and tell them what to do with their lives."

But you can, of course. Most people aren't so complicated. They only like to think they are. And I loved being Mr. Blue. It felt good to write the words on the screen and click on *send* and know they'd appear in the paper the next day. And the money was all I had to live on. It was the only writing I did. Other stuff I blanked on, but I'd pick up a letter from some poor lost soul and it stimulated some cortex in me—some deep avuncular impulse—and I rattled off advice to them, no problem. As Marley's ghost said, we wear the manacles we forge in life. And I felt I had the key.

～～～

Dear Mr. Blue,
I'm 20, a star pitcher from Round Lake (don't print that) now at St. Wendell's, and all my dreams are coming true, next week I have a tryout with the New York Mets, their head scout thinks I'm a shoo-in, but I'm paralyzed. I can't throw a strike to save my soul. I'm throwing and throwing and throwing and my curve isn't hooking and my fastball is about 55 mph and I'm ready to throw in the towel. I wonder if hypnosis could be my problem. Two weeks ago I was hypnotized by a wonderful young woman whom I dated a few times last year (a nurse) and I seem to recall her saying to me, "When you awake, you won't be able to pitch worth shit." It was after a

party at her house, we were sitting on her porch drinking Cokes, she asked if I'd ever been hypnotized, and I said no, and then I was staring at her, she was naked and twirling a baton, and ever since then I've found myself walking past her house late at night and feeling strong urges to submit to her will. This tryout is my only chance at the Big Leagues. I could become the next 30-game winner and sign a $250 million four-year contract or I could get a job uncrating tomatoes and carrots in the produce department at Piggly Wiggly. One or the other. I've thought of calling Denise and saying, "Okay, make me a major leaguer and I'll marry you." I always thought of hypnosis as a cheap trick. But now I am in the force field of a devil woman who controls my fate. Help! I desperately need help.

—Desperate

Dear Desperate, What are you waiting for? Shower, shave, put on a clean shirt, get Denise, and go to the jewelry store. A $25,000 ring should be about right.

Dear Mr. Blue,

I gave up a life of individual fulfillment for the mindless drudgery of motherhood, and though my children loathe and abuse me, I feel truly blessed. Thanks to my duties as laundress, scrubwoman, chauffeur, cook, and cheerleader at soccer and basketball games I have no life of my own. All I know is that my babies (14, 16, 19) are happy and enjoying the good things of life that I myself never had. Nonetheless, I do crave one little thing and that is the opportunity, once a month or so, to put on a leather outfit and leather boots and get on a motorcycle and ride with a gang of other moms, cruising through the Norman Rockwell suburbs, the manifolds banging like gunshots, and see children cringe and duck for cover. Are there

**clubs where a nice middle-aged lady like myself could go and ride a bike?**

**—Mrs. Mom**

Dear Mrs. Mom, Yes, indeed. There are Road Mama clubs in the Twin Cities, Duluth, Fargo, even in Rochester, home of the famous Mayo Clinic. Pediatric cardiologists, OR nurses, ophthalmic technicians, women who are calm and caring through their work shift and then go home to be good mommies and best pals, but on Saturday night when the sun goes down, these babes put on the leather and jump on the hawgs and go looking for ass to kick. Fifty or sixty of them rumbling through the hamlets of Olmsted County. Mayo's Marauders, out for cheap thrills at high speed. All week they care for the sick and raise healthy children, and one night is theirs to piss away in senseless frivolity. They are better people for it. Those who stay in the harness day after day wind up taking out their aggressions in other ways. This is better.

Dear Mr. Blue,

I am 19, a sophomore at St. Olaf, about to fly to Beijing for my semester abroad, and I've fallen head over heels for a guy I met at a campfire last Tuesday. He got drunk and passed out with his pockets full of melted marshmallow and I took him to my dorm room and got him cleaned up and gave him Advil and cared for him as he slept off the hangover, and I fell in love. I think we're soul mates. I can't bear the thought of leaving him for six months. Should I cancel everything?

**—Absolutely in Love**

Dear Absolutely, No. You're very young and still discovering your powers and learning to be your own person, and what you need now is to get out and have experiences and become a responsible and self-reliant woman. Romance is great fun, but it doesn't advance your cause right now to get tied up with this guy. A big love affair is no shortcut to the adult world. There are many regretful young women with two small children living in tiny dingy apartments who know the truth of that. Say good-bye to him, shed a bucket of tears, fly away, and learn how to make yourself happy as a solo.

# 20 🦃 Turkey Cont'd.

**Dear Mr. Blue,**

It's me. Brian. A.k.a. Turkey Lurkey. My beloved mom died. In her sleep, which was lucky, because she never slept much. Now she's gone to a better world, and so have I. I broke up with Katherine and got in touch with the Trappists and became a novice and—to make a long story short—I have decided I am more attracted to men. I think Nhunu and Katherine were sent by God to prepare me for Ted. He's the other novice, and he and I shared a room for two weeks and fell in love. (Or I did.) It was amazing. He and I are both Virgos and we're both St. John's alumni and major football fans and turkey hunters and now we're on the Trappist team and have each other and are terribly happy. But he doesn't want to "act on" his feelings or "come out." He prefers to pray for guidance and see what happens. He's scared, is the truth. You know what a big thing homosexuality is to some people. His dad is on the school board and his mom is president of the Friends of the Library, and he doesn't want to become That Gay Guy. I say it's now or never. We got in a big hissy fight over this and he stomped out of the refectory crying and I am so mad I could spit. After all I've been through, finally I find the real thing and the son of a bitch won't even wear my ring or let me kiss him on the lips. What gives?

—Brian

Dear Brian, Either you're in love with him or you're not. I say you're not, because if you were in love, you wouldn't be asking me what to do. True love is an imperative, and people jump off the cliff for it. We know this from Puccini. It's nobody's business who you love, but of course everyone will find out eventually so you and Ted may as well hire a brass band and march through the monastery holding hands. If you're really in love, throw yourself at him. But don't imagine you're in love if you're only in heat. Not the same. I almost made this mistake in Denmark, Brian. I flew over to see a great woman after I'd been having a rough time in New York—basically, my whole career went into the toilet—and I think the pressurized jet-liner raised my libido and I landed in Copenhagen and we tumbled into bed and there was so much jiggery-pokery in the next 48 hours, it felt like *Amore.* We drove around looking at little villages with red-tile-roof houses and ancient whitewashed churches and hiked along the beach and ate herring and drank shots of aquavit and I thought, Maybe this is it, but I saw my own foolishness in time and escaped without harm. Life is not about flying. It's about falling and then picking yourself up.

~~~~

**Dear Mr. Blue,**

**I am the poet who broke up with the alcoholic mommy-obsessed turkey caller after he got to ripping me and calling my work "self-indulgent drivel" so I kicked him out. He was an energy vampire and purveyor of despair whose mission was to kill my every creative impulse. He left and I'm glad. But now I realize that he took quite a bit of my stuff with him. He's in a monastery. How can I get my poems back?**

**—Moonflower**

Dear Moonflower, We're all artists and we're all critics. Each of us has beautiful creative impulses, and each of us comes equipped with a bullshit detector that looks at emperors and thinks, Naked. Your boyfriend saw you as naked. And you may very well have been. Don't attempt to contact him now. Do as Fitzgerald, Whitman, Frost, Updike, and God knows who else did when they lost their manuscripts—they sat down, tried to reconstruct from memory, and wound up writing something better.

≈≈≈

**Dear Mr. Blue,**
I'm the Texas guy who wrote you about wanting to write books. You told me to go ahead, but my wife pushed me into politics and I got elected. Hot damn. The euphoria lasted for about fifteen minutes, and then I found myself trapped between a desk and a credenza and a bunch of drones pushing papers at me and talking in their weird metallic voices. What a fascinating life. (Not.) And about 2,700 times a day you have to stand and press the flesh with goofy strangers and breathe in their germs that I suspect are the cause of this irritable bowel syndrome I can't seem to get rid of.

If it were up to me, I would be out at my ranch writing novels. I have one in mind, called "Runaway Home," in which a fella sets out alone on a life of adventure in an RV and meets interesting people along the way, a rancher, a Mexican trucker, a short-order cook, a waitress, and so forth. He roams the country, meeting people and solving their problems by leaving behind a nice chunk of cash in a plain brown envelope. (He's quite wealthy.)

My wife, however, loves being married to a big shot and walking into a big room full of people staring at her like she was the Tattooed Lady. She loves to do these little dinners at which she presents a Lucite award to some blowhard for his service to the cause of literacy and he stands up and blows for half an hour and everybody sits and grins and thinks about their ovaries. Here's my question. Can a political guy write a novel anyway? Where's the escape hatch around here?

—Curious George

Dear Curious, Go ahead and write that novel, but put it aside for three years and then have your wife check and make sure it's okay. The plot you describe sounds like a snooze fest to me so be sure to put some shooting and rassling in there and maybe heavy drug usage and incest. People nowadays want a book that makes beads of perspiration pop out on their foreheads, and dang it, it's getting harder and harder to accomplish that, what with all the weird stuff on television.

Dear Mr. Blue,
Okay, he came back. Mr. Turkey. And he brought my poems back. And a lot of his own stuff. I can't believe that a guy who spent three months in a Trappist monastery could accumulate a station wagon full of boxes and shopping bags! I told him I'm taking him back conditionally, and now, three days later, my apartment is a welter of garbage. What to do?

—Moonflower

Dear Moonflower, Tidy housekeeping is not where romance begins. And many wonderful tidy men are already in relationships with other tidy men. Mr. Turkey never learned to be a good roommate, I guess. Some men learn this in the monastery but I guess he wasn't there long enough. And standards of housekeeping do vary. Some people feel that sheets should be washed every week; others feel that if the bed smells a little, hey, we're asleep, what's the problem? Most women like curtains or drapes, some men prefer tinfoil taped to the windows. Why fight over it? Dismiss him, if you like, but remember: there is no relationship between two people that does not include considerable irritation.

~~~~

**Dear Mr. Blue,**
**My poet lady friend and I are back together and, thanks to you, she's quit nagging me about neatness. But I'm wondering if, while I was in the monastery, she was faithful to me. I found a poem in which she refers to "reflection of your sweet manhood hung down dreamily as I lean out the window and smoke." Am I just being petty? I can't seem to let go of this.**

**—Turkey**

~~~~

Dear Turkey, She wrote that poem about something that happened a long time ago. Be happy, move forward, live memorably, etc.

# 21 ❧ Mr. Blue's Happiness Quiz

**Dear Mr. Blue,**
**Would you please reprint your Happiness Quiz from a couple years**
**ago. That was a classic.**

**—Alone**

**P.S. My husband passed away a year ago Tuesday.**

Dear Alone, Gladly. Here you go.

Read the following ten items and circle the ones that apply to you.

1. My girlfriend is Born Again and won't remove her clothing but she will kiss me until I am climbing the wall and whining like a dog.

2. I've been dating Bob for eighteen years and he is still "not sure" about us and my heart is in a twist.

3. My cat died one year ago last Wednesday and I still feel emotionally shipwrecked, and my friends are sick of hearing about it, and after ten years of sobriety, I'm back on the joy juice again.

4. My wife is God's Apostle on Earth and the Voice of Authority on every subject and corrects everything I do or say. She is like a horsefly in my life, I go sit in the car for a little peace and quiet. But it's January and the temperature outside is twenty

below. Below zero. We live in a suburb of Duluth. I moved to this godforsaken place as a favor to St. Judy so she could be close to her family. When I remark on the cold, she says, "What's your problem?" Everyone up here is like that. I live in a dark shithole of suffering.

5. I am the child of affluent agnostic liberals who gave me no sense of values whatsoever and their moral relativism has led me into a life of meaningless sex and addiction to crack cocaine and sometimes I drive through the ghetto in search of some boojie. I wrote a book about it and then my computer was stolen, containing my entire book manuscript and I am devastated, numb with horror, and my mind is a blank.

6. I have everything I ever wanted, a good family, a showplace of a home, hundreds of friends, satisfying volunteer opportunities, and yet I am taking Percodan, Paxil, Xanax, Diloxil, and some mellow yellows now and then, and I also like to shoot horse.

7. I am a candidate for public office.

8. I am on the run from the law, living in paranoia and fear and also having an identity crisis. I am a Hell's Angel on the outside, but on the inside I'm a little boy who goes to bed with Tigger and Piglet and Roo. What if I am arrested and the police open up my saddlebags and see my stuffed animals and assume that I have drugs stashed inside and so they rip my babies to pieces? I will be devastated.

9. I am the hostage of my conservative upbringing in the snake pit of Baptist theological back stabbing, haunted by guilt, unable to break loose and enjoy life and express the free-spirited "party girl" side of me. I met a man in an Internet chat room and in two weeks he has become my world but I'm afraid to meet him for fear he cannot accept my bovine personality and the black leather Bible with study helps and concordance that I carry everywhere I go.

10. I am lying, semisensible, in a tiny cubicle in a geezer warehouse, drugs flowing through an IV in my arm and mushy music dripping from the ceiling. I am full of bitter rage and too weak to even swing my legs over the side of the bed. But I have a loaded pistol under my pillow, which I intend to use to win my escape. Where to go, I don't know.

Circle the items that apply to you. Circle any that ring a chord, even if not accurate in every jot or tittle. Face up to what's really going on in your life. Be honest.

If you circled fewer than four (4) items, you're doing pretty darn good. If you circled two (2) or fewer, I'd say you're definitely happy. If you circled none, I'd call you a big fat liar.

The Happiness Quiz drew more mail than Mr. Blue ever got before. Even when I told Incredulous to forget about the uncle who "accidentally" left the bathroom door open and exposed himself to her as a child, which, thirty years later, she uncovered in therapy and told her family and none of them was interested in hearing about the self-loathing she suffered by having seen Uncle Ted's thing or accepting what he did to her—the quiz drew more mail than that. It drew more mail than my dismissive reply to Suspicious.

**Dear Mr. Blue,**

Last January, I lost my cat when he went out the back door when my wife was taking out the garbage. He was an indoor cat and she let him out. I can't stop thinking about him and also I can't help but think that it's hard for an older (15) cat like Mr. Pokey to get through a door and disappear without the person who opened the door being aware of this. I just wonder if this was an assisted death. I found his skeleton in the flower bed in the spring. My wife is sticking to her story. What do you think?

—Suspicious

Dear Suspicious, Who cares about your stupid cat? Not me. I've got real problems. Go soak your head.

A torrent of abuse rained down on me from cat lovers, but the quiz drew even more mail. More, even, than my ill-tempered diatribe against Republicans as "bullet-headed ideologues devoted to prisons and sterile office parks and McMansion developments and pumping oil and destroying the Alaska wilderness to power their SUV's while taking away funds for homeless children sleeping in doorways to pay millions to fat-cat farmers and ranchers firmly attached to the right hind teat of federal welfare."

Dear Mr. Blue,
I am married to a woman whom I worship and adore and the other day she took your Happiness Quiz and I saw where she wrote in the margin, "My husband is a good man but something about him quenches my spirit." I was deeply hurt. I got in my car and drove up north to a fishing resort in Canada and I've been here for ten days feeling empty inside. What's the point?

—Defeated

Dear Defeated, A man should not enter into matrimony if he doesn't wish to be known. The woman of his dreams, the light of his life, is also an authority on him, his best critic. Go home and purge yourself of ill feeling by doing something useful such as cleaning the bathroom. Fill a bucket with soapy hot water and get a mop and a stiff brush and twenty minutes later you'll feel better. Guaranteed. Tomorrow is a new day.

## 22 ❧ Lonely Guy

Trillin's novel *No Parking* was on the *Times* list of "Twenty Most Significant Books of The Past Two Years" and Updike was all over the place with his *Collected Notes* while I sat in Deadwood Gulch watching the dust motes fall through the sunbeams, hearing Time slip away, feeling sour and jowly and snappish, a real pill to be around. Jesus wanted me for a sunbeam and I felt like a major storm front.

One night, in the grip of whiskey, I called Katherine in St. Paul and told her I was depressed and her mood brightened instantly. "How awful for you," she said with real interest. "I wonder if I have long to live," I said. "I've been unfaithful to Iris, unfaithful to myself, seduced by money and fame and now I'm involved with the Mafia and could wind up with a bullet in the head." She thanked me for confiding in her. I told her that I wished my remains to be returned to Minnesota and my friends to hold an appropriate memorial service. No eulogy. But maybe something from the *St. Matthew Passion*, "*O Haupt voll Blut und Wunden,*" and maybe "*Jesu, meine Freude,*" and read from Ecclesiastes and maybe something from *Life on the Mississippi* about floating on a raft—we both broke down and cried at the thought of it. I asked her if she had a boyfriend, and she said yes and they were thinking of getting married, as soon as they could figure out the ceremony.

~~~~

I tried to write for *The New Yorker*. I sat in diners on Eighth Avenue and drank oil-slick coffee and eavesdropped on conversations ("You heading home?" "No, not yet.") and took notes on people ("fat man

50 bleached hair reading *Vanity Fair* & eating sugar doughnuts") and tried to think of how to use this in a story but mainly I hated being alone. A jeweled city at night and how it calls to you but you venture out alone down Columbus Avenue past the sidewalk cafés and little bars around the Museum of Natural History, you yearn to be a couple. How sweet it would be to be a couple—to have a faithful companion to see and hear the same things you do—*and how this would assist you as a writer!*

> Dear Iris,
> I'm going through a bad patch right now and wonder if you could take a couple weeks and come out here. I miss you. We could sit at the glass-topped table under the canopy and eat our supper and have a glass of wine and watch the sun set and the lights come on. We could even haul a mattress out there and sleep. I miss you a lot.
> **Love love love, Larry**

I could imagine Iris and me, holding hands, walking down Columbus and suddenly Placido Domingo strolls into view—*and because I am with her, everything is more vivid to me*—the great tenor in his black silk shirt and blue blazer and gray fedora, towed by a black poodle, and we stop by a stationery store, pretending to window-shop, meanwhile eyeballing the maestro as the pooch stops to sniff around a NO PARKING sign for a spot to make its deposit. A tall dame stops and speaks to Domingo: Who is she? I know her. She was in a movie. I can't think of her name but Iris does. "It's Clover Williams," she says. We watch the great man unfold his charm, touching the actress's sleeve and flashing his fabulous smile like a carpet salesman, all the wattage that has lit up *Carmen* and *Parsifal* now bestowed on one lady in a green-and-white jogging suit—yes! Clover herself, luminous, slightly tousled, playing a scene of romantic comedy before our eyes! And the dog, knowing what the comedian is meant to do, squats and looks lovingly up at the lady and shits magnificently, a fine steaming pile of greenish poop. And the hero, with a gallant smile and great verve, picks up the shit in a Baggie and tosses it in a trash basket, with no diminution of his charm. And now she gazes into his face with her special radiant look and the story is clear: she knows he is Placido Domingo and he thinks she is just another leggy American beauty and she knows he thinks this and—she doesn't mind! Clover is happy to put stardom aside and enjoy flirting with a grand master. She would rather be flirted with than fawned over. A man's unabashed interest is reassuring to her. His accent is thick as clotted cream. She touches his arm now and speaks in an urgent voice and suddenly his charm dims slightly. She has complimented him, but the compliment was the wrong color or was one size too small or maybe he thinks she thinks he's Pavarotti, a real deal breaker. That's it. She says how great he was as Marco in *Les Moins Chères* and that isn't a role he sings. Pavarotti does. A faint chill descends, propriety takes hold, he bows slightly and prepares to move on. She senses her mistake, leans toward him on tiptoes, speaks softly and urgently. The dog, done with its low comedy, sniffs her in the very place that Domingo might want to sniff her as well, and she puts her hand on the dog's head but does not shove it away. The dog is saying, "Come home with us. He's a wonderful lover. It'd be a night you'd remember. The guy is slick. And I'd get to watch." And now you understand why a man goes into opera: it's not only for the music but also for what can happen afterward. A tenor stands onstage advertising his tenacity and prowess and ladies line up at the stage door. Sex. The great steaming mystery. The love of being naked in a dark room with another and the cool sheets and lying down and the hundreds of ways there are to lie together. The whole vocabulary of nakedness. This is what Puccini was thinking about, and Mozart, and Strauss. All the time they pretended to address God or death or the soul, they were showing off their legs. A little scene on Columbus Avenue can illuminate so much of Western art. And now a third party enters. An aging lady—a lady Domingo's age—a real turnoff, a stout lady in a black cape and pointy boots, a shock of gray ponytail, she looks as if she might be the opera critic of *The Nation*, she steps up and addresses Domingo as a fan, mincing, ducking her head, like a lowly serf curtsying before the count, and now the great tenor makes his escape. With a grand beneficent smile and a sweep of his hand that includes both women, he speaks his final line and tugs on the comedian, and they turn, and with a little backward wave of his hand, he flees south to the safety of his apartment. The aging lady attempts to speak to the star, who looks at her with such hauteur as could stuff a toilet and stalks east and the poor lady heads north, and Iris and I turn to the west, witnesses to a priceless little play, and being two, we can savor the thing and replay it a couple times from separate angles, whereas when it's just me myself alone, as it is tonight, I leave the scene desperate to tell someone, but who cares? If it were the two of us, we could talk about this scene all evening. Alone: What's the point?

# 23 &ge; Dr. Liebestod

After watching Domingo's failed seduction of Clover Williams, I was so desperate for company, I went to a comedy club called Goober's on 112th, where a stand-up lady was performing to a bar thinly populated with Columbia students hitting the Cosmos. "Great to be in New York, a city where something is always happening, most of which you wouldn't want to be involved in personally," she said in a husky lady-comedian way. I ordered a beer and sat and watched it fizz. She stood on the tiny stage in brilliant light, tall and lean, jeans, T-shirt, a thatch of wild blond hair flying around. "Some New Yorkers go around the city with imaginary friends, and it's not necessarily an imaginary friend they get along with real well—they have to yell at them sometimes." There were little pinpricks of laughter, but she didn't care, she went careening along, punctuating the jokes with a sneer, a toss of the head, a twitch of the microphone. "People say that New Yorkers don't know their neighbors, but this depends on the construction of your building. Some newer buildings like mine—your neighbors are a radio show you can never turn off." My eyes got focused in the dark: she was working a crowd of sixteen people, but her eyes betrayed no sense of failure. She barreled along like a true artist, enjoying her own sense of timing, the perfection of the jokes, the purity of the act of doing comedy for no good reason: "You see all these dogs running around with people chained to them scooping up their poop, like slaves. The dogs look really prosperous, the people look sort of embarrassed. No question who's in charge there." A guy my age sat alone at a table in front of her, working on a drink. A faded guy who looked like he'd been camped here awhile.

"No speed limit signs in New York. I guess they figure it'll work it-self out." The sadness of drink and solitude was loud in this man, his slump, his hands plucking at his sport coat and tie, his fingers toying with the lit cigarette in the ashtray, trying not to smoke, taking a puff, not wanting to, smoking some more, not wanting to be alone, not wanting to drink so much, drinking more. I sat directly behind him, looking at Miss Wonderful, who was peering at me in the shad-ows. Was I an agent scouting for someone for a movie for HBO? A friend of Steven Spielberg's? The sport coat man was peering up at her, and when she stepped off the stage, his face brightened and he sat up straight, and then she walked past him to me.

Comfort comes in many forms, including the intercession of strangers. The comedian sidled over my way and I smiled and of-fered her a chair and she sat down and asked where I lived and I said, "The Bel Noir," and she said, "Oh, I used to know someone who lived there," and I said, "If you don't have other plans, come up and we'll have a drink—I'm a writer—I'd like to talk to you about tele-vision—" And she came up, and we drank some Scotch, lying in ad-jacent chaises, looking at the city lights, talking in a languorous manner, and I leaned over and kissed her. A sweet simple kiss. A kiss meant to unlock the doors and send you skipping and dancing into never-never land to do things you were told never never to do and enjoy them.

So into the bedroom we went and everything was fine. Better than fine. Exquisite. And then her cell phone rang.

"I'm sorry," she said. And she answered it.

We were both naked as jaybirds and our bodies were entwined but she reached over and snagged the phone out of her jeans pocket and flipped it open and said, "Yes? Oh, hi. No. No problem.—It went fine.—Yeah, it was pretty crowded.—Oh, really?" Then she whis-pered to me: *My agent.*

Meanwhile, my unit was making itself scarce.

She yakked with whoever it was for a good long time, rolled over and lay on her belly, looking out the window, and discussed some movie project involving someone named Packer or Parker. And when she was done with whatever it was and clicked off her phone, I was done, period.

She surveyed the situation and said, "I know a good sex therapist," and before I could say, "I'll be all right. Just taking a break"— she whipped her cell phone out and—"Dr. Liebestod? Diana. Remember when you told me you make house calls?"

There's New York for you. You can pick up a phone and get anything you want at any hour of day or night.

Dr. Liebestod arrived fifteen minutes later, carrying a duffel bag. She was a large lumpy woman with black horn-rim glasses. A real potato. "Let's have a look," she said.

"I think we can figure this out ourselves," I said. I tried to tell her, I'm up for casual sex, but to me, casual implies *easy*. You know? Not something laborious and complicated—

"I assume he's been fellated," she said to Diana, who nodded.

"It's important to get a good seal," said the doctor. She opened my bathrobe and stared at my dormant member.

"Oh boy."

It was the sort of thing you would say if you found three inches of water on your basement floor and the cellar door open and a big raccoon up on a shelf, eating your mom's raspberry jam out of the jar.

"I like to get paid in advance," she said. "When things get hot and heavy, people sometimes forget." So I made out a check for $220 to Liebestod Real Life Therapies, Ltd. She folded it and thanked me and gave me a long penetrating look.

It was 3:30 A.M. I was regretting the whole evening. In fact, I was way beyond regret. I was thinking seriously about celibacy as a way of life. *Older Man seeks monastery. Temperate climate, Christian preferred, vow of silence a big plus.*

"Hey, we'll get you operative in a jiffy," she said. "Heat. That's the surefire aphrodisiac."

"Maybe I should take a rain check," I said.

"Nonsense. When you fall off the horse, get right back on it." And she reached into her bag and pulled out a leather skirt. "Put it on," she said. I did, and sure enough, there was a definite sense of warmth in the underworld, a stirring, an indwelling.

"How's that doing?" said Dr. Liebestod. "Just fine," I said. She leaned down to look up my skirt. "Looks good," she said. "We're almost ready for the condoms." There was definitely some uplifting going on. A wonderful feeling of manhood. I was ready to go. Diana lay on the couch and nickered.

"I'm glad to wait around in case you have any questions," said Dr. Liebestod, but I had none and neither did Diana and I heard the door click shut as I climbed aboard.

~~~~

**Dear Mr. Blue,**

**I am planning an evening at my apartment with a woman I've been dating for a month and I'd like our relationship to move to the next level and am not sure whether to serve martinis or pour a white wine. What's your thought?**

**—Anxious to Please**

~~~~

Dear Anxious, Back when our hairy ancestors lived in smoky caves and fought with rocks and clubs and stank of putrefying sores, they liked to squat around the fire and eat extremely rare meat and exchange myths and one myth was that fermented grain alcohol is a sure route to fabulous sex. You have to be pretty drunk to believe this. For one thing, alcohol creates billows of gas, and passion is a fragile mood, and heavy tail-gun fire is likely to kill your chances. As the Irish say, "May the wind always be at your back but not coming out of you yourself personally."

The matter of dosage is critical: a woman is a slight creature, not a Percheron, and a big glass of hooch may overshoot the mark and make her green around the gills and reduce her level of judgment to where her affection for you doesn't mean all that much. It's much smarter to make yourself appealing and win her interest: the reward will be greater than if she is limp and semiconscious. Making oneself appealing is what led to civilization as we know it: poetry, music, sport, learning—it all began as romance. Women sang, made food, wove fabric, grew flowers, men competed in footraces and jumping contests, composed odes, mastered bodies of useless knowledge, all in hopes of impressing the opposite sex. Seat the woman on your couch, offer her a glass of sparkling water, and beguile her with your wit and elegance, and see where that leads you. If you run into problems, put on a leather skirt. Without going into a lot of detail that might sound like boasting, let's just say: it really works.

# 24      Iris Strikes Back

A few days after the adventure with Dr. Liebestod, I got a letter from Iris.

Dear Larry,

My dad asks if we are getting a divorce and I tell him I honestly don't know. He thinks you're the bee's knees. They opened up the lake cabin for the season and chased the squirrels out of the bunkbeds. Aunt Boo backed out of going, said she felt "light-headed," and now she seems to have gone completely bonkers. She has packed her bags and won't tell anyone where she's going, just not to worry, the Lord will provide. She sits on the porch waiting for her "ride." She will be 82 in August. Meanwhile, Dad and Mom and Gene and Marge all say hello and wish you'd come home and go fishing.

I have decided to dig up all the hosta, which I have always hated and put in hydrangeas or something else colorful. What a glorious summer. Bob and Sandy are going to California to help the farmworkers. I ain't going anywhere.

xoxox Iris

And then Mr. Blue got a letter from Iris. No doubt about it. IrisW@mama.org.

Dear Mr. Blue,

My husband is seeing other women, which strikes me as pretty dumb of him, but I know better than to think I can change him. I love him dearly for his gentle eyes and sweet smile. But he has a problem with telling the truth and this is a sad fault in a mature man.

I'm not angry at him exactly. I don't feel heartsick or confused. I have a good life and I don't intend to let this pebble of a problem overturn the carriage. We could easily divorce, but I can't imagine life without him. My best friend says I should go ahead and have an affair. Go to a bar and pick up somebody. A night of passion with a total stranger. I feel so ill informed. What to do?

—Lady Liberal

I was flummoxed. My Iris, thinking about shacking up with some guy she meets in a singles bar? What kind of deal is that?

I wrote her a hasty letter.

Dear Lady Liberal, We all feel our youth slipping away and wish we were better loved. It's sad about your husband. But don't let his foolishness lead you down some one-way road to grief. You get liquored up and suddenly some wacked-out drifter starts to look like Cary Grant. Direct your attention to the home front. Get your hair done, rejuvenate your skin, learn the old art of seduction and one of these nights your old husband will walk right in and drive the shadows away. You wait and see.

I pressed *send* and a moment later it bounced back, *undeliverable,* and I dashed off a note for the cleaning lady ("Water the trees on the terrace, Laverne") and grabbed a cab to LaGuardia and paid a king's ransom to get on the first flight home. It was packed. People shoving onboard and stuffing the overheads with bags the size of German shepherds. I took a middle seat between a lady with a small sullen dog and a big guy whose shoulder and arm were in my space. The dog's name was Snuggles. We sat for forty-five minutes and I was worrying about Iris's barfly friend and the pilot came on the horn to explain that we were experiencing a minor instrument read-out problem. "I can't take this much longer," said the big guy. Finally, we took off—shakily, it seemed to me—and the man in front of me reclined his seat back so that my femurs were driven a couple inches into my abdominal cavity. The big guy downed a couple beers and examined a pornographic magazine in which weight lifters humped women with breasts like artillery shells. Meanwhile, the lady with the dog complained to me about her sad life, the perfidy of her children, the broken promises of plumbers and electricians, a rare lymphoma that was eating at her vitals, the chemotherapy that had drained her of the will to live, her troubled children who were no comfort, et cetera.

I said, "My wife is out scouting for gigolos in the watering holes of St. Paul, Minnesota." She paid no attention but went on and on about her lab tests.

The dog nipped at me when the plane ran into turbulence and the big guy fell sound asleep and his head lolled around and came to rest on my shoulder. He said things in his sleep that made me uneasy, like "I know you care about me" and "I'm your little muffin man." The dog looked as if it might go berserk at any moment. The lady looked over at the man dozing on my shoulder and said, "I didn't used to be okay about homosexuality but I am now ever since my brother Shelly came out. I think it's up to you who you love and nobody should ever try to make you feel bad about it. If a heavyset fella is who makes your heart sing, then more power to you." I said nothing. What should I say? If I can help a guy get his rest and serve as an object lesson in tolerance for a dying woman, then shouldn't I accept this chance to be useful? I have nothing against homosexuals. I can even see the advantage to it. You could share clothing, you could pee together at a urinal and talk baseball and golf and enjoy rare steaks and none of this nonsense of Discussing the Relationship and one of you bursting into tears and saying, "Why are you this way?" It just stands to reason: *it's easier to love someone who is more like yourself, such as same gender, for example.* And if he isn't pleasing you sexually, you'd just say, "Shape up, clown." And he would. When you think about the miseries of loving women, you wonder if there isn't Another Way. Unfortunately, men have poor social skills. And their bodies aren't as interesting. Show me somebody who is aroused by the sight of a man's chest and I'll show you someone who is wild about coffee tables. Doggone it, every time I put my hand in Iris's shorts, I get a thrill.

I got home to Sturgis Avenue and she seemed pleased to see me. She was on the phone but kissed me and waved me toward the old wingback chair in which a pile of placards roosted that read: WIPE OUT COMMUNITY VIOLENCE: BE KIND AND RESPECTFUL TO ONE AN-OTHER. I looked around the living room for signs of Another Man, as I filled her wineglass with a fine Vouvray I'd purchased for her. She was in the midst of a lawsuit against the city of St. Paul, something about the dignity of lunatics. She said, "I have walked into a wasp's nest of lawyers." She looked quite enthused at the prospect of battle. She fixed me a bean wrap and then we fell into bed and rode the Tilt-a-Whirl and afterward she said, "That was nice." Which was high praise from Iris.

How're your parents? *Fine.* How was the cabin this year? *We missed you.* And the state fair? *Not the same without you.* You still have hockey season tickets? *Of course.*

"I worry about you," she said, nestled against me, warm and naked. "Loneliness is a contributing factor in insanity, you know."

Loneliness is a vicious circle, I know that. You get to brooding about it and you become poor company.

"Work has always been more important to you," she said.

"I have no work," I said.

"That's the problem, isn't it. Same thing happens to my poor old geezers with the grocery carts. They're just trying to be useful, poor boogers. Going around stuffing their garbage bags with cans and bottles and scraps of cardboard—they're just carrying out a filing system that they alone understand and they wish somebody else did."

∿∿∿

**Dear Mr. Blue,**
**I am an orthodontist, 31, good-looking, athletic, and though I have dated many so-called attractive women, I've never been in a relationship. I simply don't care for women who let themselves go. You take her to a gourmet restaurant and as your eyes adjust to the light, you notice the ruptured canker sore in the corner of her mouth. Or the hairs sprouting between her eyebrows. Or the zit alongside her nose. I just can't feature myself spending time with anyone with so little self-respect. Am I off base here?**

**—Eric of Edina**

∿∿∿

Dear Eric, You need women for education, flawed or not. The maiden with little snow white feet, the one with black black black hair, Barbry Allen, the gypsy girl, Kathleen Mavourneen, Jeannie, Fair Ellen—each woman prepares you for the next. You learn the basics from Lady A and you graduate to Lady B, who is grateful to her predecessor, as are C and D and E, and by F you are a quite a fine fellow, mostly recovered from your sulky adolescence and rapacious narcissism and prepared to carry on a conversation, brighten your corner, do light housekeeping, and every so often perform amazing feats in or near the bed. In my case, I married Lady A and then met B–F and now am returning to A, but the effect is the same: educational. And finally you wind up with your true love.

And maybe you turn to her and say, "Remember that little bar in the West 60s where we went after we saw *A Chorus Line* and there was that pianist with the bad toupee playing the white piano?" and she says, "That wasn't me. You were with someone else." But secretly she's grateful to that woman for teaching you what she taught you about dwelling in harmony, which takes practice. Practice, practice. You, sir, are way behind.

~~~~

Iris and I lay in bed and drank wine and when it got dark we lit a couple candles. It was just like the old days except we were heavier and wrinklier but in candlelight you don't notice anyway. We watched *Appointment in Chicago* with James Mason as a corrupt judge, Studs Terkel as a boxer turned reporter, and Stella Stevens as the dancer who loves them both.

"I wish you'd been at MAMA when we dedicated the activity center," she said after the movie, hoisting herself up, plumping the pillows.

This was a place for the elderly insane to come for a hot lunch and use the toilet or sit and doze or play checkers or read a magazine. It was on West Seventh near the drop-in center for single mothers in recovery and near the Salvation Army and the Dorothy Day Center, so there were a lot of drunk and crazy people coming and going, which irked the mayor who was trying to encourage sidewalk restaurants and boutique brew houses and small theaters—the St. Paul Lifestyle Quarter—but Iris and her ilk were bringing in the tired, the poor, the wretched refuse, the tempest tossed, and when you sit under your Campari umbrella with an $8 glass of Pouilly Fumé and a $24 plate of mushroom risotto, you don't want some old toothless hag to lean over and ask if she can have your baguette, please.

Anyway—there was a crazy old man named Gus, a card-carrying

member of the Communist Party U.S.A. He had the card pinned to his red plaid shirt along with about fifty protest buttons, some of museum quality. Gus was a favorite of Iris's. She liked poor people with Attitude. Old winos who go through the Union Gospel Mission chow line and complain about the lack of seasoning. Gus had given Sandy a hard time about the magazines that the activity center would provide, she having ordered a couple dozen such as *Mother Jones* and *Harper's* and the *Utne Reader* and Gus wanted *Playboy.* Anyway—there was a grand open house attended by the demented geezer community and a dozen Hansons, the kind and generous family who put up the dough for the place, and their friends and admirers, and the MAMA crowd, and a few innocent bystanders. Unbeknownst to MAMA, Gus had organized a clients' strike.

Yes, a clients' strike. MAMA and the Hansons were providing these crusty old flea-bitten snot-ridden wretches with a place to park their grocery carts and come in and take a load off, and Gus had organized the demented in a strike. The first demand was "The center shall be under the direction of the people who need it, not the wealthy elite, and shall be renamed the Eugene V. Debs Center for Social Change." And the second demand was: "Let us see tits." Gus and his revolutionary crowd bided their time until the mayor came to the podium to render his remarks about our multicultural society, and then Gus started pumping his fist and chanting, "We Want Tits, We Want Tits."

Iris laughed. I hadn't heard her laugh this hard in a long time. "Gus is drunk, of course, on that Salty Dog wine, one of those screw-top wines, the kind that doesn't go *with* your meal, it *is* your meal, and the bottle fits nicely in your pocket so it won't fall out when you fall down. Which he does. What a goofball. Poor old people, hacking and wheezing, flapping their gums, brain cells fried, all of them chanting, 'We Want Tits,' and Sandy trying to shush them and she gets hold of Gus and he pulls away and his shirt gets ripped and Gus knows enough to fall down and start yelling bloody murder, and the Hansons, who really are *extremely* nice people, look around at each other and think, What in God's name have we just gone and spent four million dollars on? So there's a lot of donor regret going on, and the cops arrive in two patrol cars and they find an old man on his back with a rip in his shirt and his left eyebrow slightly sprained, but you know how cops are these days—very professional, everything by the book, so they start filling out forms and they call the EMT wagon, and Gus is now the star of the show, they're taking his blood pressure and vital signs and the cops are collecting the names of eyewitnesses, and Gus is screaming about Vietnam, the Palestinians, Cuba, Nicaragua, Salvador Allende, the family farmers, the coal miners, Wounded Knee, the whole shopping list, and now a crew from Channel Five Eyewitness News arrives and instead of boring speeches by do-gooders, they've got themselves a wounded old man, and they hoist the antenna for their live cam and one of those TV ladies with beautiful molded hair begins her live report, talking about the irony of poverty in the midst of affluence, and she holds the microphone toward Gus—his lifelong dream, freedom of speech in front of an actual audience—and he hoists himself up from his bed of pain and cries, 'Fuck you, all of you.' It was hilarious. The Hansons are Lutherans, you know, and Mrs. Hanson leaned over and said to me, 'This is not our sort of thing at all.' So they head for the exits, and the next day they offer us an additional million dollars to take their name off the building. Which strikes me as kind of spendy, but . . . I say, never trust people with charm."

We had a lovely two days, we two. We made a truce. She didn't object when I took her over to La Reserve in Minneapolis and ordered a fine Château Haut-Brion, and I didn't object when she talked about the emergency nursery for parents in crisis and the transsexual hotline.

"Why don't you stay longer?" she said. "A year or two?"

"I hate to leave New York in defeat," I said. "Soon as I have me a success, I'll think about coming home."

I'd gotten undressed and was brushing my teeth, and Iris walked into the bathroom stark naked, holding a condom with a snake head painted on the tip.

She explained that it was for birth control in the Amazon rain forest. With all those vast tracts of rain forest being destroyed to make coffee plantations, the forest peoples are left homeless, but without the trees there is more light to read by so literacy has gone up, and with all those rainy days, there is plenty of time to read, and plentiful coffee, which has led to more sex, so they need birth control, but then they found that the Amazonian plumed egrets were eating the condoms and choking to death, so they put snake's heads on them, which seems to scare off the egrets but also scares off the forest people, who are superstitious about snakes, and so the birth rate has gone through the roof.

She handed it to me. "Put it on, I want to see how it looks."

I said, "I need to get hard first."

"Well, why don't you?"

That's my Iris. On our kitchen wall is the sign:

DEFINE THE NEED.

DEVELOP A PLAN.

COMMIT RESOURCES.

So I did. I committed my resources and we completed the project and the next morning I performed some follow-up and flew back to New York.

# 25 🦋 Papa's Poems

I stayed away from *The New Yorker*, hoping to avoid Tony Crossandotti, and then one day, he knocked on my apartment door. I looked through the peephole and there he was. He looked like he could snap my neck like a pea pod. He wore a white suit and a pearl gray shirt and a green tie. I was going to stand there very quietly and wait for him to go away but he put his eyeball up to the peephole and said, "Open up, dog breath, or I'll open it for you."

So I opened.

"Sorry," I said. "The doorman didn't ring up and tell me you were coming."

"I know all the doormen up here," he said. "They know who to tell and who not to tell." He strolled out on the terrace as if he owned the place and looked out toward Broadway.

"You must get to see a lot, living up here. Lot of nookie in those apartments. You got a good pair of binoculars?"

I shook my head.

"Here," he said. And gave me a pair. Brand-new. I put them to my eyes and saw a woman with red hair standing at a window, weeping. She was fully clothed and in the process of tearing up a piece of paper. I could see the return address on the envelope: San Luis Obispo, CA.

He said he would like a cup of coffee with milk and sugar. So I went and got it for him. When I returned, he'd taken off his jacket and his shoulder holster and was relaxing on a chaise, the holster and a blunt-nosed revolver sitting on a glass-topped side table. I set the coffee down beside the revolver.

"My grandpapa came over from Sicily and got into the landscaping business. He loved flowers and trees. And he was agreeable to burying dead bodies that people brought to him. It was a service. Sometimes people get into a bind. They've got a body and what do you do with it? So they'd come to his landscaping concern and give him a hundred and he'd toss the corpse on his sod truck and it was gone, it was taken care of, they knew they could trust him. That's how he operated. All those big mansions on Long Island with the nice green lawns running down to the Sound. He did all those lawns. They were fertilized by the mortal remains of losers. Nature's way. You lose, you die, you become part of something better. It sure beats getting fitted with concrete shoes and feeding the lobsters.

"He was a simple man, my grandpapa, and he did business the Sicilian way. If he liked you, he couldn't do enough for you, and if you crossed him, he would rip your heart out of your chest and eat it. It was that simple. He was a stand-up guy. You always knew where you stood with him. If you could see the sun shine, it meant he liked you. If you were dead and your eyes and mouth were full of dirt, it meant you'd done a bad thing.

"What you're probably wondering is how we got our hands on the premier literary magazine in America, right?"

I said that I only wanted to know whatever Tony thought I should know and no more.

He said that his poppa won *The New Yorker* in a poker game with a rich guy named Fleischmann, who was three sheets to the wind and couldn't tell his jacks from his jackhammer. Harold Rossi was Poppa's buddy from their army days in Paris, when Poppa was on General Pershing's staff and running a wholesale liquor business on the side. Gin and bourbon were rare in France, and the doughboys had no taste for fine Bordeaux, and Poppa did very well in wartime, as did Harold Rossi, who edited the army newspaper, *Stars and Stripes*, and was one of Poppa's better customers. They both returned to New York and kept in touch after the war and Poppa opened a drinking establishment in midtown, and that was where the poker game took place. It was four in the morning and Mr. Fleischmann was going down like the *Titanic* and trying to go home and they kept propping him up and pouring gin into him and he was out of cash and writing IOU's and on this one hand Rossi folded and Fleischmann stayed and Poppa won the pot with a pair of fours. A heart and a spade. Two double deuces. And he scooped up the pot and looked at Fleischmann's IOU and said, "What's the New Yorker? A hotel?" And Rossi said, "It's a magazine. Don't worry. I'll take care of it. Except my name's Ross now." This was in 1928 or so.

"Poppa got interested in writing and he wrote a memoir about growing up in Nebraska and sent it to *The Saturday Review* and the editor took a very negative attitude and said, 'You're not from Nebraska' and he laughed. Poppa didn't like to be laughed at. You're aware of the fact that *The Saturday Review* is no longer in business?"

I was aware of that.

"Poppa wrote poetry, too. He was in Leavenworth, Kansas, for a few years and joined a poetry club and—I got one of them here in my billfold." He handed me a sheet of white paper, folded. On it was neatly typed:

Whose woods these are I think I know.
He got whacked half an hour ago.
He will not see me stopping here
To write my initials in the snow.

Tonight I drank a quart of beer
And now there is no toilet near.
I take a leak beside the lake.
What a relief! What heartfelt cheer!

Finally I give a shake
And button up for goodness sake.
The only other sound's the beep
Of semi horn and hiss of brake.

The woods are lovely, dark and deep,
And I had promises to keep.
I put the son of a bitch to sleep
And buried him among the trees
With his head between his knees.
Sleep well, you little creep.

"What do you think?" he asked. "Pretty good, isn't it."
I said I thought it was good.
"I got more," he said. He handed me another.

This is just to say
I have buried your friend
who you asked me to take care of for the weekend
and who
you were expecting to see
this morning
Forgive me
he was dead
so stiff
and so cold.

Tony walked over to the railing and looked down through the leaves of the elm tree to the street and spat a big gob and watched it land and turned to me and said, "I'd like *The New Yorker* to print one of Poppa's poems. It would mean a lot to him. If they don't like that one, he's got a lot of others. I suppose that, as publisher, I could give the order, but I'd rather they printed it of their own free will because they wanted to. Could you take care of it for me?"

I said that the magazine doesn't print light verse anymore. Only serious poetry.

"What are you saying? My poppa is a joke? Huh?"

I said that I didn't consider his poppa a joke, not in the slightest, and that *if it were up to me personally* and so forth. I told him that I had no sway with the editors. None. I was deadwood around there. Nobody would listen to me for two minutes.

"You go out with Shawn on his boat."

"He likes me to come along because I'm such a nothing, he isn't embarrassed to get shit-faced and say what he thinks. Some guys can only confide in their valet. That doesn't mean he takes my advice about poetry."

"So what would it cost you to put in a good word for my old man? If you're a nobody, you got nothing to lose."

"Let me think about it," I said.

"Poppa doesn't only write poetry. He writes fiction, reviews, whatever you want."

"Send it to the poetry editor, Alice Quinn," I said. "She would be the person to speak to."

"I ain't talking to her. I'm talking to you." Tony was standing very close to me right now and his left arm was around me, sort of massaging my back. He was smiling a ferocious smile. He handed me two more of Poppa's poems. One was about snowflakes and the other about fall leaves. *O what a sight is this, the maple tree so tall / Its red and yellow leaves come suddenly in fall—*

"Let me think about it," I said.

"What's there to think about? Either you're a stand-up guy or you're a dirty louse. Take your choice."

"It's not that simple," I said. "I can show these to them and they'll probably just reject them."

He shook his head as if I were a small child who was persisting in saying that two and three is six.

"You don't understand. This is Poppa. My poppa. He wants to have a poem in *The New Fucking Yorker* magazine before he up and croaks. You get it?"

I said that I understood that part perfectly. But I am not the person to speak to about it.

"You are the one I am speaking to," he said. "You are the one standing there and I am the one over here with the words coming out of his mouth."

"I wish it were so simple," I said.

"It is exactly that simple," he said. "Either you're my friend or you're dead meat, and I guess you just made your choice, asshole."

He left without saying good-bye.

That evening, a city inspector came and looked at my terrace and found sixteen violations of code involving hoses and faucets and electrical wiring and wrote up $9,400 in tickets and another inspector came and flushed my toilets and said they would all have to be replaced.

I saw Trillin at the office and mentioned my meeting with Tony and he said, "You didn't tip your doorman enough for Christmas. Otherwise he'd have told Crossandotti that you'd gone to New Jersey for the weekend."

"What do I do now?"

He pondered this for a moment, the Trillin eyebrows rose and fell, and leaned in and whispered, "St. Paul is a safe place. You might need to be there for a while."

I hustled around the corner to the Tradesmen's & Mechanics' Library and sat at a table in the rear, facing the door, waiting for Tony. Nobody had ever been gunned down before for rejecting a poem, I would be the first.

### AMERICA'S FIRST LITERARY REVENGE KILLING.
#### "NOTHING LIKE IT," SAY PD VETERANS.

The poetry world was rocked by yesterday's murder of an aging *New Yorker* writer, apparently for his rejection of a poem. Larry Wyler, 56, who had suffered from a bad case of writer's block for years, was gunned down as he sat at a table in a library on West 44th Street, holding a copy of *A How-to Guide to Nude Photography*.

The book was not damaged, according to librarians.

Mr. Wyler's wife, Iris, of Sturgis Avenue in St. Paul, was not available for comment. A friend who answered the phone said she was out at a bar with somebody.

According to Alice Quinn, the poetry editor of *The New Yorker*, Mr. Wyler had no responsibilities in the poetry department.

"Whoever expected him to get a poem printed in the magazine was barking up the wrong tree," she said. She felt that the killer was not a poet.

"Handgun ownership among poets is low," she said. "Most poets tremble at the thought of attending a literary cocktail party—it's hard to imagine one of them walking into a library and pumping hot lead into a guy."

And then Tony walks in. I swear the guy has lookouts on every corner.

"I'm gonna give you a second chance," he says. "I got a package that needs to get to Chicago. How about you take it to Chicago for me?"

"What is it?" I said.

"You don't want to know."

"Okay. I don't want to know. How big is it?"

He said it was about the size of curtain rods.

"I don't want to know what it is," I said. "I want to think it's curtain rods."

"It's curtain rods, all right. Trust me."

"I mean, I don't ever want to know. Never. Cocaine or heroin or whatever it is. Promise you'll never tell me."

"It's nothing illegal, but whether it is or not, I won't tell you," he said.

"Thank you."

He said it was a package for a friend of his and the friend did not trust the mails. That's why he needed a personal courier.

Fine. I could carry a package, I said. "But it's not curtain rods. Give me some credit. I'm not an idiot. Just tell me it's not heroin."

"It's not heroin. No way. Let's stick with curtain rods. That's all you need to know."

"Oh my God." I stood up and walked to the circulation desk. The librarian looked up from her table where she was typing cards for the card file. "I used to be a writer," I said, "and now I'm a drug courier. My boyhood ambition. To write for *The New Yorker* and be a mule hauling heroin on a plane. Do me a favor. If you see my mug on the front page of the *Daily News*, don't think ill of me. Okay?"

She laughed.

This happens when you're a humorist. You tell the truth and people laugh at you.

Tony clapped a hand on my shoulder. "It's legal," he said. "I swear. Hey! Do I look like a drug dealer? Huh? Do I?"

He didn't, actually. He looked more like an assassin. So I said, "Okay, okay, but don't tell me what's in there because I don't ever want to know. Even if I beg you to. Not even a hint. I do not want to know."

He made the motion of zipping his mouth, locking it, and throwing away the key.

He gave me the box of curtain rods and a plane ticket and I took the C train to my apartment to get my shaving kit and I left the curtain rods on the train. I swear it's the truth. Dumb as it sounds, that's just what I went and did. I walked in the front door of the Bel Noir and the moment the doorman said, "Afternoon, Mr. Wyler," I clapped my hand to my forehead and thought of the curtain rods riding north to the Bronx. My fingerprints on the box.

No curtain rods in that box. Too heavy. I figured it was a high-powered rifle with a scope. Some maniac would get it and sit in his kitchen window and pick off a couple dozen innocent people and terrorize the city and the box would be found and it would be curtains for me.

I looked at the telephone and asked myself if I was going to call 911 and tell the cops, "There's a rifle in a long cardboard box on the C train." I thought a long time and didn't get a clear answer to that question.

# 26 · Alaska

Mr. Shawn sent me a note:

> It's been eight years since we've seen
> anything by you in the magazine and this is
> just to say that you should not feel pressure
> of any sort and whatever you're working on
> should not be rushed in any way. I'm confident
> that it will turn out to be absolutely amazing
> and will silence the naysayers around here who
> think you're sitting in there eating bonbons
> and tweezering your eyebrows. Take your time
> and follow your own instincts and if we must
> wait ten more years for it, know that the wait
> will be worth the prize.

I wrote back.

> Dear Mr. Shawn,
> I am a grown man in despair. I must give up
> the fight and return to St. Paul. I am not good
> enough to survive in this town. That's the
> truth. Thanks for your faith in me, but you
> were wrong, sir. I am a loser.
>                   Larry W.

He took me out to a steak house for dinner and we had the 36-ounce rib eyes and a couple of double Scotch and sodas. "You got to buck yourself up. Get back to the basics, kid," said Mr. Shawn. "For my money, that means Alaska. You fly into Anchorage and get a bush pilot to fly you out in a float plane and drop you off on a lake with no name, where there's nobody within a hundred miles, and you spend a month there, fishing, sleeping, thinking, killing mosquitoes, and about the time you forget what day it is, you hear the plane coming back to pick you up. You return to New York a new man. You'll be the man you were before you got lost."

"I am too fragile to go to the wilderness. I can't bear loneliness anymore. I want to go back to Minnesota."

All through my twenties and thirties, I had trudged along the literary ridgeline, enduring blizzards and gray days and ice storms, and New York was my reward for all that suffering, a place where you don a tuxedo and starched shirt and go dancing at the Rainbow Room on a revolving floor with a big orchestra and a girl singer and a boy singer doing Gershwin and Porter, and a nice lobster dinner and baked Alaska, and if it's cold and snowing outside, well, you just tell your limo driver to wait for you under the marquee on 49th Street and you jump in the backseat and speed home.

I had zero interest in seeing Alaska, but Mr. Shawn thought I should go, and when I saw the messages Tony Crossandotti was leaving for me, I thought maybe I should, too.

```
What's up with the poem?
Do you need a new copy? T.C.

Let me hear from you today about the curtain
rods. What happened? I need to know. No
kidding.
   Time is of the essence. T.C.

Call my cell phone number in the next six
hours. It is 2:30 p.m. T.C.
```

```
    Poppa asked me today why his poem isn't in
the magazine this week and W. S. Merwin's is.
Who the hell is Merwin? I read his poem about
palm trees and was not impressed.
    Evidently Mr. W. S. Merwin has guys who are
better than my guy (you) at getting stuff in
the magazine. You lied to me about the poem
and you lied to me about the curtain rods. Two
strikes is all you get in this ball game. T.C.
```

I had sent the poem to Alice Quinn but she was in the south of France. I faxed the poem over there. No answer. I phoned her and left messages. I called Philip Levine, John Hollander. I called W. S. Merwin and begged him to talk to her. I begged Mr. Shawn to print the poem.

"Don't come crying to me," he said. "Deal with it yourself."

"I don't know how, I'm from Minnesota. We have no Mafia there."

"He's a bully. If you run from him, he'll walk all over you. Stand up to him. Look him in the eye and tell him to go fuck himself. And be prepared to sock him in the nose. That's the only way to handle it. Didn't your father teach you anything?"

I pointed out that my father was a golfer and a Republican who never hit anybody or used rough language of that sort. He hired goons to do it for him.

No word from Alice Quinn. Trillin was in Kansas City, accepting a Brotherhood Award from B'nai B'rith. Powers was on Maui, vacationing with money he'd gotten from the Guggenheim Foundation, the lucky stiff. Salinger was at a men's conference, with Robert Bly, speaking on "The Bitch Goddess and How to Fight Her with Fire & Water & Word."

Finally, Tony painted a message on my door, in red letters: I DO NOT FORGET.

Time to go to Alaska.

Mr. Shawn had put it to me straight. "I don't want you to turn into a stylist like White and devote your life to painting Easter eggs. Him and Strunk have screwed up more writers than gin and Scotch combined. You take that *Elements of Style* too seriously and you'll get so you spend three days trying to write a simple thank-you note and you'll wind up buying a nickel-plated .38 and robbing newsboys out of sheer frustration.

"Damn it, be assertive. There is an I in *writing*—two of 'em in fact. Put your foot down on the gas and shoot the yellow light and get where you're going. Don't sit and go nuts weighing the alternatives. Get out there in the Alaska wilderness and climb those mountains and look at death and spit in its eye. Don't you come back here and write some fitful 1,500-word showpiece of puissant sensibility and irony and couth, some half-assed feuilleton. Sit your butt down in a one-room shack with a paper and pencil and a bottle of rock 'n' rye and write your damn heart out and come back here with 100,000 words and none of them modifiers and I'll print the whole damn thing, and if the gentlemen at the Century Club don't like it, let them stamp their slippers and shake their wattles. You understand me, boy?"

So I flew to Seattle and sat in the airport and a girl sat down next to me. Her name was Alana, her blond hair was drawn back in a sort of Parker House roll and her high cheekbones were flush with vitality and her lips were broad and full. I didn't want her to be attracted to me but she was. And, as it turned out, she was seated next to me on the plane to Juneau. "I can't talk to you," I said. "I'm writing for *The New Yorker*, I have to focus on my experiences so I can write." She practically fainted when I said *The New Yorker*. Her bedroom back in Malibu was decorated with magazine covers, she said. "I'd love to be an experience someone writes about in *The New Yorker*," she remarked. I said that I was already in a relationship, one that begins with the letter M, and had no interest in fooling around. "Life doesn't always turn out according to plan," she said.

It was a rough ride. Juneau was socked in by clouds and Alana put down her book, something called You 2, and she started whimpering as the plane hurtled down through 10,000 feet of murk into a narrow mountain pass, jagged ridges visible at three o'clock and nine—the wheels lowered, the ground still not visible, and then the plane began to shake violently—I caught a glimpse of a pale flight attendant weeping and holding a rosary to her lips—the cockpit door flew open and the copilot stuck his head into the lavatory and cast up his lunch—a serving cart tore loose from its moorings and careened down the aisle, scattering ice and hot coffee—the plane rolled over to one side, then the other—there was wailing and gnashing—and Alana took my hand and told me she loved me, and she felt we must affirm life in the face of death—and she unbuttoned her blouse as the plane groaned and rolled and we groped and kissed passionately as it pitched and bucked and her blouse was off and my face was crimson with lipstick when finally the plane bounced twice on the tarmac and rolled to the terminal and I zipped up my fly and staggered into the terminal full of profound feelings and Alana and I took a courtesy van to a place called Dave's Wilderness Lodge and got the $230 Pinecone Room and we tumbled into bed for more turbulence and afterward soaked in the Jacuzzi and swapped our life stories and drank two bottles of pinot noir and ate three cheeseburgers and two baskets of fries and slept for twelve hours and awoke to a wilderness breakfast of steak and eggs and I kissed her good-bye and hiked up the Chilkoot Trail. I went about a hundred yards up and sat down in a grove of spruce and then I came back to the Wilderness Lodge. Alana was still there, in the Pinecone Room.

"It was a good experience for you, wasn't it," she said. "I certainly felt it had literary qualities."

"Well, I don't know. It strikes me as unreal."

We stayed there for several nights.

"This is awfully nice of you," I said. "But I'm losing respect for myself by not going into the wilderness."

"I want to be as meaningful for you as any other wilderness experience," she said. "And it's okay if you use my real name and everything."

Two weeks, day after day, night after night, Alana and I shacked up at the Wilderness Lodge. I had a dream in which Iris was searching for me. I lay naked and motionless in a cold mountain stream, sucking air through a reed, as a helicopter came zooming in low over the trees, *whupwhupwhupwhup*, and Iris leaned out the door with a bullhorn and yelled, "Larry, you big skunk!" I ran away into the woods, and crawled under a blanket of wet moss, and she dropped leaflets that said, "How could you do this, Larry? How could you be so cruel?"

I walked up and down the trail a little but I have never been good at the identification of birds or trees, and I didn't meet any trappers or woodsmen who weren't drunk, and after two weeks, the Alaska piece seemed to be mostly about me and Alana and my childhood among serious golfers whose entire political philosophy is, Cut Taxes, and who never read books, just golfed and drank, and how I wanted to be a writer in order to get free of them. I only wrote about 500 words. It's hard to concentrate when you're with a woman so single-minded as Alana. Hard to sleep, too.

One day, I locked myself in a closet and wrote and it was going great and then I looked at the page; it read—BIQ SUATRO MEECH KWERTY NISK REMPLON NAMLEREP TRIXLY SWISK THEB BRILIP PO ENNER SKWILM.

After two weeks, I handed what I had to a Western Union operator and climbed into the Jacuzzi.

"Maybe you should make me Inuit," Alana said.

"I don't have any idea how to do that," I said.

The woman was relentless about wanting to get into print. "We went through death together. Almost. That's your story right there. What more do you need?"

"I don't know."

Meanwhile, my stupid story was making the rounds at The *New Yorker*, with its dumb first sentence:

> "What the heck are you doing in Alaska?" the old-timer said to us at the urinal in the Malamute Saloon one Sunday night not long ago after we had come down from two weeks on the Chilkoot Trail and found the bar made famous by the late Robert W. Service in his poem "The Shooting of Dan McGrew," once a staple of amateur recitations, at least in this midwesterner's boyhood, and ordered a pint of beer.

There was quite a bit about Alana and me, and the Lodge, and "taking Mr. Scroggins to town in the pink convertible."

Mr. Shawn called me the next morning. "What does 'getting the pole in the tent flap' mean?" he asked. "And how about 'parallel parking'?"

"I can tell that you don't like it," I said.

He said, "Don't give it a thought. It was a warm-up piece. Alaska got your juices going. You'll come back to New York and find something you really care about and everything will be jim-dandy."

That was Mr. Shawn for you. The guy was a font of hope. He had unlimited faith in writers and their ability to work things out eventually, or if not unlimited, then darned near unlimited, certainly more than 65 percent.

I tiptoed out of the Pinecone Room while Alana was asleep and flew back to New York and took a taxi to 25 West 43rd Street and there was a note on my desk.

```
Wyler: Emergency staff meeting in my office,
3 p.m. Be there. Updike.
```

# 27 🦋 War Council

I found Mr. Shawn in his office, his head out the window, elbows on the sill, watching a fire blazing out of control a few blocks away. Two hook and ladders were in the street, apparatus raised, pouring water on the blaze. Billows of smoke drifted westward.

"*Vanity Fair*," he said. "One of those dang celebrity rags. Somebody must've left a curling iron on and set fire to the glossies. Used to date a woman who worked there. A nice kid but the magazine is a piece of shit."

Then he reached down behind the galley proofs, the *Webster's 2nd Unabridged*, and a picture of Dietrich, and took out a bottle of Jim Beam and a couple Dixie cups and poured us drinks.

I said, "I'm sorry about Alaska. I know I let you down, Mr. Shawn. I promise to do better. I met a woman and my head got in the wrong place."

"Mine, too," he said. "I'm leaving the magazine. Going to LA. Ever hear of a songwriter named Joni Mitchell? Quite a lady." And he sang to me—

Pickle jars and foreign cars
The sun is setting here on Mars.
The saffron in the consommé
God, I love a rainy day
It's raining on the jungle gyms
The tile roofs and spreading limbs
What can I say?
Just one more lonely lady in LA.

"So that's what the emergency meeting is about."

He nodded.

"You can't leave us in the hands of Tony Crossandotti," I said. "You just can't do it, Mr. Shawn. The man is a beast and a criminal. He doesn't understand writers."

"Neither do I," said Mr. Shawn. "You, for example. You don't learn from experience, Wyler. You're a guy who's capable of singing his little song and doing his dance and you try to make it into *The Ring of the Nibelungs*, for crying out loud. You're a clown; you're not Jumbo King of the Elephants. You go crashing around and trying to be all things to all people—and then suddenly you can't write anymore. Big surprise.

"I know about you guys. I spent my life trying to make writers look good. Salinger! Capote! Hersey! Rachel Carson! The world hailed them as visionaries! All I can say is: YOU SHOULD'VE SEEN THE FIRST DRAFT, PEOPLE! Man is conceived in ignorance and born into squalor and grief and it goes downhill from there. I was Mama and Daddy to you people, I balanced your checkbooks and fended off old lovers and the tax man and got the district attorney to overlook your peccadilloes. I saved your bacon more than once, meanwhile I took your manuscripts, which had all the elegance of wet cardboard, and pressed them into shape and you people were hailed as giants, and me? People called me obsessive-compulsive.

"Tom Wolfe called me a tiny mummy. I don't care. Fuck Tom Wolfe, the little shithead. We editors know about abuse. Writers come in here, hat in hand, hairy-legged realists and agony queens and cloud gazers, and like every writer since Moses was a child their egos are frail and feverish and if you don't keep up a steady stream of endearments they fall over in a faint and if you tell them the straight truth and say, 'I ain't printing this shit!' they never forgive you. They lie in ambush for thirty years, waiting for the chance to do you dirt. Spread pernicious gossip. Invent ever more demeaning anecdotes. Piss on your Collected Letters. Snub your children and throw stones at your dog. Hire professional sneerers to stand along the funeral route and say, 'what's the big deal about him?' as your coffin goes by. For such a noble profession, there sure are a lot of pissants in it.

"No, I've had it with the literary life. Meeting Joni changed everything. Life is too short to spend it trying to protect the inept from the insensitive. Joni and I are going to make a beautiful life in Topanga Canyon and enjoy the dappled foliage and the flickering shadows and water running over rocks, and you knuckleheads can edit yourselves." He drained his cup of whiskey and grinned and shook my hand. "Go home, Wyler. New York is too rough for you. You don't thrive on the abuse, you need to be wrapped in a quilt and fed bouillon. Go back to Minnesota. And get some golf lessons."

Updike's office was full of people when I got there and I had to squeeze in between Trillin and Salinger, who were perched on the windowsill.

"Here's the situation," said a lady with long braids. "Crossandotti told Shawn that there were too many short stories in the magazine in which people take trains. Or they go to Ireland or they come back from Ireland and sit and think about a conversation they had with somebody in County Sligo. Somebody on a train. 'Train travel is dead in this country,' he tells Shawn. 'And what's the big deal about Ireland? Fuck the Irish. You need more stories in which people fish and hunt and get laid.' So Crossandotti went out and bought *Field and Stream* and he's merging *F and S* with *The New Yorker*. Next month. It'll be called *The New Yonder*. It'll be about hunting and fishing but in the large sense."

"Hemingway wrote about fishing," I said. "So did Faulkner. I've just recently been in Alaska."

"How can he do this?" said Trillin. "Even for a publisher, this is insane."

The lady laughed. "Publishers care about writing the way bears care about butterflies."

"What can we do?" said Powers.

Pauline Kael stood and glanced slowly around the room. "Imagine this as a movie," she said. "You've got yourself a nice little town and this gangster moves in and pushes people around to see how far he can go. And then somebody comes in and sizes up the situation and walks across 44th Street and faces the bully down. And somebody in this room is that person."

"Well, shoot," I said. "It sure seems to me that we can't sit by and let this fella wreck a magazine like *The New Yorker*."

Trillin said, "There's a pistol in your desk, Wyler. Head over to the Algonquin and when he's not looking, perforate him two or three times and vamoose." Updike pointed out that, being a tall person, I could get a good angle.

When I got to my office to pick up the gun, there was a note on my door:

Wyler: Understand you drew the assignment to
shoot yrs truly. Well, I'm waiting. Tony

# 28   Oh, I Was Good

Alas, poor Yorick. Life has brought me to the unthinkable Here and Now. I used to live in St. Paul, a sensible and prudent place. We ate kale, exercised, drove defensively, invested in long-term securities—and I come to NYC and my brains are about to become the Carlsbad Caverns.

Once I lived the life of a millionaire and paced my terrace high above the city lights and thought my writerly thoughts and now this—

Oh, I was good, I was even sometimes almost great, and the crowd was on its feet, cheering, and I was ahead on points and pacing myself nicely, thinking about the victorious locker room scene—the champagne, the gratitude of my supporters—and then in the tenth round, a vicious left hook intersected with my jaw and the crockery broke, and I was on the mat with my mouth full of resin, and men with jackhammers were tearing up the avenues of my mind.

Tell me about your troubles, dear reader, and I will tell you mine. I can't write for shit. And Tony is going to kill me.

# 29   Meeting Tony

Updike called around nine the next morning. I'd slept on the office floor and was stiff and hung over. "Go splash some cold water on your face and take care of business, pal. We took a vote. You're our shooter. If you don't do the job, who's going to? There is a tide in the affairs of men that, taken at the flood, leads on to fortune. So take it. Crossandotti is over at the Algonquin. I'm afraid you've lost the element of surprise. The desk clerk says he's waiting for you with a pistol in his pocket."

"Okay. I'm on my way."

"Don't screw this up."

"I'll try not to. I promise. I've been remiss and I'm awash in guilt, but I believe I can still shoot straight. Though I wouldn't mind going to a shooting range for a few hours. But I won't. I'm sorry I even said it. I'm going to fill my mind with murderous thoughts and go right over."

"It's extremely important. Everybody at *The New Yorker* is counting on you. American literature is counting on you. Harvard. Princeton. The Academy of American Arts and Letters. The Poet Laureate of the United States, Mr. Louis Jenkins, called me up this morning personally and said he's counting on you to carry out the execution. Off the record, Jimmy Carter wants you to whack this bastard. The faculty of Harvard voted in favor. Arthur Sulzberger, Jr., Elie Wiesel, Desmond Tutu, Susan Sarandon—and Michiko Kakutani from the *Times*.

"Miss Kakutani called? About *me*?"

"She didn't mention you by name, she sort of inferred you—"

I was thrilled, of course, to think that the chief justice of book reviewdom was aware of *me*.

"Consider the trigger pulled," I said.

"We don't want to open up *The New Yorker* someday and find a photograph of two guys in a boat on Lake Mille Lacs holding up a stringer of walleyes, do we?"

"No, sir."

"Or recipes for venison sausage? The magazine that was home to Edmund Wilson and Richard Rovere, telling people how to make sausage?"

I promised to do what I said I'd do.

"We're counting on you. Michiko's counting on you. Jimmy. Desmond. Did I mention Barbara Bush? Her, too. Don't hang us out to dry, pal."

"After I kill him?"

"Yes?"

"After I kill him, could I call you John?"

"Yes," he said. "Certainly."

I hung up and the clock said 9:08 and then I looked again and it said 11:02. There was drool on my chin. I had dozed off. *How could I?* I jumped up, cheeks burning, and ran out the door and crossed 44th Street and walked into the Algonquin, where the lobby was empty except for Tony Crossandotti, who was sitting under the Benchley portrait, surrounded by a couple dozen empty beer bottles and a pile of pistachio shells on the floor. He had just sprayed himself with cologne and smelled like an aging prostitute. He stood up. It was right then, standing and facing him, when I realized I'd left my pistol in my desk drawer.

"I was afraid you had deceased," he said, "or gotten engrossed in a long book."

"I decided not to," I said

"You have broccoli on your lapel," he said. He brushed it away with a pinkie. He was cool as could be. "How long since you ate? You been carrying broccoli around on your lapel since last night? I would think someone would point this out."

"You just did," I said, "and I'm grateful."

"I am disappointed about the poem," he said. "You can't do the Crossandottis one little favor for crissake? This is unthinkable. The world runs on little favors. New York does not operate according to government. Get that through your fucking head. New York runs on *favors*."

"I have great respect for the Crossandottis and in all due respect, I don't do favors for assholes like you."

"I don't think I heard you clearly." His breath smelled of beer and pistachios.

"Assholes like you, Mr. Crossandotti. People who take a good magazine and beat the shit out of it."

"Let me give you a word of advice," he said. "You maybe shouldn't have come here, seeing as you're so upset. You maybe should've taken the ferry to Staten Island or headed over to France on a Guggenheim for a couple years. You could easily get yourself shot in the ear hole for saying things like that. Not by me. I'm a pussycat. I wouldn't harm a flea. But maybe some person who's loyal to me might hear about what you said and he'd come after you and excavate your head off." There was an odd vibrato in his voice, a sort of throbbing in the pineal gland.

"What I'm going to do for you," he said, tapping me on the chest, "is teach you about gun safety."

I said, "Mr. Crossandotti, what you're going to do is leave *The New Yorker* alone. You're not going to merge it with *Field and Stream*. You may think you are, but you're not. It isn't going to happen. There aren't going to be pictures of fish, or profiles of hunters, or *Onwards and Upwards with Deer Stands. Our Far-flung Fly-Casters.* No cartoons of bears netting salmon. None of that. We like *The New Yorker* just fine as it is."

"Hey. Thanks for the opinion. But I'm concerned about the danger of somebody banging you in the forehead. There's a lot of that going on these days. Let me demonstrate the workings of a pistol and give you a tip or two about firearm safety. Let us step into the next room so as not to alarm the tourists."

The lobby was deserted except for a man and a woman, English majors by the looks of them, taking snapshots of the venerable room from various angles, and stealing a few coasters.

"Fuck off!" Tony yelled. "Or I'll rip the lungs out of your chests. Hers first." They flapped away like terrified pigeons. Being English majors, they'd never been spoken to in such basic terms, probably.

I could see he was riled. That was my plan, insofar as I had one. Infuriate him until he was frothing at the mouth and pissing his pants and then—do something. Something sudden and violent and effective. Something unexpected. Perhaps a forefinger in the eye socket. Or something involving tripping. A sharp blow to the nose with the heel of the hand, driving the nasal bone into the frontal lobe and causing extreme disorientation. I had a number of possibilities in mind.

"Right after you teach me about gun safety, I'll call up the *Times*," I said. "I'll inform them that plans for *The New Yonder* have been shelved and that our esteemed publisher, Mr. Crossandotti, is taking a well-deserved sabbatical."

"Hey. I appreciate your interest in my company, Wyler. All what you know about publishing would about fit in a roach's left nostril, but that's okay. Believe me. No hard feelings. Come this way and let me show you how to wrest a .45 revolver away from a crazed attacker."

"How about New Jersey for that sabbatical? Hoboken or Weehawken?"

"Listen. You should know about self-defense. Life is good. You should live a long life and enjoy."

We walked into the Oak Room and he pulled out his pistol and said, "The first lesson in how to wrestle a pistol away from a guy who is stronger than you and smarter than you and who is just about to blow a big hole in your ear is not to even let yourself be drawn into the type of situation where it's you and him alone in a room with no other people, okay? That's the thing you want to avoid at all costs. Number two: don't attempt to distract him with a sudden move or coughing fit or that old trick of looking over his shoulder and saying, 'Hi, Jim!'—that is an old trick that doesn't work anymore if it ever did. Number three: don't have illusions about your own strength. Some guys, from having watched Alan Ladd movies, get the idea that they could hurl themselves at somebody and knock him to the floor. In your case, this just fucking ain't gonna happen. It would be like a parakeet hurling itself at a glass window. Strictly unproductive in the larger scheme of things."

He was about to get to No. 4 when a man walks in with a big Leica around his neck and says, "Is this the room where Dorothy Parker and Benchley and Woollcott and George Kaufman and Marc Connelly and those people used to gather for the famous Algonquin Round Table?" And Tony yells, "Who gives a fuck! Get your ass out of here or I'll blow it off you one cheek at a time."

The guy says, "I'm sorry, but what are you talking about?"

"Get your ass out of here."

The guy says, "We came all the way from Minnesota to see the Round Table. Is that a problem? Is now not a good time?"

Tony yelled, "Get the hell out!"

"I'm sorry," the guy said. "I didn't mean to upset you. I just came in to take a picture. We're *New Yorker* readers. And I love Benchley." And then he recognized me. "Aren't you an author yourself?" he said.

"Yes, I'm Larry Wyler," I said. "I'm from Minnesota as well."

"Right," he said. "You wrote that novel about soybeans. What was it called?" He turned to ask his wife, but she was gone.

Tony held up the gun so the guy could see it. "This ain't some book club you walked into, this is a gangland-style execution. This is something you don't want to be a witness to. You hear me?"

"I loved the stuff about soybeans," the guy said. "I grew up on a farm near Morris. You ever get up that way?"

"Not as often as I'd like. I wish I were there right now."

Tony is miffed. He stamps his foot.

"Hey," he says. "You ever hear of the Mafia?"

The guy said he had seen *The Godfather*, the first one, but thought the book was better.

"Brando was good and Duvall, but the rest of it was a piece of crap," says Tony. "Only guy who can write about that stuff is El-more Leonard."

"Is he an actor?"

"Elmore Leonard?" Tony looks at me. "I cannot believe this yahoo never heard of Elmore Leonard."

"Does he write for *The New Yorker*?" the guy said.

"You never heard of Elmore Leonard? You're bullshitting me."

Tony was saying something in Italian that sounded like a curse for when somebody spits in your mother's tomato sauce. Either that, or a recipe for ground glass. And he was poking the gun in the guy's ribs.

"Hey," the guy said. "I can take a hint. Don't get all hot and both-ered. I apologize for the trouble. Have a nice day, okay?"

And that was when I killed Tony, when the man said, "Have a nice day, okay?" Tony sort of lost control of himself at that point. He threw his head back and snarled and his arm twitched, and I grabbed the wrist of his gun hand and he yanked with all his strength and in the process shot himself in the forehead. The room goes *boom* and

Tony falls down like a load of fresh sod and the guy says, "What happened to him?"

I said, "He tripped on a wrinkle in the carpet. It happens all the time."

"Is he all right?"

"He's better than he's been in a long time. He's resting now. Let's tiptoe out and leave him to his thoughts."

And Tony opens one red eye and says, "You'll never write for my magazine again, Larry Wyler."

I tried to think of a witty retort—*Oh? Really? Who died and made you editor?*—and his head rolled to the side and he was out of here, he'd left the building. A powerful publishing tycoon murdered by a second-rate writer. Accidental, in a way, but in another way, quite deliberate. I certainly had bossicide in mind when I entered the Algonquin, but the manner in which it happened was unintended. So probably it'd be second- or third-degree manslaughter. My defense lawyer would argue that Tony was the one with the intent and the weapon—that Tony, in resisting my attempt to disarm him, had caused his own demise, and the jury would deliberate for ten minutes and I'd go scot-free. And that very afternoon, after stopping at the deli, I'd be waylaid by a van full of shooters and my bullet-riddled body lie on 90th Street, with punctured containers of chicken salad and tabouli strewn from hell to breakfast.

"Should we call an ambulance?" the guy says.

"The hotel will take care of it."

I leaned down and opened Tony's jacket and got the roll of bills out of his breast pocket. No sense leaving it for the cops. "Just making sure he's got cab money," I say to the guy. I'd never seen ten-thousand-dollar bills before. I didn't know Reagan's picture was on them. "I sure never expected something like this," the guy says to his wife, and then remembered she wasn't there, so he went to look for her.

The money came to $128,656. I stuck it in my pocket and thought to myself, This whole thing would make a good story, except I'd change it and make the murder more deliberate. I'd have the writer struggle with the tycoon and trip him and the tycoon's noggin would bonk the leg of the sideboard and the tycoon eyes glaze and the writer snatch up the pistol and kill him. Or hold him until the cops arrive. Or maybe kill him, but with a fork. And I wouldn't have me be a writer. Maybe a choreographer or composer. A more lethal line of work.

I walked out through the lobby. A bellman had locked the front door and pulled the drapes, and waiters had put up partitions to shield the brunch crowd in the Rose Room. "Someone dropped a sofa," the maître d' announced. A man in a black suit got off the elevator pushing a wheelbarrow. He went in and got Tony and covered him with a tablecloth and took him out to the curb and laid him in the backseat of a taxi and gave the cabbie some bills and away he went. The janitor tore up the carpet Tony died on and laid a black rug there and set a table on the rug. The place was back in business in ten minutes. That's New York for you. When we die, we leave a hole behind, a hole so large it takes them less than half an hour to fill it. I turned left on 44th Street and there was my man with the sign FORMER NEW YORKER WRITER DOWN ON LUCK and I dropped the wad of money in his lap. "What's this?" he said. "Your ship came in," I said. "Why are you doing this?" he said. "Consider it back pay," I said. "Thank you," he said. "My pleasure," I replied.

When I walked in the front door of my apartment, the phone was ringing—it was Updike. He said to meet him at Zabar's.

I waited in the cheese section, right by the entrance, where there's more traffic. He arrived, looking cool as could be, in a black raincoat. He said, "We're grateful to you, Larry. Alfred and Michiko and

Helen and the Academy—All of us thank you for the way you took care of business. The Crossandottis are gone. I'm taking over *The New Yorker*. Mr. Shawn is going to LA with Joni Mitchell. And you'll be heading back to St. Paul."

"St. Paul?"

"That's your home, isn't it?"

"Mr. Updike, I'm a writer. A citizen of the world. The English language is my home."

He laid his hand on my shoulder. "You'll be happier in St. Paul. You're not a New York guy."

"Hey. Come on. I just killed somebody!"

I told him that I couldn't be happier than I was right now. That while I, as a Christian, am opposed to homicide, nonetheless the death of Tony Crossandotti was for the good of journalism—and that while I, as a friend of Mr. Shawn's, would miss him, nonetheless, as a realist, I would toady up to whoever was editing the magazine.

"I'd love to keep you, but if I do, I've got the rest of the publishing Mafia after me. The Murdochs, the Newhouses, the Forbeses, the Grosvenors, the Hearsts, the Gucciones and Hefners, DeWitt and Lila Wallace. They'd be sending goons after me by the busload. They'd turn 43rd Street into Beirut.

"This is a big city but it's naked," he said. "You're safer in St. Paul. Nobody's going to go looking for you there on account of they're not sure exactly where it is. They keep getting it mixed up with Omaha." He stuffed a ticket in my pocket. "And besides, your writing is a little on the feminine side, kid." And he slapped me. Playfully, but it hurt. "Nice knowing you," he said. "Enjoy your winter." And he was gone.

I walked outside in a daze and there was a squeal of brakes and I threw myself into a doorway, expecting a burst of hot lead, but nothing. Only a car full of teenagers.

I got blind roaring drunk in The Dublin House that afternoon. I beat the house record for consecutive whiskeys, the bartender told me, a record previously held by Brendan Behan, and he gave me my prize, a double on the house. I was a crazy man. I staggered around Riverside Park singing "Rainy Day Woman" and throwing my shoes up into the trees, terrifying the little kids in the Hippo Playground, and finally a mommy called the cops on her cell phone and I was hauled down to the precinct station. I threw up as they took my mug shot. Not a proud moment in my life. The desk sergeant told me to pull myself together. Wash my face with cold water and gargle with Listerine.

"I am down in the dumps because I've been fired by *The New Yorker* magazine after shooting the publisher through the forehead," I explained.

His name was Halloran. A little bald guy with a Groucho mustache. "You're from Minnesota, aren't you?" he said.

"Right."

"The K-shaped one. Near Chicago, right?"

"Right. About five hundred miles from there. Not that far nowadays."

He said he could hear Minnesota in my voice, the way I pronounced the *r* in New York. "So you know someone from Minnesota, then?" I said. He had an uncle in St. Paul, he said.

"Odd you should mention it. That's where my wife lives." I showed him a photo of Iris from my wallet. "Quite a looker," he said.

I explained that I was living in New York and she was in St. Paul, but it was a temporary thing. I still loved her and everything.

He said he wanted to give me a word of advice. He said he wasn't a churchgoing man, but sometimes a guy needs divine intervention, and maybe I had come to that point, he figured.

"I know all about the Crossandotti business and I say good riddance and thanks for the memories and let sleeping dogs lie, but—if

I were to hear that you missed that 11:40 plane to Minneapolis tomorrow morning, I would have to throw you into Rikers Island. And there you are apt to meet people you'd never want to know. Don't make me do it. This is your Get Out of Jail Free card, kid. Don't waste it."

I promised to go home to Minnesota and never again let myself get into such a sorry condition. "Good," he said. "Remember, we got your mug shot on file. The one with food coming out of your mouth. Believe me, it's not you at your best. Nothing your mama is going to frame and put on the top of the piano." He tapped me on the chest. "If you ever get in trouble again anywhere in America, that picture is the one that'll be in the papers. People who thought of you as an author will look at that picture and think different. Go. Don't sin anymore." I went home and packed my bags. I called a real estate lady and put the apartment up for sale. I walked out on the terrace and thought long thoughts about my future.

I had behaved badly. I had shown no common sense whatsoever for a long time. I was a guy in a horror flick who goes down the cellar to see where the raspy breathing is coming from. The beast in the cellar is booze and when you hear it breathing, you should turn around and get out of there.

Bad enough to go around throwing your shoes in the trees and scaring the kids on the teeter-totters. Does a guy need to find out what comes next in the story? Does he need to wake up in the gutter clutching an empty paint thinner can? Or wind up living in the backseat of a 1972 Buick and listening to talk radio? Do you need to be shipped off to a nursing home because your vital organs have turned to sawdust and lie in the dialysis ward and watch TV all day?

No, I do not want that. Not for me, thank you, Lord.

RIP Tony Crossandotti. Good-bye to Manhattan and 25 West 43rd. I am done with all of that for now. I will return to Minnesota, a good place, home of humorous, charitable, modest, soft-spoken people. A state on the same longitude as Italy, so the same slant of light that moved Raphael and Michelangelo illuminates our trees in the afternoon. A state of passionate hockey teams and world-class choirs. I took a cab to the airport and got on the 11:40 flight. Practically empty. I had 26A, B, C to myself and pulled up the armrests and slept. I return to St. Paul, where, God willing, I shall gain some clarity in my life.

# 30 ❧ Sobriety

I thought about calling Iris from the airport, but was afraid she'd be not happy enough to hear that I'd come back home. I didn't want to have to plead my way into my own house. So I took a cab downtown to the Embassy Suites, the one with the duck pond in the lobby. The cabdriver was a large feverish man who was irked at the presence of other cars on the road. "Where you coming from?" he said. "New York," I said. "Big town," he said. "But I'm from here," I said. I told him I was moving back. "You're nuts," he said.

I had him drive down Sturgis Avenue past my house, which was dark except for the upstairs hall light. No cars parked in front. I have nothing in this world but you, my love. Nothing but you. You're my music and my wine, you're my roof, our love is the only good book I ever wrote. I said, "Stop here." He stopped. I walked up the driveway and looked in the garage. All the grocery carts were still there. The crazy people were in their loony bins, or dead and in the ground, but Iris had promised and her promise was good, death or no death. Harry, Wally, Evelyn, Luverne, Agnes meant nothing to the world at large, but they were real people to my wife. So maybe there was hope for me. I got to the Embassy Suites and up to room 502 and it felt grim. To come home and plop down in a hotel and look up the hill to the cathedral with the beacon on the dome and know that my darling could see it too and that I wanted her more than she wanted me.

The cure for the blues is to go to sleep and wake up in the morning. A good night's sleep can change everything. Don't base your life on what you think at 3 A.M. Go to bed early and be asleep in your bunk as the train chugs over the Donner Pass of the soul, and awaken fresh and happy in San Francisco.

Iris kissed me when I paid a call that afternoon. She offered me tea. Her old DFL poster wasn't on the wall. A landmark, gone. She had thrown out a lot of stuff, including some of my old LP's. "Maybe things are over between us and we just don't know it," she said.

I expressed shock.

"How many years do we need to spend finding out how we feel about each other? Either we're married or we're not."

I could not believe that she would toss my LP's. The Grateful Dead's *American Beauty* with "Ripple" and "Brokedown Palace" and the Bernstein *Messiah* with William Warfield and the Leo Kottke *6 & 12 String Guitar* and the Coasters and the *St. Matthew Passion.* That was the music of our life.

And then she dropped the bomb. "I'm seeing somebody." I thought my heart had stopped. Like somebody'd poured Liquid Eraser on me.

"He's only a friend. We have dinner and stuff. But I like him a lot."

I had to sit down.

"I want to be honest and tell you what's going on with me," she said.

"Fine," I said. "Would you like to take a nap?"

"You mean, have sex?" She shook her head.

"Just lie down with me for old times' sake."

She rolled her eyes and I took her hand and we toddled up those well-worn stairs. She had stripped the bedroom bare except for the old bedstead and a bedside table and lamp.

She lay down on the left side and I on the right, as usual. She lay on her back, her hands clasped on her belly, her eyes closed, more or less as you'd lie in your coffin at the reviewal, waiting for everyone to close the door and leave you alone so you could begin your well-

earned rest. I told her that I was coming home and she could take her
time deciding about me but I was there. She was very quiet. Then
she said, "Did you remember it's our anniversary today?" "Yes," I
said, and I had a small package to prove it. Wrapped in silver paper,
with a blue ribbon, a book of love sonnets, the covers made of dark
chocolate. And a card: "Come, my beloved, let us go forth into the
fields; let us go out early to the vineyards, and see whether the vines
have budded, whether the grape blossoms have opened and the
pomegranates are in bloom."

"I don't think they are yet," she said.

"Oh. Okay," I said.

~~~~

I called Frank Frisbie the next morning. "It's Larry," I said. "I'm in
town for a while and—I don't know if you knew this or not—Iris
and I are sort of in a separation kind of thing right now—"

"Actually Iris told me. I heard you were having problems. I'm
sorry."

"Oh," I said. "You two see each other often these days?"

"No, but I know she's worried about you. Your drinking, especially. Have you ever thought of going to AA?"

"Never gave it a thought."

He wanted to tell me all about a book he'd read about alcohol and
how it affects the neocortex, where neuron impulses are stored, and
also the amygdala, which gives emotional weight to memories.
Memory is one of the sweetest pleasures of life as you get older. Alcohol short-circuits this stuff, he said.

I told him I don't drink anymore.

"Oh? What happened?"

"Nothing. I just stopped."

"Were you in a program?"

"No. I didn't want to be in a program. That was my second reason for quitting." He seemed disappointed. Here he had the answer to my problem and I'd gone and turned the page.

"The reason I called is I'm wondering if you know about any apartments in your neighborhood, " I said. "Iris refuses to move up the hill so I figured I would."

And he did know of one. A studio, furnished, on the first floor of a big brick manse on Summit Avenue. He met me there an hour later. "The Humphries house," he said. A three-story château with a drive and portico and pitched slate roof. "Emmaline Humphries was in love with F. Scott Fitzgerald when they were kids. She was the inspiration for Daisy Buchanan. Scott came back here in 1939, the year before he died, to see her. He was on his way back to Hollywood. He was on the wagon but he was a wreck." Frank gave me a pitying look. "Sometimes people fritter away their chances and then wake up and it's too late."

He handed me a copy of Emmaline's diary that the historical society had published, and his latest book, *The Lavender Muse*, and the phone number of the owner of the Humphries house. I rented the room for $600 a month. Furnished. I moved in the next day.

Frank thought it was sad that I used to write for *The New Yorker* and now was back in St. Paul, living alone in a rented room. I had to tell him that I was okay. Really. I simply moved on. In America, we do this. If New York disappoints you, try Minnesota. If whiskey gets you in trouble, try herbal tea. If you shoot a publisher in the forehead, do something constructive about your marriage.

"What are you working on these days?" he said.

"I am working on living my life," I said. "Living life is all I can handle for now."

I sat on the front steps of the Humphries house and thought about how nice a glass of cold white Bordeaux would feel in my hand right now. Wine in hand, and Iris there, seated prettily on the rail, and I say a funny thing and she squinches her eyes and kisses me with her Bordeaux mouth.

A lovely picture, but we don't live in pictures, do we—no. I believe I can live without alcohol, and so I am trying to do. I have had enough, thank you. I drank a lot because I enjoyed it. Then I didn't enjoy it as much. So I stopped. As simple as that. We puritans over-dramatize these things. We want there to be lions stalking us, whereas it's only some old coyote. Not utter degradation: just poor choices.

Dear Mr. Blue,

I'm 65 and was married for forty-two years and then, two years ago, Sandy and I got a divorce. It was amicable, based on personal differences, and we remained friends and still square-danced together Wednesday nights and sat together in church. Some people thought this strange but I never stopped loving her. Last night, after the dance, she said she wanted to "clean the slate" and she confessed that in 1974 she had an affair with our (then) minister, Bernie. She apologized, and said it felt like a boulder had been lifted off her heart.

I feel angry and depressed. The thought that, after betraying me, she stuck around and cooked all those Sunday dinners and put up the Christmas decorations and organized family trips to Yellowstone. I think of those family photographs. She, an adulteress, standing beside me in front of Old Faithful. It makes me sick. And that her sister Lois certainly knew about it and said nothing.

I tracked down the minister in Sun City, Arizona, and got his wife on the phone and told her to ask Bernie where he was poking his sausage back in 1974. I got a truckload of pig manure, the kind that's fresh and green and runny, and dumped it on Lois's lawn late one night with a great big sign, A D U L T E R Y.

**But I don't know what to do about Sandy. She says she feels "cleansed" and wants to talk about getting back together on a new footing of honesty and trust. But how can I after what I've been through?**

**—Bewildered**

Dear Bewildered, Put the past behind you, which is where it is anyway. The story of Sandy and Bernie and the sausage exchange is an ancient story and not so interesting as a new chapter could be. In another twenty years, you could forgive her easily, but you don't have that long to live, so do it now. Just do it. She is a part of your life and it's too late to be replacing cornerstones at your age. She loves you, and you love her and face it: you're no great prize. People imagine that they can keep starting over anew: well, guess again. Better make do with what you have. It's never too late to wake up and face facts.

Two days later I looked at *The Lavender Muse: Gay Poetry from the Puritans to the Postmodernists*, and there, amid the homoerotic photography of dewy-eyed men with molded chests and damp golden tendrils, was a picture of my own great-great grandfather Emory King!—his handsome face was opposite Walt Whitman's poem "As I Lay with My Head in Your Lap, Camerado." I was so mad I could've spit. Emory King was a private in the First Minnesota Infantry who fought at Bull Run, came home, married, had nine children, and farmed near Windom. The clear inference was that Walt had lain his head in the lap of my ancestor and vice versa ("I stroke your fine hair, so delicious, it is the grass of the soul. I touch you in all the hairy places, O aficionado, O compeer! O mirror of my Better Self, my darling, my Other Inner!") and the literal truth is that Emory King was nowhere near Whitman's lap, he was wounded at Bull Run when Whitman was still lounging around Greenwich Village, and Emory took the train home to Minnesota and married and settled down. No heads in my family ever lay in Whitman's lap, and yet there is Emory King, photographed in 1861 as he was about to go to war, looking pretty darned handsome, and the reader is left to assume that he was Walt's main squeeze.

Frank answered the phone, and I burned right into him and told him what a liar he was and he gave me some hoo-ha about the dead losing their individualness and becoming part of the Whole and I sort of lost interest. I realized I only cared about Iris and getting her back somehow.

# 31 ❧ The New Millennium

It was the end of 1999, and 2000 was coming, the new millennium, bringing chaos, computers shutting down, the electrical grid going dark all over the country, planes falling out of the sky, mass hysteria, so people stockpiled flashlight batteries, LP gas, brown rice, water, and Katherine wrote a Y2K poem:

Shadow on the snow
Of a great white owl
Awaiting
The long Lucifer night
When
The neon Venus tears
Of the bituminous dada city
Will stop
Flowing
Forever,
Perhaps.

Then it was New Year's Day and nothing happened and nobody said any more about it.

I spent the holidays in my room, thinking.

The Humphries mansion was prairie style, staunch, proud, without any Pre-Raphaelite swirliness or Victorian gewgaws, and my apartment was their dining room, 25 x 25, green walls and wainscoting and a 13-foot ceiling and a fireplace, and above it, in faded gold letters on a black panel:

In every heart is kept a shrine
To the beloved dead
To whom we raise the summer wine
And break our daily bread.
Live each day fully, o'er and o'er,
As if each were the end,
Until death knocks upon the door,
Our quiet and faithful friend.

The bed was in the center of the room. I lay there and looked up at the brass ring in the ceiling where their chandelier had hung. Around the corner from here, Fitzgerald sat on Mrs. Porterfield's boardinghouse porch smoking cigarettes on those 1919 summer nights mooning over his Southern girlfriend Zelda. He was 23. He had missed out on the Great War, had endured for a few months an office job in Manhattan. Zelda was in Birmingham, Alabama, dancing with other young men, and Fitzgerald was trying to stitch together *This Side of Paradise.* The Humphries family was rich—Mrs. Humphries was a Hampl, she came from beer money—and Emmaline was tall, with upswept hair and a patrician nose and keen eyes, and she was still in love with Scott that summer.

He was hanging out with his friends on the Porterfield porch not far away, smoking cigarettes and talking about becoming a great writer. The boy did not lack for confidence. She sat in this room eating dinner with her family on those summer 1919 evenings, and thinking about him.

She wrote in her diary: "The One whom Fate intended to be My Life's Companion is mooning over a flighty southern deb who appeals to his weakness and can only do harm to his artistic soul. He needs a strong woman, not a moon maiden; a woman who can lend him some discipline even as she admires his gifts. Why is such a Man so incapable of looking out for Himself? Why so enslaved to lightning-bug sentiments that He goes off willy-nilly to seek out His own destruction? O my Dear if only you Knew—how little time there is in this bright world. Though you are ever in my heart—we are propelled onward by onrushing time and soon you will board the train and speed East to claim its Treasures and I will stand here at the window and look for the spark of your cigarette in the dark hollows of Mrs. Porterfield's front porch."

One February morning, Iris called me to say she'd gotten up at six, and the radio said it was five above but her thermometer said eleven—"Is it warmer on the south side of a house, do you think?" she asked. "Or maybe I need a new thermometer." We talked about the weather forecast and suddenly I felt that I really had come home. For her birthday, March 8, I gave her a sparkly burgundy colored dress with spaghetti straps and a daring low-cut neckline with rhinestones, like a marquee. She put it on for me and then she took it off. I stayed the night. Ash Wednesday we went up to the cathedral to get black smudges on our foreheads from the thumb of an old priest who didn't ask if we were Catholic, he just told us we had come from dust, and I knelt on the cold floor and put my forehead against a Catholic pew and prayed for God to save me from arrogance and the easy disdain for things I know nothing about and all stylish angst and also to protect my intention to not drink and to make me ever thankful to be occupying this space, living in this skin, especially if Iris's skin is next to it. And in that spirit, I entered into Lent, the forty days before Easter, and the next week was our annual late March heartbreaker blizzard, fourteen inches of snow, icy roads, schools closed in Renville, Bird Island, Wabasso, Sacred Heart, Tracy, Walnut Grove. The blizzard made it onto national television. *Midwest lashed by winter storm*—film footage of snow blowing sideways. The next day she called to say, "There's a guy offering to shovel the roof for thirty dollars. Should I let him do it?" Sure, I said. It can't hurt. "You never used to shovel it off." That's because I knew that if I did, I'd fall and break my neck and have to go around in an electric wheelchair with a steering device between my teeth. But if he wants to, that's fine. A cold week, molecules slowing to a crawl, and then she called me one morning to help her start her car, and I did: got in the old Cougar and pumped the gas pedal three times, turned the key and gave it a jolt, waited ten seconds, second jolt, fifteen seconds, then turned the key and finessed the gas and resurrection occurred, the engine roared to life. She thanked me. "No problem," I said. She was in a hurry, otherwise she'd have gone to bed with me, I just knew it.

# 32 🐚 Spring

The snow melted. Roofs dripped. Patches of mud appeared, the flotsam of spring, a child's mitten, a chunk of blue plastic, a soap bubble ring, a Frisbee, a brown dog dish, ten thousand dog droppings. Formations of geese heading north. A lake formed on Sturgis Avenue and a car raced through it and kicked up a sheet of brown water. Kites flew from the school playground, red and yellow and green ones, sedate kites with long tails, upwardly mobile, striving, and a couple berserk ones, leaping and diving, self-destructive, ground obsessed. Little green shoots popped out of the ground. Iris asked me to get rid of the spiders in her kitchen. And the next week buds appeared on the lilac bushes, a light haze of green in the tops of trees. The meadowlark was heard, and the killdeer singing, "Killdeer, killdeer" and the song sparrow singing, "Sweet sweet sweet," and the robins singing, "Cheer up, cheer up, cheer up." The air was sweet and mulchy. Iris called to say that the toilet was plugged and she couldn't unplug it with the plunger, so I went over and did it for her, which I felt was a particularly intimate moment and a sign of great trust.

Crocuses arose through the debris of dead leaves. In the flower shop on Selby Avenue, a flood of Easter flowers, lilies and tropical flowers, flowers in the colors of ladies' lingerie. Jesus came to Jerusalem and was welcomed as the Savior but before the week was out, he was no longer welcome, which was okay by him because he'd come to die for the sins of the world, so that we might believe in his Resurrection and enter into his paradise. This happened on Friday. And on Sunday, his disheartened followers came to his tomb and found the stone rolled away—one defeat after another! Jesus murdered and his body desecrated. Then he appeared in disguise to two disciples walking to Emmaus who were talking about the crucifixion, and Jesus said, "What crucifixion? Who? Anyone I knew?" Little girls in bright spring coats and Easter bonnets and white gloves appeared, attended by their drab parents. Iris called to ask if I believe in the Resurrection and I said, Yes, I think I do. She does not but will wait before making up her mind. It was warm. A long string of sunny days. The air full of pheromones and goldenrod. People walked outside in shirtsleeves who were not accustomed to this. A great burgeoning of dandelions; the whine of the lawn mower was heard. A few more warm days and all of nature opened up, leafed out, prospered, just as I hoped my own life might, that I wouldn't always be this little naked scared person crashing through the woods. In the western sky just after sunset, Jupiter, Saturn, Mars, Venus, and Mercury, all five, aligned on the horizon. Iris called to tell me that the word "planet" comes from the Greek word for "wanderer," the Greeks believing that the planets move freely in the sky, unaware that they obey strict rules, like everybody else. We wish we were free but actually we're in orbits determined by various factors, none of them our choice. "I didn't know the Greeks thought that," I said. "Interesting." In the yard next door, a naked young woman glistening with oil lay on the grass, not quite naked—there were three teeny scraps of cloth and five strands of translucent fishing line and a few beads of perspiration and that was all. She wasn't beautiful so much as vulnerable: a meal for coyotes. Iris called to ask if I had seen the story in the paper about the survey that shows that one out of seven adult Americans cannot locate the United States on a map of the world. I had. "It's like not being able to locate your own hind end using both hands," she said. "What is wrong with people?" So we talked about that for a while. There were two days of soaking rain. Daffodils and tulips came in bloom, and a crab apple tree in back of the Snow Bird Café. Goldfinches came to the feeder. A mole appeared in Iris's backyard and I flooded him out with the garden hose and helped her plant tomatoes in the rock garden, the Big Boys and the Paradiso, the Crimson Defender, the Pride of the Prairie. A dozen little interlocking terraces shored up with stones, and tulips there and now tomatoes. On the street someone had parked a purplish van with rusted fender skirts and a flat tire and a sign in the window, $800 OR BEST OFFER.

There I was in a rented room on Ramsey Hill, the neighborhood Iris didn't approve of, not a hill so much as a ledge, from which people on the heights look down upon the floodplain and feel exalted and grateful. Streets of old monumental homes, Romanesque and Greek Revival and Queen Anne, built by the barons of the 1880s with their lumber and railroad and brewing and dry goods loot, then left to molder in the Depression and postwar years, then snapped up in the antisuburban backlash of the seventies by young liberal couples who slaved to restore them to their original grandeur. Having accomplished this, they went and got divorced. After you've spent four years stripping and sanding and painting and restoring wainscoting, you need someone to blame and you choose whoever's nearest to hand. They sold the house and split the cash and went off to condos in Tampa and Tucson with new partners, who they soon came to realize were all wrong for them, having never gone through a renovation, but then it was too late.

The new buyers settled in to enjoy the genteel life. They hired people to tend their children and clean their houses and other people to listen to their problems. Iris did not want to live that life.

She asked me one night, "Are you in treatment?" I shook my head. "I notice you don't drink anymore. Are you sick?"

No, I don't drink, that's all. For me, drinking is Dionysian. It's wildness. There is no moderation in wildness. The purpose is not to wash down the risotto or get a pleasant buzz; it is to dance all night and show the petit bourgeoisie our bare buttocks. But Dionysianism takes a terrible toll and a man should heed that still small voice that says: if you don't wish to go to Chicago, then don't get on this train.

I have had enough. Time to put it away and see what else there is to do.

~~~~

The scarlet tanagers arrived, yellow-throated warblers, vireos, grosbeaks, and the indigo bunting. Fishing season opened on Mother's Day. Iris found a wood tick in her hair, and I offered to conduct a body search for more, which she declined, but I sensed some interest. The bushes grew lush, and the trees: a long canopy of green boughs overspread the street. Long white limos cruised by, hauling girls in pink formals and boys in white tuxes to the prom, and a few weeks later, they graduated to the strains of "Pomp and Circumstance" and the next morning there were streamers of toilet paper in the trees. A daylong rain washed the paper out. A good soaking rain. Iris and I lay in my bed in the Humphries house and listened to the hush of rain in the bushes. We arrived in this bed by way of a dinner at Zander's on Selby, mussels and beet salad and a bowl of black bean gumbo, and a long loving conversation about old choral days. The New York bus trip remembered, Holy Trinity, the mighty *St. Matthew*, the chorus of *Bless yous*, the park in the dark. From there it was not far to go to spend the night together. We lay content in the clean air and had breakfast at noon, scrambled eggs and hash browns with pork sausage and hot salsa, rain coursing in the gutters and pouring out the waterspout and a great long rolling clap of thunder like somebody dropped a pile of lumber. She asked me if I had read *Anna Karenina*. I had not. Nor *The Brothers Karamazov* or *Jane Eyre*. So much to look forward to.

On Memorial Day, I drove north with Iris, her father, and Uncle Gene and Uncle Lee to put in the dock at the cabin. The water was freezing cold and I being the youngest male was delegated to wade

out up to my testicles and a few inches beyond, carrying one end of
the dock and setting it on the iron posts sunk into the lake bed, my
legs numb, my nuts, too, and fasten the bolts onto the posts. "Atta
boy!" her father cried. My ceremonial welcome back into the family
fold after the years of wandering in New York. He looked around at
the beach, the dock, the old white frame cabin, and recited:

> Breathes there a man with soul so dead
> Who never to himself hath said,
> "This is my own, my native land!"
> Whose heart hath ne'er within him burned
> As homeward his footsteps he hath turned
> From wand'ring on a foreign strand—

"There's no running water yet," Lee told me, "in case you were
wondering." This reminded him of the joke about the Norwegian
bachelor who had no running water, and the lady asked him, "But
how do you bathe?" He said, "I just take a bar of soap and go out in
the crick and wash up." She said, "But what about in the winter?"
He said, "Well, the winter isn't that long."

There was some feast day at the cathedral when we came back to
St. Paul, the Knights of Columbus standing around by the side door
in their plumed hats and their sashes and red satin knee pants and
the shoes with silver buckles and the swords. "Let's make love," I
said. So we did. Our fourth time since my return. I was marking the
notches on my scabbard.

# 33    Mr. Blue on Duty

**Dear Mr. Blue,**

This is a dumb problem, but I'm 33, educated, and my friends say I'm attractive and fun to be with, but I haven't had a boyfriend for six years. I'm night manager at a video rental store, and I get a lot of feeble invitations around closing time on Fridays and Saturdays from guys with skin problems and an Arnold Schwarzenegger movie and a 12-pack of Coke and turning them down is like drowning puppies. But there was this nice older guy—he rented Steve Martin's *Roxanne* and lingered at the counter and we chatted about movies and so forth, and I sensed interest on his part. I have his phone number on file here. Should I call him? Or am I mentally disturbed? I am self-conscious about the weight I gained over Halloween when I ate all the candy that the trick-or-treaters didn't come for because I left the dog out in the front yard. I'm also embarrassed about having this stupid job.

—Anxious

O Anxious, this is no dumber than the human predicament itself. I have taken so many wrong turns and been so careless with precious things and managed to lose, or break, or leave out in the rain so much that I loved. And now I would rather walk barefoot across broken glass than be married to anyone other than my old lady. Call Mr. Roxanne and tell him you neglected to give him his bonus jumbo box of buttered popcorn and ask if you may deliver that now. He'll say yes. Buy the box of popcorn and take it to his house. Ring the bell. Smile when he opens the door. There is so much in a smile. Put something in yours.

~~~~

Dear Mr. Blue,
I am a lighthouse keeper married to a ship's captain. We are in love though he is gone for months at a time, and I am here alone on a rocky island. Yesterday, in a sealed envelope marked PRIVATE, DO NOT OPEN that lay concealed at the back of the kitchen cupboard behind our fondue set, I found pictures of him in a bunny suit standing next to a strange woman, also in a bunny suit. She has red hair. They are both holding the bunny heads in their hands and smiling at each other. They appear to be in a parking lot in a foreign country. The picture is dated eight months ago. He never told me about this. I feel devastated. What to do?

—Faithful

~~~~

Dear Faithful, When you entertain jealousy, my dear, you are taking a 300-pound dog for a walk and there's no telling where it may lead you, especially when you're on an island. Go swimming naked in the cold, cold sea and that'll get this off your mind. Many men have gone to clubs where young women are paid to dress up as rabbits. Your husband is a principled man who believes in the rabbithood of men, too. Let it be. Put the pictures back. Send a beam across the wave.

~~~~

# 34   Pressing My Case

We went to the Guntzel family cabin for a week in July and Aunt Marjorie and Uncle Gene were there, and Lee and Florence, and Reverend and the Missus, Iris's folks. We took off the sheet of plywood nailed over the front door and I walked in and got tears in my eyes to see it after all these years. The old wooden rocking chairs on the screened porch. The blue linoleum with Egyptian temple border. The woodstove and dish towels with cross-stitched flowers and the saying 2 GOOD 2 BE 4 GOTTEN, the ancient cooking pans, the totally mismatched collection of knives and forks and spoons. The faint aroma of fish and motor oil. The plaque on the wall: "The more you complain, the longer God makes you live." Grandma's white wicker chair, the porch swing where Iris and I used to drink gin and tonics in our youth. Gene had grown a mustache. A major news item. *CERAMIC TILE SALESMAN SPORTS FACIAL GROWTH: DETAILS AT TEN.* A simple gray mustache. "Forget to shave?" asked Lee, the family comedian. The Rev popped open a beer, for himself—another news item—and offered me one. I shook my head. We sat on the porch. Gene passed around pictures of their trip to Rome, the Piazza del Popolo and the Forum and the piazza in front of St. Peter's, each with Marjorie standing to the side, like a guide, which reminded Lee of the big bathtub in their hotel room in Naples (Florida) and he and Florence climbed in and he accidentally hit a switch plate with his elbow and the water foamed up, frothing and churning, and he leaped up in a panic and knocked over a bottle of bubble bath and the foam filled the room and spilled over the balcony. "It just got so we couldn't take the winters anymore," Florence explained to me. She complained about her grandchildren, who all carry pagers, and the family has twelve different phone numbers between the five of them and there's a daily schedule on the fridge as long as your arm and the parents bring home bags of work every night. Florence sighed and shook her head. Lee looked at me and said, "Nice to have you back. Guess you got New York out of your system, huh?" He paused one beat and said, "You know what they say: getting married for sex is like flying to London for the free peanuts and pretzels." I enjoyed their company: men who knew how to set the timing on a Ford V-8, who knew what Anzio was like, and how to rid your tomatoes of bugs, and how the big grain elevators were built without interior or exterior bracing. There was no slander in their conversation, not much gossip, a general reticence about themselves, but if you inquired about how to lay concrete, they might give you a whole seminar. Optimists. "My father, Hilmer, bought a brand-new Buick for himself when he was 94, and he got the extended warranty," said the Rev. "So you two going to get hitched again?" he said. "I wasn't aware we got divorced," said Iris. Marjorie said that the New Year's Eve before she and Gene got married, he fell asleep on the couch and snored so loud it scared the tar out of her. "I never heard anything like that except at the picture show," she said. "I didn't know if I could sleep next to that for the rest of my life or not!" A tremendous thunderstorm rolled in, black clouds boiling up like mountains to the west, and buckets of rain and volleys of thunder and lightning, every tree in the woods lit up clearly, the line of little white cottages. "Wettest June in history," said the Rev. "It was in the paper." Over breakfast, he read the Scripture verse for the day from the *Our Daily Bread* calendar—"Consider the lilies of the field: they toil not and they spin not and yet I say unto you that Solomon in all his glory was not arrayed like one of these. If God shall so clothe the flowers, how much more shall he clothe you, O ye of little faith. Take therefore no thought for the morrow; for the morrow shall take thought for the things of myself"—which nobody there believed for one minute, but it sounded nice, like something a person ought to consider someday.

As soon as we got back to St. Paul, I went to Dayton's to buy some raiment and rode the escalator and it crisscrossed with the one coming down and there was Katherine riding down, she didn't look at me, her hair was dyed red, she wore a tight black miniskirt. I guessed she was still with Brian. I was wondering when Iris and I would get back together. I hated to think that we might not. The gains in life come so slowly and the losses come on suddenly. You work for decades to get where you want to be and it can all be wiped out in one moment when you check in the rearview mirror to see if you need a haircut and you don't see the lumber truck pull out in front of you. I got a haircut. I fixed supper for her. Bought Sri Lankan oregano and Slovenian cinnamon at the spice shop and added them to the tuna hotdish, the manna God gave to His people in the Minnesota wilderness, and we ate it, and afterward we made love, our kisses reminiscent of lands we had never seen.

I lay thinking about oregano and she murmured, "I have to go to sleep."

"Go to sleep then."

"Good night, Larry," she said, sitting up. "Thanks for making love with me." She gave me a kiss, the kind that leaves no doubt: *There's the door, buster.*

So I was dismissed.

I drove up the hill, Summit Avenue, feeling no less exalted, determined to press my case.

I will say in my own defense that Iris needs me quite a bit. Yes indeed. These liberals are in need of lightening up. Iris can sit drinking fine coffee on a sun-speckled day in June with the nectar of lilacs and cut grass in her nostrils and still brood about the unmet needs of the American people and work herself into a froth of quiet desperation.

She needs a guy like me who will flirt with her, steal a kiss, coax her into bed, tell her the joke about two penguins on the ice floe, sing "Some intertwined centipedes do it/In the winter even Swedes do it/ Let's do it, let's fall in love".

I took her to lunch. She brought along a book. Frank Frisbie's *Fair Henry*. The annotated edition. "There is so much in it," she said. "It's like a fable. I'm absolutely astonished. Someone we know, an old classmate, and here he's written an American classic." My heart burned. Dammit, woman. We are a marriage, every marriage is a conspiracy. Disinclude jerks like him and adhere to your old lover here.

"Why are you so quiet?" she said.

I denied that I was quiet. I pointed out that we were having a conversation about various things including Frank Frisbie and his book that he wrote quite some time ago and that she was gaga over.

"I just wish we could be friends," she said. "Do you still want to be married?"

"Sure," I said.

"Do you? You don't seem happy." And then she told me her big news.

"I'm happy," she said. "I quit MAMA, you know. A year ago."

I didn't know.

"Too much monkey business. Talk, talk, talk. Too many unnecessary meetings. The paperwork. Every time you turn around, there's another form to be filled out and they get longer and you look down at the bottom, it says, 'Penalty for misrepresentation, a fine of $10,000 or six months in jail, or both,' I love the 'or both' part. And of course if you actually read the whole thing line for line, you'd never get any work done. And my weekends started getting eaten up. It was time to move on. So I went into massage therapy."

Silence.

"Didn't I tell you all this?"

Nope.

"I thought I told you."

I said, "This isn't the sort of massage where there are colored flashing lights around the doorway and you wear a pink negligee—"

"How do you know about that?"

"I have friends. They tell me things."

No, it wasn't that. It was the sort of massage you go to school for nine months to learn and get a license and people come in for an hour, mostly ladies, and you turn down the lights and put on a Chilean flute CD and they lie on the table under the sheet and you tell them to take two deep cleansing breaths and you go around the table twanging their muscle groups and pressing the connective tissue and getting the lymph nodes pumping.

"The real benefit is just that people get to relax. It's siesta time. People pay me to give them permission to stop working for an hour. And people need to be touched. They crave it."

I said nothing.

She looked at me for a long moment. "Are you seeing someone else?" she said.

I am a lonesome monk in a cloister, kneeling on the cold stone floor, I said.

She talked about trust and how fragile it is.

"You can't eat trust for breakfast," I said. "You need me. I love you."

"You've changed so much," she said.

"I haven't changed one bit," I said. And I snatched a fly out of the air and popped it in my mouth and ate it. An old trick and a good tactic for changing the subject. She rolled her eyes in disgust but we went to the St. Paul Chamber Orchestra concert the next Saturday night and they did the Bach *Magnificat* with the St. Olaf Choir and it stirred something in us, some old ardor, and I wrangled her into bed, and that was sweetness itself, and then quite amazing, two old veterans quickened by such sharp desire—mounting up—spurring each other on—intoxicated by the familiar touch and smell, and as we lay afterward, naked, at rest, she said, "That was lovely."

# 35 🐝 Chasing Iris

**Dear Mr. Blue**

It's me. Brian. Remember? I left the Trappist monastery when Ted tried to kill me with an ax and somehow (don't ask me how) I wound up back with my old girlfriend Katherine and within 48 hours we were busy planning our wedding. I love her so much. She's been depressed for the past year, and when I mentioned marriage, she brightened right up, and started talking about the ceremony and choosing the poems. I feel that marriage requires a ritual, that you shouldn't do it down at city hall like you'd apply for a dog license. But when I mentioned that maybe I'd like to do some turkey calling at the wedding—in the spirit of celebrating life—she got all snippy and huffy. I don't see how she gets to inflict her poems on everybody, and I can't do my thing. And I want my ex-girlfriend Nhunu to be there to share the day with us, and Katherine says, "Over my dead body."

—**Turkey Lurkey**

Dear Brian, There is much to be said for a church wedding. There are clear cues and prompts and the nervous couple walks through it with the Lord's help and comes away moved and edified by the old words about love and honor and sickness and health and there is no need for original poems or for turkey calling. You can do those at the drunken revels that follow. Call me an old fool, but writing your own wedding is a short road to pretentious silliness. God bless you both and give you a long happy life together.

Hot summer days, quiet except for the whining of insects and complaining children and dogs panting in the shade. Magnificent clouds and hawks hanging in the sky. A boy whizzed down the sidewalk on a skateboard. He had so much metal in his face, it looked like he'd been rolling around in the tackle box. On the 4th of July Bob and Sandy came for supper with their friends Bruce and Kirsten, and Bob cooked burgers on the grill, over an inferno hot enough to smelt iron, and they came out hard and black, raw in the middle. Bruce was a slender man with nice hair. His dark glasses were parked on top of his head all evening, which I got tired of looking at. Why not put them in your pocket? They seemed to be cutting off circulation to his brain. Kirsten wore a black blouse with a plunging neckline. She said that she and Sandy and Bob and Bruce were going to observe their 25th wedding anniversary with a "Celebration of Connection" at Mounds Park and would Iris and I perhaps like to join them in this? There would be music and food and we would recommit to each other. "You're going to read Whitman, aren't you," I said. "Yes," she said. "I celebrate myself and sing myself, and what I assume you shall assume, for every atom belonging to me as good belongs to you." I said I didn't think I wanted to do that. Iris said she thought we were pretty well connected already. I turned to her, tearily, and kissed her. We walked to the river to watch the fireworks on Harriet Island. A crowd of neighbors I hadn't seen in years, grown old, gotten divorced, lost jobs, children gone away in anger. The mayor arrived and was heartily booed and smiled and waved. An interminable wait and then the rockets' red glare and the bombs bursting in air, which was also full of mosquitoes. Independence: not the best thing we could have hoped for, I guess, but what are you going to do? That night, the heavens opened in a downpour.

She asked me out on a date the next night. We went to Walker Art Center and a benefit for a Physically Challenged Artists Program. The crowd was gathered in the lobby, an enormous rectangle with glaring white walls, around a bundle of old newspapers on broken glass with a velvet rope, *Prose Rectangle.* A troupe of dancers in black underwear and tiaras were skimming around in a free-associational way and a poet in a wheelchair was crying out into a microphone, "It soared, a bird, it cried a swift pure cry, soar silver orb it leaped serene, soaring high in the ether, in the bosom of radiance all soaring over and about the all, the whole, the endlessness of the thing" et cetera. It was a Walker sort of event. Art that nobody actually enjoys but you find it interesting to be with the sort of people who go to that kind of thing.

Frank was there. I told him that Iris had quit MAMA.

"Yes, I know," he said. "A year ago."

"Surprised me that she'd go into massage therapy. But maybe she's good at it."

"She is."

I blinked.

Iris wore a black silk blouse cut so low you instinctively cupped your hands, thinking you might have to make a diving catch.

And the frizzy-haired dork standing next to her was looking straight down the front of her shirt as if he was the chairman of the 4-H Breast Judging and trying to decide between these two semifinalists.

The crowd clapped for the poet, and Iris made a beeline for the chardonnay and Mr. Frizz followed her. At the wine table, she turned and smiled at him and he patted her on the shoulder, and right there I felt a primal male urge to plant one on his kisser and then his cell phone went off. He whipped it out and walked toward the front door, in conversation—NO, THAT'S OKAY, I WAS HOPING YOU'D CALL. WHAT'S UP?—primping, adjusting his balls, just one more phone bozo announcing his presence in the world—and I followed him. YEAH, I'M AT WALKER—and he stopped and turned and tripped over *Prose Rectangle* and his cell phone skittered across the floor like a hockey puck and Iris said, "Let's go home." I followed her, at a trot.

It was good, making love two nights in a row. Doggone it, maybe we men are right about sex not being the answer; sex is the question, yes is the answer, and it blows away a ream of troubles, especially when it's your old beloved. Oh, miracle of miracles. Authentic rapturous passion between two old pros. You lie in bed afterward in a warm daze, tired, rapturized, like a salmon who made it back to the headwaters, like an old stallion who has fulfilled his destiny one more time, and life begins anew. In the dark, the judges are holding up their scorecards—8.1, 9.0, 9.0, 8.9—but that doesn't matter so much, what matters is that the war is over, the roads are open again, the ice is gone, spring is here, and you have discovered, for the 863rd time, the great beauty and simplicity of your life as an animal here on earth. You rise naked from the bed and go down to the creek for a drink of water and far off in the distance other males sound their cries of manly joy and wonder and you reply with a deep, chesty roar and the forest is quiet. You drink your water and return to the warm nest of percale and eiderdown and fit your naked self into the dozy curve of Madame's body where she lies swooned on her side and you smell her dew and roses and absorb a simple thought about marriage: this woman is all women, and when you chose her, you became Jay Gatsby and Robert Jordan and Prince Andre and Raskolnikov and Ishmael and embarked on a life of imagination, which adultery cruelly violates, and breaks up the music in your head, and also it's a hell of a lot of work to scout up something inferior to what you and she can create at home. You have roamed the Western world in search of the perfect tuna sandwich; your wife makes a good tuna sandwich; your powers of imagination are what make it perfect.

~~~~

Iris called to ask if I wanted to take a vacation with her this summer, but we couldn't think of any place to go, so we stayed in St. Paul. "Whatever you'd like is fine with me," she said, "it makes no difference, so you choose, I can be happy either way." We did make our wedding anniversary canoe trip on the St. Croix River and lay on a sandbar island in our swimsuits and I told her the story of Emmaline Humphries.

Emmaline kept a flame burning for Fitzgerald until he died, all used up, in 1940 at the ripe old age of 44. She clipped the reviews of his books, stories about him and Zelda dancing the night away in New York and Paris and Cap d'Antibes, and when they returned to St. Paul briefly in 1922 for the birth of their baby, she helped them find a house to rent and a nurse. Six months after they left town for good, she married a classmate she barely knew who was a good dancer and looked good in a brown suit. He turned out to be a lush, too, except he didn't write The Great Gatsby, he just sat in his office in the First National Bank and looked out at the Mississippi and in 1934 he went fishing on White Bear Lake and fell overboard, drunk, and drowned, and was washed up on the beach two days later. Emmaline went back to live in her parents' house. Their money was mostly gone and her mother, though a Hampl, had taken in four roomers on the third floor, young men come in off the farm to try to become bookkeepers or teachers—any job offering a white shirt and a tie. Emmaline cooked and cleaned. When Fitzgerald came back, washed out, sweet and sad in his papery skin, she met his train at

Union Station and they walked to the river and sat and talked. According to him, he had been on the wagon for six months, was doing the best work of his life, he wanted to come back to St. Paul.

"He sat and wrote our life story in the air from all those dear memories of that shining world we inhabited in the long-lost summer. He looked out at the river and closed his eyes and imagined how his life might be, frugal and disciplined and filled with simple pleasures. He would finish his movie writing and buy a house on the River Road and rent an office downtown and write two more books and go to the movies and eat popcorn and take long walks through the old neighborhood. His face shone as he said, 'People can change. I know this! A man can pull out of a tailspin and land safely. The ship can find its way back to port. A fever rages and then it abates and the sick man sits up and walks to the window.' And all the time he talked, he never touched me or looked at me. He was talking to his memories. I walked him back to the station and kissed him and he promised to write me a letter soon and half a year later he was dead."

# 36 ❧ Nothing but You

Iris was sick with a bad cold that week, hoarse, feverish, nose running, so I went over to the house early in the morning and made coffee and brought it to her in bed along with the newspaper. She liked that. She really enjoyed being waited on. *Boing* went my little brain: the lady who spent all those years helping the deranged and friendless gets pleasure from being brought coffee and the newspaper and maybe a warm croissant from the bakery. *Why didn't I think of this twenty years ago?* She loves to be waited on.

The slow rate of learning is discouraging to the older man, but thank God for illumination at whatever hour.

So I started slipping in early every morning and making coffee. One morning, Iris said she was going away for a couple of months. I had been ignoring the conversation, which I am pretty good at, like a yogi walking barefoot across burning coals, and I was reading a letter to Mr. Blue from a divorced man whose ex-wife (they are still good friends) starts dating his old high-school classmate and he goes nuts, and Iris was talking about the Minnesota Association of Massage & Aromatherapy, which she was active in and then she said, "They've offered to send me to Miami to study alternative organizational methods so I could work part-time next year lobbying for them at the legislature."

"That's great," I said.

"Are you sure?"

"Sure."

"You wouldn't mind my going?"

"Should I?"

"Of course not."

The association was active in promoting massage as a form of preventive medicine and wanted to be accredited for Medicare and Medicaid. Just because somebody is poor or elderly doesn't mean they should be denied the health benefits of being rubbed with oil and listening to Tibetan flute music, does it? And then it dawned on me that I couldn't let her go. I might lose her.

These things happen. Everything is breakable. A lady lands in Miami for a few months and she happens to drop in at a daiquiri bar and is introduced to a Cuban aromatherapist with glimmering swept-back hair who puts hibiscus over her left ear and teaches her to execute the samba *one-two one-two-three* and the tropical night throbs with mandolins, the stars, the moon, the white egrets, and they go to his apartment and mix their aromas and set up housekeeping and the poor sap back in Minnesota is left to walk around with a heart full of broken glass.

I told her, "You can't go. I have nothing but you. You are what I have on this earth. My life is all about you." She was grateful to be kept, though like a true Minnesotan, she said, "Well, if that's what you want, okay."

# 37 ❧ Election

It was a splendid fall. The day before Labor Day, we went to the Minnesota State Fair, the Fair of all Fairs, the Holy Midway and the Grandstand and jams and jellies and quilts in Home Activities and 4-H and animal barns, cattle and swine and sheep and fat people strolling around looking at the animals' rear ends, fat people with hair you wouldn't believe looking at the tails of their entrees. "I need some centrifugal force," cried Iris, so we climbed aboard a huge cylinder called the Salad Spinner and it spun, pinning us against the wall for two minutes, until we could barely remember our multiplication tables, and then we ate deep-fried walleye on a stick. And paid 75 cents to see the World's Largest Piece of Toast under a tent, toast the size of a tennis court. And did not go to see the Maggot Man. He costs two dollars and he eats worms and maggots from a pail. We'd seen him years ago back when he had more of an appetite.

"Isn't this great?" she said. "Didn't you miss this?"

I did. How did I avoid coming here for all these years? Some people don't go because it's the same old stuff every year but that, of course, was exactly why Iris and I loved it. Christmas is the same every year, and Easter, too, but people don't skip them on that account. The great white Horticulture Building smelled of apples and grain, and the fish swam in their tanks in the Conservation Building and they were walleyes and muskies, sunnies, perch, bullheads, just as when I was a little kid and wormed my way to the front of the crowd to see. Machinery Hill spread out above the racetrack, bright red and yellow and green combines and tractors and corn planters and silos. Back in the era of candy cigarettes and milk in glass bottles and washing machines with wringers and telephone exchanges named Juniper and Central and Harrison, these extravagant exhibits were just the same, the church dining booths, the butter sculptures in the Dairy Building, the DeZurik Sisters singing "Minnesota, hail to thee, hail to thee our state so dear. Thy light shall ever be a beacon bright and clear" and yodeling the refrain.

I called Iris the next day and got her machine. A recording of Pachelbel's Canon and then her voice: *Thank you for calling Starflower Bodywork. This is Iris. My hours are noon to seven p.m. Monday through Saturday and I offer an excellent deep-tissue nonsexual massage for $70 for the hour, $100 for 90 minutes. I'm located near West 7th Street and I accept cash, personal checks, or credit cards. Leave your name and number and I'll get back to you just as soon as I can. And have a wonderful day.*

"It's me. Your husband. I'd like an hour. How about lunch tomorrow?"

So she met me for lunch at a Vietnamese café. We ordered spring rolls and chicken soup and I asked her how she was and she said, "Never better."

She said she had gradually come to realize, as an Advocate for Moral Action, that in politics it's easy to come to dislike people a lot, especially good people. She liked massage therapy, as an antidote to grand pronouncements. You didn't have to talk. You stood in the dark and put your hands on the stranger on the table and felt her force and summoned up your own and got yourself grounded and then went to work in a ritual that never varied—head, back, legs, arms, front, neck and shoulders, head—and if she talked you talked and if she didn't you didn't and meanwhile you did a small miraculous thing for one person per hour and for now this felt like it was good enough.

"What happened to you in New York?" she said.

What happened was, I had a big novel and everybody was clamoring for me to do something for them. The kiss of fame. Something happened in my inner ear, a sort of ringing set in and waves of nausea. It was hard to keep my balance. I just plain went beyond my limits and tried to live a fantasy and life had to grab hold of my ankles and pull me back. And then I lost that story in the Portland train depot. And I went into a steep dive. I drank an awful lot of whiskey and gin. Face it. A lot of New Yorkers sit in dim rooms discussing their existential problems and the plain fact is: you drink too much and don't get outside enough. So do something about it, okay? Take the stone out of your shoe and walk straight. Duh! But I didn't. I spun my wheels, trying to live the Republican life. Upward mobility. You follow *Amber Waves of Grain*, a megahit, with *Purple Mountain Majesty* and *Fruited Plains*, and you work your way up to the top and wave your hanky to the peons down below.

Just like my daddy. He started out in the district managership that Grandpa gave him, moved up to regional manager, to vice president, while keeping the peons in line and doing reprehensible things that his liberal arts degree didn't prepare him for, and was given plush perks, an excellent parking spot, travel on the company jet, a key to the platinum bathroom, where nobody peed except men as good as he or better—and then became CEO and was chauffeured to work and had a bathroom all his own and lived in Golden Valley with Mother and me, and thence to a gated community, Versailles View, in a seventeen-room château with a staff of three that prepared a dinner of medallions of beef with the tips of young asparagi and a fine muscular red wine and a masterful meringue, and at 70 Daddy moved up to chairman of the board and at 75 he sat down and wrote his memoirs via a PR man, which he paid to have published (*A Life of Quality*) and now he putt-putts around the golf course and waits to go to Republican heaven, where there is no pain, no grief, no taxes, and no goddamned liberals.

It doesn't work that way for most people.

In real life, you succeed and earn some money and then life kicks you in the pants and you learn about life, enough so that you figure out how to be happy, and then it's about time for the lights to come up and the credits to roll.

~~~~

It was a magnificent fall. Trees golden in the soft dusk, the blue sky spotted with clouds. The sensuous and poignant hour of afternoon. Smoke in the air and the smell of apples and wet grass. Piles of leaves. The oaks turned maroon and ocher, the maples yellow.

> Loveliest of trees, the maple now
> Is turning yellow on the bough.
> It stands among the trees of green,
> All dressed up for Halloween.
> Now of my three score years and ten,
> Sixty will not come again.
> Subtract from seventy, three score.
> It means I don't have many more.
> And since to look at things sublime,
> Ten years is not a lot of time.
> It's rather sobering for a fellow
> To see the maples turning yellow.

The maple trees stood blazing yellow, crying out for music and romance, and then the wind blows and they're gone. Mr. Ziegler next door died in September. He told Iris he was going to learning to play the mandolin. He said, "I've decided to do the things I like while I'm young enough to do them." A week later he fell down from a brutal stroke, the executioner's ax fell on his forehead. And on Halloween, a child dressed as the Grim Reaper, holding the sickle, knocked on the door and asked for candy. A fire truck came screaming up Sturgis Avenue to a house where a child had left a doll in the oven and her mother put in pizza to bake at 425 degrees.

Dear Mr. Blue,

I am 29 and engaged to be married to a man I fell in love with at a dance, but lately we haven't gone dancing and he seems unhappy most of the time, cold and grumpy, easily irritated, liable to kick furniture. It seems like we have one big fight after another. Yesterday it was about my not wanting to go to a fishing movie with him. I find fishing movies rather boring and prefer romantic comedies. He got all huffy and said, "Well, maybe we ought to call off the engagement if that's what it's like." What can I do?

—Feeling Fragile

Dear Feeling, You and the Fish Man are in the courtship stage, a sweet period of life, and if he cannot be friendly and attentive and endearing now, then he is a bad bet. The guy is behaving like a lout. Cold and grumpy and irritable are not good indicators. Making crucial discoveries like this is what an engagement period is for. Don't ignore what you learn. At the moment, I am in a courtship period with my wife, and I know enough not to go grumping around the house kicking furniture.

# 38 ❧ V-I-C-T-O-R-Y

In November 2000, I moved back to Sturgis Avenue for good. We spent the month at home suffering over the Florida voter fraud and the long grim slide toward the Bush presidency, watching the dreary little shtoonk as he minced past the TV cameras, fawning courtiers in tow, smirking toadlike at the glorious free country whose handsome house, the mansion of Adams and Jefferson and Lincoln and the Roosevelts, he would soon occupy, appointed by five Republicans on the Supreme Court, and thus this narrow-minded tongue-tied frat boy and casual executioner would win four years' opportunity to inflict what damage he could on our decent society.

Iris and I camped at the dining room table, the *Times* spread out before us, soaking up the tragedy, drinking coffee by the quart, as the Republicans stole the election, simple as pie.

"This is just unbelievable," she said for the 1000th time.

The tragedy is that a man who personified the worst about America was elevated to leadership. A small man became president. Meanwhile, a procession of disheartened Democrats presented themselves at the door. Bob and Sandy were in and out, with fresh grim details. Bob was hitting the sauce hard; he looked rather low and rugged. Sandy was on the verge of hysteria. Eirdhru was having a hard time. He told his parents he wished he had never been born. He wandered around our house performing random acts of vandalism, telephoning Uzbekistan, tearing up my *Duino Elegies* into tiny shreds and clogging the toilet with it. A wretched child.

And yet in the midst of so much misery, Iris and I became sweet lovers again, just as my parents did on the Day of Infamy. We found comfort in each other. That is what George W. Bush did for us. He made us a couple again. Disaster is an opportunity to change direction. If some tinhorn tyrant closes off the streets and declares martial law, then it's time to become country people and learn to plant tomatoes. Don't beat your head on the Wailing Wall. Let the Mongols win and we shall bury our dead and go sing a New Song unto the Lord and make a new life that is jazzier and ballsier and more delicious than these bushers can imagine. Give us Calvin Coolidge and we will bring forth Louis and Bix and Ernest and Scott and Josephine Baker. Give us Richard M. Nixon and we will give you Dylan and the Dead and Lawrence Ferlinghetti.

Thanksgiving arrived, the celebration of the survival of the fattest, and I offered a toast (ginger ale) to George W. Bush, the patron of our meal. Iris's mother, who serves a fifty-pound turkey injected with six pounds of liquid butter, had been informed that we weren't coming and, great martyr that she is, the Queen Mother said, in a small wounded voice, "That's fine. You do as you think best." So we did. We sat in our pajamas eating Chinese barbecue ribs and sushi from little white boxes and watching *Citizen Kane* and *The Caine Mutiny* and *Mondo Cane* on The Movie Channel.

The first Sunday of Advent, and the minister said to make a place for Jesus in our lives and the choir sang, "Wake, oh, wake to tidings thrilling, the watchmen all the air are filling, Arise, Jerusalem, arise." St. Paul got all twinkly and friendly.

We celebrated my conception day, December 7, and that evening the air was full of snowflakes as if God picked up the globe and turned it upside down. Cars slowed. People stopped. The great hushed moment. *Look, it's snowing.*

# Epilogue

The other day, I was telling Iris a story about when I was a kid and worked for truck farms in the summer and I couldn't think of the word for that thing you carry the dirt in, the thing with the box and the little balloon tire and the two handles. I could not, could not, could not think of the word *wheelbarrow*.

*I wondered if I was losing my marbles so I phoned Dr. Johnson and made an appointment.*

Though I don't think Johnson was his name. It was some Polish name. He was a swarthy guy with tinted glasses and he drew blood, had me piss in a cup, banged on my knees and ankles, squinched my knuckles and kneaded my neck as if sizing it for the noose, had me stand naked with eyes shut and watched me sway, listened to my poor pounding heart, thrust his hand up my hinder and examined my adenoids, and all whilst he did these things his flinty green eye was locked on me, squinty, drawing a bead, and he said, finally, "You've got Pedersen's." Premature Pedersen's syndrome. Memory loss, loss of motor, dementia, death.

"Of course it's always premature," he said dryly. "It always comes earlier than we think it should."

"Never heard of it," says me.

"Discovered in Norway in the eighties. Older guys who everyone assumed acted like that because they always had been 'that way' and besides they were drunk—forgetting their keys, forgetting names, not conversing or responding to questions—they discovered it's a syndrome. Named it for the first proven case."

"Huh. Isn't that something?"

Bad news comes to us in beige rooms, carpeted in brown, with bad art on the walls.

He asked if there were anything he could do for me.

"Find my car. I forget where I parked it."

He looked at me with real concern for a moment before he realized I was joking. A piss poor sense of humor, if you ask me.

I grew up in the forties and fifties and now in the double aughts my mind put out to sea.

I came home, shaken to the core. The secretary on the 79th floor of the South Tower, she was lucky in a way, she died quickly and escaped this sour morbidity. She was on the phone with her mom, talking about her cat and her date with Bret, and when she swiveled around to reach for the cup of cappuccino on the credenza, there was the silver airliner heading straight toward her at 543 mph and half a second later she wasn't.

What mind?

I am losing words. Looking for my glasses—the little monkeys—after a while I say, Bag it! And stay home and forget about it. The rathskeller, the benefits, the frangipan. Who cares? Songs are gone. Yes, we have no bananas. What we lack in our heads we must make up for with our feet.

She comes home for the meal of the evening. My wife. The woman in the blue skirt. She is mad at me. Finally she explains that she got a haircut and a makeover and dyed her hair red and I didn't notice. Well, I had other things on my mind. Do I want to go to a movie? No. I want to think.

This is sad. Surely it constitutes some sort of travesty.

I don't know what to think. In two years, I could be completely gerflossed, helpless, needing somebody. I won't remember where I live or where my bed is or the toilet and I will require a saint to care for me.

I thought of writing to Mr. Blue myself for a word of advice, but I knew what he'd say. Be thankful. Life is a gift. Every day is a gift.

I sit enjoying my coffee and looking at the mail. I look at the newspaper. War going on in the Middle East. Nothing new there. I don't do the crossword anymore. Too hard. Emu I can get or Mimi from *La Bohème* or Ike's Mamie or Auntie Mame. The simple ones. They are writing those things for geniuses now, of which I am not one. I clip photos out of the paper and study them for familiar faces. Is this a bad thing? Once I saw a picture of Mr. Shawn. He was fishing with Jack Nicholson, two guys wearing shades and sitting barechested on swivel seats and drinking beer, grinning, looking good. Looking good, Mr. Shawn. I loved that man. I read *The New Yorker* a little but I don't remember much. Guess my brain is full. A curious organism. Billions of little neurons, more than there are stars in the cosmos, they say. Of course I have no idea who they are. Or who you are, for that matter. Years ago, this would have troubled me, but no more. Now I'm quite content with my little corner of the living room. I can see the copulo, or whatever it is, atop the cathedral, and hear the cars go by on Sturgis Avenue. I let the phone ring. Iris handles all of that. Bob and Sandy come by to visit and I try to be pleasant. Don't hear from Katherine or Frank anymore and I don't ask why. Ours just to do and die. I sit and look at the patch of sunlight on the carpet, the pattern of the carpet full of minarets and crenellated lines and filigree. I'm happy. I must write down that word, *crenellated*. You never know. For lunch, we have BLTs today. That stands for bacon, lettuce, tomato. Probably it stands for other things, but today, here, to me, it represents a sandwich. The name of the tomato genus is *lycopersicon lycopersicum*—the description in the seed catalog is rather poetic: "They grow in heavy clusters like rich jewels—rosy red, marbled in gold, with broad shoulders, free of blemishes with meltingly smooth mild-tasting sun-warmed sweet flesh. You'll revel in the incredible flash of tomato flavor." This, along with fried pig fat, green iceberg lettuce, and mayonnaise on a kaiser roll. What a thing to look forward to. Then the nap. A fine idea. Take off your shoes and lie on the couch with a comforter pulled up over you and away you go like Wynken, Blynken, and Nod.

If this is death, I say, GIVE ME MORE LIBERTY JUST LIKE IT.

Of course there is the problem of word loss. A sad infidelity.

Knock knock. *Who's there?* Dementia. *Dementia who?* I have no idea. Ask me again. *Dementia who?* You gotta be crazy.

I haven't discussed my little Pedersen problem with Iris, but surely she knows—otherwise, why is she so nice to me?

She brings me coffee in my favorite cup and takes me in her arms. She calls me Baby. We were going to have a baby. Then we didn't. Long long ago.

I am that child. It took a long time but here I am. Arrived at last.

I love her so much. She walks in light. She is entirely beautiful and fitting. She suits me so well. After all these years, she is the most suitable person I know. Praise the Lord. Thank you for your mercy to me, a sinner. I am going to go lie down now. If the phone rings, it isn't for me. That much I know.

# THE END

# For more cleverly hilarious works by Garrison Keillor, look for the 🐧

### Love Me

The enterprising Larry Wyler is frustrated with life in St. Paul and his marriage to an earnest Democrat out to save the world. His best-selling novel, *Spacious Skies*, earns him a ticket to Manhattan, a million-dollar apartment with a fabulous terrace, and an office at *The New Yorker* magazine among the writers he admires and the legendary editor William Shawn. But that doesn't save Wyler from writer's block after his follow-up novel, *Amber Waves of Grain*, bombs badly. ("Why did I write so much about soybeans in the first chapter?" he wonders.) An invitation to write a newspaper advice column, "Ask Mr. Blue," provides a much needed distraction. It's a low rung on the literary ladder, but writing commonsense advice to the lonely and the frustrated initiates Larry's own long recovery. He doles out wisdom to **Exasperated**, whose wife gives up her judge-ship for figure skating; **Nice Lady**, who is abusive to the obese; and **Secular Humanist**, who suddenly notices his girlfriend is Amish. Slowly, painfully, Wyler finds a measure of clarity for his own life, and then he sets out to win back his wife's affections.

*ISBN 0-14-200499-5*

### Good Poems

An anthology of poems selected and arranged with marvelous style. *Good Poems* includes poems about lovers, children, failure, snow, death and transcendence, and the color yellow.

"The unerring ear that has earned Keillor admiration on public radio translates perfectly onto the page." —*The Houston Chronicle*

*ISBN 0-14-200344-1*

## Explore Lake Wobegon with these titles

### Lake Wobegon Summer, 1956

*Lake Wobegon Summer, 1956* depicts the most harrowing time of life in Lake Wobegon—adolescence. With his trademark gift for treading "a line delicate as a cobweb between satire and sentiment" (*The Cleveland Plain Dealer*), Garrison Keillor brilliantly captures postwar America and delivers an unforgettable comedy about a writer coming of age in the rural midwest. *ISBN 0-14-20093-0*

### In Search of Lake Wobegon

In the twenty-five years since Garrison Keillor first brought it to life, the rural Minnesota town of Lake Wobegon has become a national treasure. In this lavishly produced photography book, word and image combine to illuminate the real Minnesota town's life, landscapes, and people who inspired its creation. *ISBN 0-670-03037-6*

### Lake Wobegon Days

A portrait of small-town American life emerges in a novel of humor, sadness and tenderness, songs and poems.

"*Lake Wobegon Days* is about the way our beliefs, desires and fears tail off into abstraction—and get renewed from time to time . . . this book, unfolding Mr. Keillor's full design, is a genuine work of American history."    —*The New York Times*
*ISBN 0-14-013161-2*

### Wobegon Boy

John Tollefson, the son of Byron and Mary of Lake Wobegon, leaves Minnesota for upstate New York, to manage a public radio station at a college for academically challenged children of financially gifted parents. He makes a pleasant bachelor life for himself in New York. Yet, he feels rootless, restless, joined in no struggle, with nothing at stake. Can a romance with a historian named Alida Freeman give his life the nobility and grace it lacks?

"A masterful portrait of the sort of small-town world that many of us Americans believe we grew up in, or would have liked to. . . . A wonderfully readable tale."   —*The Washington Post Book World*
*ISBN 0-14-027478-2*

### Leaving Home

Revisit the beguiling comic world of Lake Wobegon. In this collection of Lake Wobegon monologues, Keillor tells readers more about some of the people from *Lake Wobegon Days* and introduces some new faces.

"*Leaving Home* is a book of exceptional charm . . . delightful . . . genuinely touching."    —*The Wall Street Journal*
*ISBN 0-14-013160-4*